Amber

Also by Stephan Collishaw

The Last Girl

Stephan Collishaw

Amber

SCEPTRE

Copyright © 2004 Stephan Collishaw

First published in Great Britain in 2004 by Hodder and Stoughton
A division of Hodder Headline

A Sceptre Book

1   3   5   7   9   10   8   6   4   2

A CIP catalogue record for this title
is available from the British Library

ISBN 0 340 82693 2

Typeset in Sabon by
Palimpsest Book Production Limited,
Polmont, Stirlingshire
Printed and bound in Great Britain by
Clays Ltd, St Ives plc

Hodder Headline's policy is to use papers that are natural, renewable and
recyclable products and made from wood grown in sustainable forests.
The logging and manufacturing processes are expected to conform to the
environmental regulations of the country of origin

Hodder and Stoughton
A division of Hodder Headline
338 Euston Road
London NW1 3BH

For Marija

Prologue

'Here's a tale,' Vassily said, his hand stroking his thick dark beard. 'There was a trader from Egypt who had in his possession a beautiful jewel. He arrived at the court of Timor the Lame in Samarkand. Amir Timor was away in battle and so it was to his wife, the young queen, that the trader was introduced.

'When the wife of the Amir Timor first laid eyes upon the jewel the Egyptian was carrying, she knew she must have it to present as a gift to her husband when he came home. The great Amir Timor was a ruthless soldier but he was also a lover of art and prized all things beautiful.

'The trader, seeing the young queen, fell instantly in love with her. When she asked the price of the jewel, he told her she could purchase it with a kiss and that no other price could match its value.

'The queen was distressed. She reasoned with the trader, but the young man was infatuated with her and would accept nothing else.

'The queen brought him two eggs, one white and one brown. She laid them on the table before him and said, "On the outside these two eggs look different, but when you eat them they taste the same. So it is with women."

'But the trader brought her two glasses. In the one he poured water and in the other vodka. "They look the same," he said, placing them before her, "but when

I drink the vodka it sets fire to my soul. So it is when I look at you."

'The young queen was defeated by the trader's logic and allowed him to kiss her. His kiss, however, was so full of passion it burnt a mark on her cheek. When her husband returned home from battle the queen presented him with the jewel. But Amir Timor noticed the mark on her cheek and his wife was forced to explain.

'Amir Timor flew into a violent rage. The Egyptian trader, hearing of his fury, jumped to his death from the top of a minaret.'

Vassily paused.

'Sometimes, great beauty is a terrible thing.'

Vilnius, 1997

Chapter 1

Vassily was slumped in an armchair beneath a standard lamp, a blanket tucked around his thin legs. It was painful to look at him, to see the damage he had suffered. His strong figure had been ravaged. His beard, once so full and wild, hung limply on his chest. It was late in the evening and I knew he would be tired, that I should go soon. But when I tried to make my excuses, he laid one of his hands, still large, on my knee and prevented me.

'I'm dying,' he said.

There was no hint of self-pity in his voice. He paused a moment and looked into my eyes. I struggled to find something to say, but no words came.

'There is something you need to know,' he continued, 'something I should have told you many years ago, but didn't.'

He paused again, watching me intently, trying to read, perhaps, the expression on my face.

'Should have, but couldn't.

'There was a bracelet,' he said, after a few moments. 'I feel, perhaps, I should tell you this story in a spirit befitting legends and fairy tales . . .'

His breath came unevenly. When he took the glass of water from the table beside him, his hand shook. Drawing the glass to his lips, he took a small sip, just enough to wet his mouth.

'Once upon a time there was a bracelet. It was

exquisite, with a history as glorious as it was beautiful. Ah, what a jewel that was, Antanas, comrade, more beautiful than anything you have seen. More beautiful than any of the jewels we have worked on through the years. And how did it fall into my hands, this bracelet? Because, after all, it was not something a poor bastard like me could ever have afforded. That is a story!'

I laughed softly. That is a story! How many times had I heard those words from his lips? Vassily was a great teller of tales. In the years we had known each other he had told me many stories and taught me all I knew about jewellery. But Vassily did not smile. He looked up at me ruefully and then turned his eyes away.

'That is a story,' he whispered.

He seemed about to say something more. His mouth worked but no words came out. He swallowed them back.

'It was in Ghazis,' he said finally, his eyes darting away into the shadows, 'the *kishlak* in the Hindu Kush. You remember it, yes? Of course you do. For so many years now we have avoided talking about that time – that place. But the time has come when we must, before it's too late.'

My scalp prickled. I had a sudden urge to stop him, to get up and say 'Well, just look at the time', and 'I mustn't tire you', and 'Tomorrow I will come again', but Vassily continued.

'It was just after midday. The air was thick with heat even there in the mountains, where, in the nights, it got so cold, so bone-crackingly cold. I was with Kirov and Kolya. We had slipped away from the unit, which was standing guard for the Agitprop Brigade, and disappeared into the narrow backstreets of the town. Kirov had arranged to meet a merchant there.'

6

The room felt suddenly hot, unbearably so, and the scent of death hung heavily in the air. I got up. Striding across to the window, I drew back the thin curtain. From the oblong of darkness my face gazed back at me, blurred, panicked.

'Do you mind?' I said, but Vassily was not listening.

I opened the window a crack and inhaled deeply the cool night air. As I pressed my forehead against the sharp wooden edge of the window frame I felt it bite into my flesh. I pictured Ghazis. The heat, the noise, the whirl of figures, the squeal of music from the loudspeakers they had erected by the Agitprop Brigade's armoured personnel carrier.

'The man we met in a dark corner of the market was one of Kirov's informers, a dirty, repulsive-looking Tajik.' Vassily ran a hand across his face. His voice was muffled, as if it came from a great distance. 'The hair did not grow on one side of his scalp and his ear seemed to have melted off his head. He had been caught in one of our raids a couple of years before.'

Closing the window, I turned back to Vassily.

'It is late,' I forced myself to say. My voice was thin and shaky. I cleared my throat. 'You're tired. I will come back tomorrow.' I attempted a smile.

The uneven flow of electricity caused the bulb in the standard lamp to flare up before it settled back down to a dim glow, barely illuminating a metre of the small room. Vassily looked up. His face was shrunken. His skin hung in dark folds. His eyes, which had once glowed with life, now gazed wearily into the distance. For a moment I thought he had not heard me.

'Tomorrow I may be dead,' he said.

'Don't be silly . . .'

'The tale must be told, comrade. Sit down. For too

7

long I have kept this secret. For years I have hidden it deep in my heart. Buried it. But it has eaten me away from the inside.' His hand clutched his belly, where the cancer had almost done its work. 'It has devoured me. Let me finish my story.'

I lowered myself back down into the chair opposite him. By my arm, on a low table, was a bottle of vodka, untouched. Vassily was unable to do more than wet the inside of his mouth without suffering discomfort now, and out of respect for him I had not opened it, despite his urging. I longed for a drink. Longed for the oblivion it offered.

'The Tajik led us down a dark passage to a door in a courtyard. It was quiet in the courtyard and we followed Kirov through. My hands were trembling. It was quite possible we were being lured into a trap, that the mujahidin were inside waiting for us. The doorway led on to some steep stairs. Kirov had climbed them and stood at the top. I could hear low voices. He turned and called for me to come up – it was for me, after all, that this had been arranged.

'At the top of the stairs was a large room. It was barely furnished; you know what their rooms were like. Hashim was there, by the window, looking out across the market. The windows were open and the noise of the market drifted in. The air was thick with dust, the stench of sweat, oily smoke and diesel fumes.'

Vassily eased himself forwards in his chair, the blanket slipping off his knees on to the floor. For one moment his eyes glowed again, as they used to.

'We sat on the carpet and Hashim took out some pieces, some stones – nothing significant. I began to think it had been a wasted journey; began, even, to fear that it was a trick after all. And then he took out a leather pouch and came over to me. He took my hand and shook the bracelet out on to my palm.

'Let me describe it to you, Antanas, comrade, as first I saw it, held it in my youthful hand. I remember the moment as if it were yesterday. The sun cut through the awnings, through the window of the room. The noise and the smell, the hustle and commotion, fell away. The jewel was of the most perfect, clear amber, and it glowed in the sunlight as if it were ablaze. It was oval, huge. Ah, but I'm holding back, I know.'

Vassily laughed. He was perspiring heavily and his hands shook as he held them before him, imagining perhaps the bracelet still in his hand.

'I could describe the band, the intricate gold lace-work that glittered as I drew it close to my eyes. Ha! I'm teasing you – myself – for the delight, what caught my breath, made me gasp, was inside the flaming oval of amber. The most beautiful specimens.

'Hashim grinned as my mouth fell open, seeing them. He nodded as I turned the bracelet to examine them from the underside.'

He paused again and wiped his brow with the back of his sleeve. He was looking at me but I could see that his gaze was elsewhere, back in that room in eastern Afghanistan almost ten years before. His hand clenched into a fist, as if he were gripping the jewel.

'The most beautiful specimens. Two beetles, perfectly preserved. Caught as the resin oozed from the bark of that ancient pine, millions of years ago. Fucking. Yes, caught for eternity, enshrined in their fiery temple, in the act of love.

'The gold work was stunning, no doubt about it, but that was of little interest to me. It was those beetles. The bracelet. I had heard of it, had read of it years before. Its history was not unknown to me. I could not believe what I held in my hands. You must understand this, Antanas, my comrade, you must understand the madness that possessed me when I saw it.'

He reached out and touched my knee. His gaze had returned to the present, but there was a haunted, almost tortured expression on his face.

'It's OK, my friend, it's OK,' I reassured him.

'You don't understand,' Vassily said, dropping back into his chair, looking suddenly exhausted. 'And how could you? We have not spoken about those days.'

'It's not important.'

'It is.' Vassily's face creased with anger. 'I am a coward, and I have never been able to tell you. I loved you, you are my brother, I did not dare do anything that would . . .'

His voice trailed away. He reached for the glass and this time, as he took it, his hands shook so much the water spilt down the front of his shirt. I leant forward and steadied his hand.

'When I returned home from Afghanistan,' he continued, 'Kolya and Kirov were both in prison.' His eyes flicked up again, looking at me, full of remorse. 'Everything had changed. Ghazis changed everything. I could not sell it after what had happened.' He hesitated. 'I had arranged to meet our contact, who sold the jewellery we smuggled from Afghanistan, here in Vilnius. We were to meet in Vingis Park, at a concert celebrating independence. I could not do it. I buried the bracelet instead; buried it along with the past. I took you from the hospital and tried to forget about it all, but it never went away. It stayed here.' He thumped his chest. 'Ghazis . . . Everything.'

I shifted in my chair, uncomfortable, my hands

trembling, longing for a drink. The vision of Ghazis clouded my mind, like the smoke that had drifted from the village, clogging my lungs. I wiped a bead of perspiration from my forehead.

'I really should be going,' I tried again. But Vassily ignored me.

He sank back against the pillows. His skin was grey and glistened with sweat. His breathing was rapid, shallow, painful. His hands trembled on the arms of the chair.

'You must find Kolya,' he said urgently. 'He will tell you all about what happened. Take him to the bracelet and he will tell you all.'

'I'm not interested, Vassily,' I said.

I longed to get out. My chest felt tight, constricting my breathing. My head spun and I noticed that my own hands were shaking.

'You must, comrade, my friend, you must. Promise me. I am a coward still, I know. I should tell you myself. The whole tale. Promise me you will find him?'

He looked into my eyes, beseechingly. I squirmed under his gaze.

'But how am I supposed to find Kolya?' I asked, irritated and bewildered by his demand. 'Or take him to this bracelet?'

Vassily reached behind him and pulled out a crinkled envelope. He handed it to me carefully.

'It came not long ago,' he said. 'It is a letter from Kolya.' He pressed the envelope into my hand. 'It seems he is back in Vilnius. He's been in Kaliningrad for some years, from what I hear. When he was released from prison, he came to see me, demanding money. "His share," as he put it. He was a total mess; prison had only made his problem with drugs worse. I gave him some money and he disappeared. For years I heard nothing from him, then a few months ago I received this.' He indicated the letter. 'He's back in Vilnius for medical treatment. He needs some money. I haven't got anything to give him, but perhaps, after all, the bracelet can do some good.'

Reluctantly I took the envelope from him. I sighed, and slipped it into the pocket of my jacket.

'The letter doesn't have his home address on it,' Vassily continued, 'but there must be some clue here – the clinic perhaps. On the back of his letter I have written how the bracelet can be found. Promise me you will find him. He will tell you what I am not able to. The bracelet cost so much. The price was too great.'

The door creaked open and Tanya, his wife, slipped into the room. Seeing Vassily looking so pale, his hair slick with sweat, the blanket around his feet, she hurried over to him. Questioningly she looked at me, as she pulled the blanket up around his knees, and wiped his forehead.

Vassily gripped my hand.

'We have been good friends, no? The years have been good ones? We have forgotten together. We have laughed together. You will not hate me, when you hear the story, *tovarich* – comrade, you will forgive your friend?'

I squeezed his hand. 'Of course,' I said. 'Of course, my friend.'

'I have stayed too long,' I added partly to Tanya, partly to her husband, who still held on to my hand. 'It is late. I must go and let you get some rest.'

In the dark passageway, as I opened the front door of their apartment, I paused. Tanya was close behind me. I touched her cheek gently. She trembled slightly,

and when she held me I could feel how hard she struggled to hold back the tears.

'He's been on edge for the last few days,' Tanya said.
'He gets so angry and it's draining the last of his
strength.'

Chapter 2

It was late October and the evening was cold. Above the rooftops, the newly risen moon hung despondently. The cathedral was ghostly pale, the streets quiet. For some minutes I stood on the cracked paving outside the door of his apartment block, my mind reeling, memories bubbling up, seeping across the floor of my consciousness, flooding it.

When the cathedral bell tolled the hour, not wanting to return home, I headed slowly in the direction of a café. Settling myself at a table overlooking the river, I reached into my pocket for a packet of cigarettes. My fingers curled around the letter Vassily had given me. Pulling it out, I examined it. Kolya's handwriting was spidery, small letters trailing away towards the bottom right-hand corner of the yellowing envelope. My fingers trembled as I screwed it into a ball. Tossing it out into the night, I saw it catch in a mesh of twigs, a little farther down the slope towards the river.

I smoked the cigarette quickly, greedily. I was agitated and angry with Vassily. An unspoken agreement had been broken, a door had been opened on to the darkness, a door I had spent years struggling to keep closed. I had little doubt Kolya's letter was just a begging letter, pleading for more money to support his drug habit. Though Kolya and I had grown up together, and he was as close to family as I had, we had grown apart in Afghanistan, wary of each other as he became more and more dependent on the opium and marijuana he was smoking. I made no attempt to contact him after my slow recovery, fearful of once more raking up memories of those times. I flicked the cigarette out in the direction of the snagged ball of paper. Behind it, the lights of the city shimmered on the oily flow of the river.

The *kishlak*. Ghazis in the Hindu Kush. Once the door had been opened a crack it was hard to push shut. Crackling images fluttered like sparks in the night sky. The sand. The dust on my tongue, coating my teeth. A cobalt canvas pulled taut across the sky. Jagged mountains. Hands slick with blood.

'Bring me a vodka,' I told the girl who had idly sidled up.

'It's quiet tonight,' I said when she returned, attempting to engage her in conversation. She looked at me sullenly for a moment, then wandered away.

In the inside pocket of my jacket I had a photograph. I laid it before me on the stained tablecloth. It was of the two of us, Vassily and me, squatting on the beach. I had come across it in an album earlier in the day and put it in my pocket to show Vassily. In the photograph I looked small and pale and he, beside me, his arm around my shoulder, resembled a bear, his shirt opened to the waist, chest hair vying with his straggling beard. He was laughing, I sombre. Behind us a wave broke heavily on the rolls of white sand.

I met Vassily in Afghanistan. I had been sent to that hellhole to do my national service. After those dark years, it was he who nursed me back to a semblance of health. It was he who put me back together again when I was finally discharged from hospital. He who taught me my trade, my love of jewellery. Vassily was a jeweller, the finest jeweller in Lithuania, a man whose talent was exceeded only by his capacity to waste it. He was a drunkard. A teller of tales. He was the closest friend I had and now he was dying.

I closed my eyes, felt his bristles against my cheek. The smell of his breath; of vodka and garlic. His laugh, as large and deep as the forests of Siberia, as warm as Odessa in spring. I slipped the photograph back into my pocket. Tossing back the drink, I immediately called for another.

At eleven I left. The streets were quiet as I walked back through the centre of the city to the trolley-bus stop. Few people braved the bitter wind. I turned up the collar of my jacket and stuffed my hands deep into my pockets. Before I reached the stop on Gedimino I heard, behind me, the rumble of wheels on the uneven cobbles and the electric click of the trolley bus. For a moment I hesitated, almost glad of the chance to miss it, to avoid going home. It pulled into the side of the road and its doors opened with a loud pneumatic hiss. At the last moment I ran, catching the doors as they were closing. They sprang back and I hoisted myself in.

Daiva was sitting on the floor in the centre of our apartment, flicking through a magazine. She looked up when I came in, and raised a finger to her lips. Laura, our baby, was sleeping. Daiva's eyes were ringed darkly, I noticed, from sleepless nights. I tried to smile, but the muscles in my face seemed paralysed and barely moved.

'How is Vassily?' she asked. She strained to control her voice, to soften the sharp tone that had characterised our conversations for so long now.

16

I shrugged.

Her eyes examined me; my cheeks were flushed from the exertion of climbing the stairs to the apartment.

'You haven't been . . .' she began.

I looked at her. Though I knew what she meant, I made her finish the question. Made her say the words once more. She faltered a moment, knowing she should not have begun but unable to hold herself back.

'You haven't been drinking again, have you?' she asked, her jaw setting in a hard, defiant line.

'My friend is dying,' I said slowly, enunciating each syllable with care, 'and all you are bothered about is whether I have had a drink or not?'

'Drinking doesn't help, Antanas,' she shot back angrily.

I opened the door on to the balcony and stepped out into the night. A slight feeling of guilt niggled at me for having used Vassily as an excuse. Just a week before I had promised Daiva I would stop drinking. She had arrived home late one evening to find me in a stupor, oblivious to the screams of Laura in her cot in the bedroom. I had managed four days before I started again.

The late traffic flowed easily down Freedom Boulevard, red lights glittering on the wet surface of the road. The television tower was lost already in the low clouds. For some minutes I stood there, as the wind blew in gusts, tousling my hair. I thought of Tanya, with whom I had shared a drink earlier, before I had gone through to see Vassily, thought of the smell of her hair, the softness of her body, the way she closed her eyes as she threw back her head and laughed.

Daiva had not moved when I re-entered the room. I put my hand on her shoulder and felt her stiffen. She flicked over a page in the magazine, then another. I

17

noticed she was not wearing the wedding ring I had made for her. The ring, embedded with a small, beautifully clear piece of amber, was on the table, beneath the reading lamp. I ran my fingers through her fair hair. She stood up and pulled away from me.

'Don't, Antanas,' she said. 'Please don't.'

'Daiva,' I said.

She stood a couple of paces from me for a moment. I tried to think of something more to say. I knew that if I apologised she might soften, might step forward and wrap her arms around me as I needed her to.

Instead I said, 'I'm suffering, you know.'

But my tone was ironic, mocking, which was not how I had intended it. Daiva turned and walked rapidly away, shutting the bedroom door behind her. I slumped down on the sofa, pulling a thin blanket around me.

Sleep washed over me as soon as my head settled against the rough cloth of the sofa arm. My eyelids drooped heavily. As I was sucked downwards, the spiral of flames exploded up towards me. The sound of crying mushroomed out of the darkness. A shriek. The sharp crackle of automatic gunfire. The heavy boom of an incoming rocket. My tongue was furred with dust. My scalp prickled. I fought to open my eyes.

'Antanas. Antoshka!'

A jagged escarpment, thin bush. Movement down there in the shadows of the ditch. A face.

'Antoshka!'

I could see it clearly now, slick with sweat, dark, fierce. I felt the hair rise on the back of my neck. My heart was pounding. My hands shook as I raised them.

Kirov's face jumped out of the flames. His eyes glittered malevolently. His thick lips twisted in a ferocious grin.

'Antoshka,' he whispered. 'I've been looking for you.'

'Shh,' Daiva said.

She knelt on the floor beside the sofa. Gently she stroked my forehead with the back of her hand.

'It's OK, you were dreaming,' she said softly, drawing me up with her voice, pulling me to safety.

I clung to her. She helped me up from the sofa and led me into the bedroom. Carefully she undressed me, throwing the sweat-sodden clothes into the laundry basket in the corner. I slipped between the cool sheets and, with trembling fingers, switched on the small lamp beside the bed. Daiva went into the kitchen and boiled the kettle. She came back a few minutes later with a cup of sweet black tea.

'Are you OK?' she said, sitting on the edge of the bed, her forehead creased with concern.

'I'm fine,' I said.

She took my hand and laced her fingers between my own. I felt the trembling recede, felt the muscles in my neck loosen. I sipped the tea slowly. Daiva settled in the bed beside me, close to me so that I could feel the warmth of her body. Beside us, in her wooden crib, the baby was sleeping. The hands moved slowly, cautiously, around the face of the clock. Daiva breathed gently in her sleep. It was only when the sky began to lighten and I heard the first trolley bus click down towards the Old Town that I pulled the sheet up over my head and allowed my eyes to close again.

Chapter 3

The summer of 1987 was hot. I was seventeen years old, nearly eighteen. School was over and the days stretched out languorously, long, sun-baked hours in which I was left to dangle. Waiting. In June I had taken my final school exams and the results had been one 'satisfactory' after another, to the distress of Ponia Marija, director of the children's home where I lived.

I had been lying on my bunk when Kolya poked his head around the door, grinning. He had come directly from her office, his results being no better than mine.

'She wants to see you,' he said.

I swung my legs off the bunk and got to my feet with a sigh. I paused for a moment, glancing out of the window at the younger children playing on the grass. Liuba was sitting by the side of the sandpit, in the shade of a large maple, watching her little sister dig a hole in the sand.

'She's just had a go at me!' Kolya chuckled. 'You're in for it now.'

I sloped down the corridor, gloomily resigned to a lecture, unable to affect Kolya's nonchalance. He had been in the children's home since he was a baby, and looked on Ponia Marija almost as a mother, while I had arrived at the age of six. I had settled in with difficulty, crying constantly for my mother, who had disappeared late one night in an ambulance and never come back.

'You're not stupid,' she said, in her office. I gazed down at the polished wood parquet, avoiding her gaze. 'It's not as if you've no brains,' she went on, more to herself now. She got up and looked out of the window at the young children· jumping and racing across the parched lawn beneath the trees. The sound of their shouting drifted through the window, and from somewhere the faint sound of radio music: Pugacheva's old hit 'Harlequin'.

'You're a dreamer,' Ponia Marija said decisively, as if the label made my lack of success somehow more palatable. She turned from the window. 'That's your problem. It always has been, since you were little. You were always sitting in some corner with your head in the clouds.'

She moved closer to me and fondly ran her fingers through my hair. I shrugged.

'I'll talk to the director of the Technical School, see if we can get you a place there.'

The director of the Technical School had, however, not been able to find room for me. As the summer wore on, burning its way steadily through the last remaining patches of greenery, I waited for the inevitable conscription papers to arrive. There was no getting out of it; there was nobody to get me a 'white ticket'. The medical tests at school had found me fit and healthy.

'It'll be a laugh,' Kolya said, grinning. We sat on the wall surrounding the children's home. Kolya was looking forward to being conscripted. He lit a cigarette and drew on it deeply, wincing, his Asiatic eyes closing to a narrow slit.

He took up an imaginary Kalashnikov and fired it, rat-a-tat-tat, in a swooping semicircle, mowing down the enemy. Liuba giggled. She was curled up in the shadow at Kolya's feet. Kolya took another drag on the cigarette and passed it down to her. She took it delicately, between two fingers, and affected a pose she must have seen on television. I gazed out across the field that sloped away from the town, towards the lake. It was just possible to hear the screams of the youngsters splashing about in their swimming costumes.

It seemed like a dream that I would be leaving this place and going out into the world. As a man. I imagined coming back to the doors of the children's home, tanned, my face lined, my uniform neatly pressed, twenty years old. I imagined the way they would greet me, how Ponia Marija would look at me – 'Antanas?' – not believing. 'My God,' she would cry, 'my God, is it you? How you have grown, you're a man!'

'But what if . . . ?' Liuba began. Her small face gazed up at Kolya, her eyes wide, her eyelashes tickling her high, broad cheekbones. 'What if they send you to . . . ?' Again she faltered.

Kolya took the cigarette from her and kicked his heel against the wall. There was a moment's nervous silence.

'I'm not worried,' he said. 'They can send me . . . I hope they send me to Afghanistan. I'll show those fucking Afghanis.'

He seized his imaginary Kalashnikov again and this time leapt from the wall, the cigarette hanging from his thick lips. He rolled on the ground and turned to us, firing a spray of imaginary bullets. Rat-a-tat-tat, rat-a-tat-tat. Liuba squealed and curled herself into a tight ball, her head disappearing between her knees. I laughed and jumped down on the other side, poking my head over with an imaginary gun of my own. Rat-a-tat-tat.

Kolya came rushing at me, a blood-curdling yell

splitting the warm summer air, the cigarette falling from his lips and dancing on the dusty earth. He hurdled the wall and fell on me, wrestling me to the ground. We tumbled in the grass, gripping each other hard. Liuba shouted and, feeling a burst of sudden, brilliant energy course through my veins, I pulled Kolya down and held him tight, glorying in the fact that Liuba was hanging over the wall watching me being victorious.

Kolya and I received our conscription papers at the same time. We took the bus to Vilnius together. Liuba sobbed at the station. She threw her arms around Kolya's neck and would not let go.

'Look after him,' she said to me, her eyes and cheeks red from sobbing.

Even Ponia Marija had a tear in her eye. Kolya and I joked, dismissive of all the tears, which we found embarrassing. As the bus jerked forward out of the crowded bay a small jolt of fear clenched my stomach. I turned and waved to the group who had come to see us off, jostled by the crowd who had arrived for market.

The bus pulled out on to the road and slowly picked up speed. Familiar scenes slipped past the dusty window; houses and trees and shops I knew intimately. The marketplace was already busy with stalls and shoppers pushing each other as they competed for the first bargains of the day. Jeans and T-shirts shipped in from the West, almost new. Oily engine parts. Fresh eggs and, in the corner near the street, a little girl with a grubby face and torn dress selling kittens from a cardboard box. It was a late summer's day, bright and warm, and it was impossible to be unhappy or tense for long. The feeling of unease, the ball of fear that lay heavily in the pit of my stomach, soon dissipated.

It was the first time I had been to the capital and Kolya and I gaped in excitement at the size of the city. We jabbed each other, animatedly, pointing out buildings, cars, cafés and bars and, above all, girls.

'Look at her!' Kolya cried. 'Oi!' He sat back with a blissful grin on his face. 'I've never seen so many beautiful girls in my life.'

'And what about Liuba?' I teased him. 'She told me to look after you and I think by that she meant keeping you in order.'

'Who? Liuba who?' Kolya grinned, eyes creasing into his high, rosy cheeks.

'Me, on the other hand,' I said, 'I'm free to pick and choose.'

I was envious of the attention and tears the beautiful young Liuba had spent on Kolya.

We swaggered through the streets of Vilnius, stopping near the bus station for a drink.

'How old are you two, then?' the woman behind the bar asked with a wry smile, looking at our fresh young faces.

'Old enough,' Kolya said, trying to imitate the rough aggression of the men we had seen in bars in our town.

The woman laughed. She leant forward, drawing her face close to Kolya's. 'Old enough for what?' she whispered, blowing the fringe of his hair away from his large square face. Her breasts rested heavily on the polished surface of the bar. Kolya's face flushed and he fell silent. We drank our beers quietly and left.

'She was too old or I would have had her,' Kolya said as we made our way to the bus stop that would take us to the base we had been told to report to.

I nodded. 'She wasn't bad, though, was she? I mean, even though she was getting on a bit.'

'Fuck off, she was old enough to be your *baba*.'

We laughed raucously, ignoring the crowd that pushed around us. When the bus came we shoved each other on, fighting through the bodies, giggling and jabbing each other. The passengers watched us good-humouredly, knowing where we going.

Chapter 4

Nobody was in the apartment the next morning when Tanya telephoned. The small red light blinked on the answerphone when I returned just after lunch. I hesitated a moment before pressing the button. Tanya's voice filtered nervously from the clumsy apparatus. She sounded fragile and distracted.

'Antanas? It's Tanya.' She paused. 'They've taken Vassily into hospital.' She hesitated again and I heard her laboured breathing above the crackle of the telephone, as if she were stifling a sob. 'Perhaps you should come to see him. They don't seem hopeful.'

For some moments, I heard the soft sound of her breath as she continued to hold the telephone receiver close to her lips. Then, quietly, gently, she replaced it.

A dim light illuminated Vassily's bed. In a steady, slow rhythm his chest rose and fell. His hands, punctured by drips, lay on the sheet by his side. I took his fingers between my own. The flesh was hard, calloused. Black hairs bristled from them. I felt the warm pulse. Life. His face was more shrivelled than it had been when I had seen him the previous day. His beard hung over the fold of the sheet. Closing my eyes, I caressed his fingers between my own. Fingers that had taught me so much.

*

'He's in and out of consciousness,' Tanya told me when I bumped into her in the corridor. 'Mostly he's sleeping, but every so often he wakes. Sometimes he is very lucid and at times not at all.'

'What have the doctors said? Have they . . .'

She shook her head but said nothing. I looked away down the corridor. We stood together awkwardly in the semi-darkness. I could see by the way her chest swelled and by the tightening of her jaw muscles that she was close to tears. She blinked twice. I laid a hand on her shoulder and she staggered slightly. We embraced clumsily, our stiff bodies colliding in the grimy corridor.

'I'd better go in,' she said.

'Yes,' I said. 'You will let me know if there is any change?'

She nodded. For a moment longer she lingered, as if there were something more to be said. I longed to hold her, but did not move. She slipped through the doorway into the ward. The nurse came and I gave her a box of chocolates I had bought from a shop on the way, and some fruit from the village; the small expected bribes to make sure the patient was well treated. A bottle of champagne had already gone to the doctor. The nurse smiled, dourly.

'Take good care of him,' I said.

She nodded, a little severely. 'Of course.'

Outside, the weather had begun to clear. I found a quiet café off the main street, ordered a coffee and lit a cigarette. It had been to Tanya's grandparents' cottage that Vassily had taken me when I was discharged from hospital after Afghanistan. The cottage was roofed with corrugated tin sheets that were brown with rust, blending naturally into the autumnal colours of the

27

overhanging trees. The door stood open, a net curtain trailing across the packed-earth doorstep. Tethered to a stake in the garden, a large dog barked furiously. A young woman stepped out, barefoot on the worn earth. Her hair fell around her shoulders, framing a handsome face. I paused for a moment, seeing her. There was something familiar about her face. It attracted me and frightened me simultaneously.

'Tanya,' Vassily said.

'You're back, then,' she said.

'*Da*,' he said, with a grin, 'I'm back, as I promised.'

His tongue licked nervously at his lips, but I could see his eyes devouring her. After a moment he collected himself.

'And this,' he said, with a flourish of his large hand, 'is Antanas, my comrade in arms, my brother and friend, as I have also promised to you.'

Tanya appraised me for a few seconds, her eyes travelling up my emaciated body, resting finally on my own. 'Vassily tells me you have been ill.'

I shrugged, sheathed still in the dark haze of the neuroleptics the hospital had been feeding me. Slowly her features worked their way into my mind, teasing out the memory of other features, of feelings numbed over the long months – years – of medication.

We followed her as she stooped through the low doorway, brushing the curtain aside. After the bright afternoon light, the gloom of the small room into which we stepped was, for several moments, impenetrable.

'*Senele*,' Tanya called, 'Vassily is back. He has brought his friend, the Lithuanian boy.'

The shuffle of broken slippers on the stone floor drew my eyes to the doorway leading off from the kitchen, through which a woman appeared, a twig broom in her hand. Moving closer, she nodded to Vassily. She examined me.

'Just look at the state of you,' she said, and despite the twist of her lips and the angry way she said this I could see she was concerned.

Tanya led me through to the back room and laid me on a large sofa beneath the window.

'Vassily has told me a lot about you,' she said, kneeling beside me.

I nodded, unsure how to respond. I found the idea of conversation difficult. She lingered a moment longer and then got up and went back into the kitchen, leaving behind only the scent of her body. I lay listening to the sound of her voice in the next room. Transfixed by it.

When I had finished the coffee, I ground the cigarette out in the ashtray and left the café. It was early enough to go back to the workshop for a couple of hours, but I could not face it. I caught a trolley bus home and waited in the gathering gloom for Daiva and the baby.

Tanya telephoned again the next morning. Daiva roused me from the sofa, where I had been sleeping. In the kitchen Laura was crying. 'It's Tanya,' Daiva said, her voice coloured with too many implications. My heart shrank and my hand trembled as I picked up the receiver. Tanya's voice was thick with sorrow, choking on the news of her husband's death. I stood on the cold tiled floor, barefoot, in silence.

'He's gone,' she said. I heard the catch in her throat and there was a short pause as she steadied herself. 'This morning. Early.'

'Tanya,' was all I could think to say. After that the

silence grew too oppressive for us both. I heard her sobbing, far away down the crackling line. I longed to be there with her, to hold her and comfort her.

Daiva stood by the kitchen window, looking out, her back to me. She did not turn as I put down the receiver. For some moments we stood like that, without saying a word. She did not offer me comfort. Instead she picked up a plate and rinsed it under the tap. Laura had stopped crying and was muttering into a bowl of porridge. I picked up my jacket, slipped on some socks and shoes and left the apartment.

For some time I paced back and forth outside, unsure where to go. It had always been to him that I turned. And now he was gone. In the end I headed for the bus stop on Freedom Boulevard. Catching the number 16 to the station on the edge of the Old Town, I made my way along the familiar route, through the old ghetto, towards the Gates of Dawn where he and Tanya had their apartment.

I was about to stop in the small beer hall close by their block when, looking up, I noticed the light in their window. For some moments I stood in the centre of the narrow cobbled lane that twisted down, away from Filharmonija Square, looking up at the third-storey apartment. Dull clouds, which had moved once more across the city, hung low and threatening now. The old grey plaster falling from the walls of the buildings was dark. Only the moss seemed enlivened. It was verdant, growing up thickly from the foundations.

Knowing I should leave her, that I should not intrude, still I pushed open the heavy wooden door and found myself in the familiar musty gloom of their stairwell. When the door closed behind me, I was in almost pitch darkness. I pressed the light switch, but nothing happened.

Slowly I made my way up the stairs. Grimy windows on the second floor let in a pale light. I stopped and peered out into the street, at the beer hall where I would have been better off going.

I pressed the buzzer and stood back from the door, so that she could see me properly when she put her eye to the spyhole. For some moments I waited. I was about to press the buzzer a second time when I heard her footsteps. She moved the flap over the spyhole and there was a moment's silence as she peered through. A key turned and the door opened.

'Antanas,' she said. She stood in the doorway, illuminated from behind by a small lamp on a table in the hallway. It was only when I moved closer that I noticed the state of her face. Her cheeks were red and her eyes swollen and dark. In contrast the blood seemed to have withdrawn from the rest of her face, leaving it deathly pale.

She allowed me to step into the apartment, then embraced me. I held her tight. Her hair smelt of the disinfectants they use in hospitals and the Russian cigarettes Vassily smoked.

'You smell of him,' I said.

She smiled. 'I smoked God knows how many of his cigarettes when I got back this morning. I feel sick, but I needed to smell him.'

We sat in their small lounge drinking coffee, and I smoked the last of the cigarettes in the packet he had left. Everywhere there were signs of him, and it struck me then how much of him there was in this apartment, unlike my own, which showed barely a trace of me. Before I left she stopped me in the corridor.

'He left something for you,' she said. 'Wait.'

She disappeared into the bedroom and emerged after

a few moments with a long, thin envelope. He had written my name on the front.

'For an hour or so yesterday he was quite lucid, although he was in rather a state. He wrote it then. He made me promise to make you find Kolya, an old friend of yours.' She shrugged.

I slipped the envelope into the pocket of my jacket. 'Thank you, Tanya.' I kissed her cheek, which was cool and paler now. 'If you need anything . . .'

'Of course,' she said. 'Of course.'

Leaving the apartment, I crossed over to the beer hall, but at the door I stopped, suddenly afraid to enter, knowing I would not find him there. Walking quickly back across the town, I went to a bar we had never visited, a modern one on Gedimino. I drank quickly to hold back the tears. Digging the envelope from my pocket, I pulled from it a thin sheet of paper. The sight of his large flowing handwriting caused a spasm of pain to tighten my chest.

'Antanas,' he wrote, 'the years have been good ones, haven't they? You must not hate me. Find Kolya. He will tell you what I have not been able to. Find Kolya. And forgive me, my little brother.'

I stared at the writing for some time. The words slowly took form and ordered themselves into phrases. But still I could not find the sense. I could not think for what he could want forgiveness. Folding the paper, I put it back into its envelope. For years it had been Vassily who had helped me hold back the flood of memories. Those years in Afghanistan were a dark hole around which we stepped with care.

The bright peacefulness of Tanya's grandparents' cottage, where Vassily had taken me in his rattling

Zhiguli, had allowed me to slough off the bleak desperation of the hospital. Tanya's grandfather sold tourist
trinkets and he put us to work producing cheap pictures
from chippings of amber.

We sorted the amber chips into coloured piles. Little
mounds of each shade dotted the card table on which
we worked. Vassily picked up a thin sheet of plywood
and laid it down on the table. With a cheap emulsion
he painted a crude black outline of the Madonna's face
and shoulders, copying a picture Jurgis had given him.
When the paint had dried, he brushed a portion of it
thickly with glue and we proceeded to build up the
image using the chippings of amber. Around the rim of
the picture we built up a luminous halo with deep orange
amber that glowed warmly. As we worked in towards
the black outline of her head, we switched to the brighter
yellow pieces, while for the face and shoulders we used
the larger dark pieces, which when stuck into the thick
layer of glue flamed bloodily red. The robe that fell
from her shoulders we fashioned with the small bone-
white fragments.

When we had finished, Vassily carefully assembled a
flimsy pre-prepared wooden frame around the picture.
A sheet of waxy paper was glued across the back,
hiding the poor-quality wood the picture had been built
on, and two small tacks were tapped into the frame.
Taking a length of string, Vassily measured it off and
cut it. Deftly, his thick fingers tied the string between
the two tacks. Once he had finished he held it up,
turning it slightly, allowing the amber to catch the rays
of the late afternoon sun cutting across the tops of the
trees and falling heavily against the peeling paint of
the cottage. The amber glowed, each transparent yellow
piece gathering its own little parcel of light.

'The best trinkets on the Baltic coast,' Vassily commented ironically.

He took the picture to a small hut attached to the cottage. Opening the door, he indicated I should come and look. Inside, stacked neatly on shelves, were more pictures. They differed in size. While some were large with stylised pictures of pine trees framing beaches, others were tiny little miniatures. A crucifixion, another Madonna, the Pope, Lenin. Most were executed crudely. The pasting was visible and the shades had been built up with little care. It was obvious which ones had been produced by Vassily. I picked up a miniature he had done of the head of the crucified Christ. In the small space he had been able to capture a look of sorrow, dark amber beads of blood trickling down from the crown of thorns.

'This is beautiful,' I said.

Vassily grinned. 'Jurgis moans I take too much time over them. And it is true, I do. They will only go for a few roubles, what is the point in working so hard on them? I don't know, I can't help it.'

He shrugged, taking a larger piece of amber from his pocket. It was orange and clear, with only a few blemishes in it.

'Look,' he said, leading me outside into the sunlight. He held up the amber so that it caught the sun. 'Isn't it beautiful? So warm; it is like a piece of sunlight solidified. From this we get the word electricity. The Greeks called it *elektron* when they discovered it, lustrous metal. And look.' He rubbed the amber hard against the ripped woollen jumper he wore and then held it over a little fluff. The fluff clung to the amber. 'Static electricity. It is a source of power, of healing, of life. It is an elemental force for good, preserved from the very beginnings of time, from the prehistoric forests which grew thickly here, across the plains to Scandinavia before the sea poured over them.'

His eyes glowed. He folded the amber into the palm of his large hand. 'I will teach you how to work amber,' he said. 'I will you teach you how to make jewels. We will be jewellers, the two of us, craftsmen of the highest order, the best jewellers on the Baltic coast. I will teach you all you need to know.'

Sleep came quickly in those days, unaided by narcotics or spirits. The tranquillity of the village and the compassionate solicitude of Vassily encouraged the slow process of healing, closing the wounds, slicking over the pale ghosts of our past. And when the dreams came, he woke me and held me through the dark hours.

Tanya was the centre of attention in the small cottage. Her grandparents doted on her, and it had not escaped my notice that when she entered the room, or addressed Vassily, his face flushed with pleasure. When he spoke to her he was especially polite and she, when she addressed him, was playfully rude. She was beautiful. When she smiled, the smile would grow from her eyes and spread down across her glowing cheeks to her lips. Fearful of the feelings she stirred in me and of hurting Vassily, I stifled my attraction to her.

In the modern bar on Gedimino I pressed the heels of my hands against my eyes and wept, my body stiff and awkward, aware of the scene I was causing. Vassily, my friend, my teacher, was gone.

Chapter 5

I did not return home until late that evening. Daiva
was already in bed. She lay silent in the darkness, and
though she said nothing, I knew she was awake. As
quietly as I could, I undressed, sitting on the edge of
the bed so I would not stumble. I opened a window
and kept a distance from Daiva so she would not smell
the vodka on my breath.

When I slipped between the sheets, she turned to me.

'Vassily?' she asked quietly.

'He died this morning.'

For some moments she said nothing, then, half turning
away, she said, 'And how is Tanya?'

She attempted to control the tone of her voice, but
it shook with the force of the repressed accusation.

'Tanya was upset when I saw her this morning,' I
said.

'This morning?' Daiva shot back bitterly, propping
herself up on her elbows. 'You didn't spend the day
comforting her?'

'No,' I said, quietly, 'I didn't spend the day comforting her.'

We lay, then, for some time in silence. I moved my
hand over to touch hers, but she drew it away sharply.

'I can't stand it any more.'

'What?'

'I can't stand this deception.' She turned her back on
me. In the light of the street lamps that glowed dimly

through the gap between the curtains, I saw her figure outlined. I felt a heavy weight settle on my chest, press down on it. I felt weary.

'I can't do this, Daiva,' I whispered, my voice tight. 'I don't want to talk now.'

Daiva sat up. I saw the stiffening of the muscles in her neck, her jaw jutting forward slightly.

Her voice was low and measured when she spoke. 'You never do want to talk about it.'

I eased myself out of bed and went over to the window. Pulling back the thin curtain, I looked out blankly into the night.

'You never want to confront things,' Daiva said.

I lifted my hand.

'Daiva,' I said, finding my breathing constricted, feeling the heavy hand pressing down on my chest, squeezing the breath from me, 'I don't want to talk just now. Let's stop.'

'I need to talk.' Her voice was furious. Quiet, low, controlled, but furious.

I balled my fist and pressed it hard against my chest. A sharp pain pierced through the muscles above my heart.

'For five years now we have been walking around each other. I have kept my mouth shut, watched you drinking more and more, sitting here in silence because I'm not allowed to talk. It's killing me, Antanas. It's killing me.'

I spun around.

'Killing you?' I spat at her. 'Killing you? You don't know the meaning of that word.' My voice rose. 'Do you want me to tell you what that word means? Do you want to know what killing means? Do you?'

'Don't you shout at me,' she said, her voice very low and tight now.

I was trembling. My pulse raced; my teeth were gritted so tight against each other they hurt.

Daiva pulled the sheet away and got out of bed. She moved silently across the room to the crib. The baby had stirred. I could hear her moving, a small snuffle. Daiva leant down, arranging the covers over her, muttering soothingly. I turned back to the window and pressed my forehead against the cool glass. Closing my eyes, I breathed deeply, trying to control the rage.

The door of the bedroom clicked and a light came on in the hallway. I turned to see Daiva entering the kitchen. I followed her. She had opened the window and was staring out, a soft breeze blowing her fine light hair away from her face, making the silk of her pyjamas shiver. Hearing me enter, she picked up the kettle. Filling it from the tap, she placed it on the hob and struck a match to light the gas. Only then did she turn to me.

Leaning back against the sink, she folded her arms across her chest. For some moments she did not say anything. I stood in the doorway, my pulse racing.

'It can't go on,' she said at last.

She pushed her hair back from her face. Her cheeks were flushed delicately pink. Her throat was the colour of marbled amber.

'I can't live like this any more.'

'You think I can?' I retorted, wounded by the implication of her words. I felt the ripple of desperation pass beneath my feet, the swell of the bubble of darkness. 'You think I can live like this?' I repeated, not knowing what else to say.

The gas flame roared faintly. A gust of wind blew through the window, billowing the net curtains, rasping the gas.

'It's not just the drinking, Antanas, although God knows the drinking is difficult enough to bear. I just can't stand how you give in to her.'

'Give in to who? What are you talking about?'

'She calls and you come running.'

'Daiva, her husband just died today.'

'And you can't keep your hands off her. Straight over.'

'You can't be serious.'

'I can't stand it any more,' she screamed. Her face was set and brutal with pain. Tears flowed down her cheeks and her whole body was rigid, her hands clasped before her, pleading. 'Go to her,' she whispered. 'Go fuck her. I don't care any more.'

'You're twisted,' I shouted. 'You're twisted, you know that?'

'You're killing me,' she whispered, her voice dissolving in her tears. She pulled her hands up to her face and buried it in them.

An intense wave of fury ripped through me. I stepped across the floor to her and pulled the hands from her face.

'You listen to me,' I said, my voice trembling with rage. 'You can't just go saying things like that. You know what you are saying is not true.'

'Really?'

'You know it isn't,' I whispered through clenched teeth. 'You should apologise.'

The kettle bubbled and began to whistle quietly. Daiva looked up and a slight sneer twisted her lips.

'Make me.'

The kettle shrilled more loudly. The rising pillar of steam jigged in the breeze from the window. My hand flew up from my side. I felt it move as if I had no control over it. It rose in slow motion; we both watched it rise. I felt the sharp sting on my palm as it made contact with her cheek. Saw her head jerk aside. Her hair flicked forwards, hiding her face. She gasped. My hand hung suspended in the air, where her face had been, the palm itching. I drew it back, rubbed it. The kettle juddered on the hob, the steam billowing up towards the ceiling, clouding the kitchen. Daiva dropped to her knees and crumpled forwards. For a moment she was silent and then a low howl broke from her. Her body trembled. She curled over into a ball, shuddering, lost in her crying.

Kneeling beside her, I felt the tears welling in my own eyes. Gently I touched her on the shoulder. I brushed the hair back from her cheek, ran my fingers across the smooth silk curve of her back. I took her arm, tried to pull her close to me. She resisted. She clenched herself tightly. A ball of pain.

'I'm sorry,' I whispered.

Above us, on the hob, the kettle shrieked. I stood and lifted it carefully, using a towel so as not to burn my fingers. I turned off the flame and stood and leant forwards across the cooker, feeling the scorching heat of the steam dampen my forehead, condense in my hair like dew on a spider's web. On the floor behind me Daiva did not move. She cried softly, unstoppably.

'I'm sorry,' I said, but already my heart was hardening, irritated by her refusal to listen. A bitter little thought niggled at the back of my head. She had won. I crushed the idea immediately.

'Really, I'm sorry,' I said. But I turned then, feeling the anger building again.

Going into the bedroom, I dressed quickly. The baby was still sleeping in the cot and I stopped for a moment by her side and leant down and brushed my fingers across the soft down on her head. When she stirred, I stepped back quickly, fearing I had woken her. I hesitated in the doorway. Daiva had not moved.

Outside, I lifted my head and gazed up into the darkness. The clouds hung low, scraping soft-bellied across the roofs of the nine-storey apartment blocks. I closed my eyes, pressed my fingers into the sockets, squeezing, until star bursts kaleidoscoped across the skin of my eyelids. A ripple of sorrow brushed across my face. Settled on it. When I lifted my fingers and opened my eyes, the dots and stars whirled across the sky, flashing among the street lamps and the brilliant sudden glow of headlights. A car engine roared, as someone revved it hard. My mind was spinning in the tail of the light particles. I felt the ground shift and open a crack. My hands trembled and my feet almost turned in the direction of the bar on the corner, in the basement of the five-storey block just off Freedom Boulevard. I stopped, Davia's voice tolling in my ear. 'It won't help. It's not an answer.'

'I know,' I said, then looked around, momentarily embarrassed that I had actually spoken the words aloud. I ran a hand through my hair. I know. Did she think I did not know? Did she continually need to tell me it wasn't the answer? Did she not understand that if there was an answer, if there was a relief from this crushing fear, this darkness, I would have taken it? Would gladly have taken it, whatever it might have been.

A sob of desperation welled up inside me. 'Oh God,' I murmured. A shower of images scattered across my mind. Scorching, brilliant sparks that settled and burnt the thin membrane of forgetting I had woven to protect myself. A scream. A shout. A body, split like a ripe fig at the side of the road. The sweet-sour stench of death. Hot dust in the back of my throat. The crackle of gunfire.

My mind wobbled, trembled, shivered on the edge of the abyss. I had worked so hard to forget those years in Afghanistan. I had manhandled a thousand rocks into the hole: my craft, friends, marriage, child, love and anger, the rubble of life, and now I turned to find it still open, yawning darkly, waiting to swallow me.

Chapter 6

The base we reported to was a sprawling site to the north-west of Vilnius. We were handed uniforms: green suits with a red band on the shoulder, boots as stiff as wood, so inflexible we could not move our feet. We laughed, tramping around the barrack room, clumsy as elephants, our heads newly shaved. Clowning, excited still.

Later we were divided into different companies and told we would be going abroad. Kolya and I found ourselves in the same company.

'Look at the belts they gave us,' Kolya said, slapping his down across the bunk.

'What about them?'

'Look how badly made they are. It's clear, isn't it?'

A small group gathered around the bunk, examining their belts.

'What do you mean?' someone asked.

'You know how it goes?' Kolya said. 'They give the good belts to those going to Germany or somewhere nice, and to those going out east . . .'

The group fell momentarily silent. We stared at the belts as though they held the key to our futures. There was no doubt the belts we had been given were of an inferior quality, even by the standards Kolya and I were used to in the children's home.

'You don't know shit,' someone said.

There were mutterings of agreement and the crowd

dispersed quietly. The clowning stopped, though, and when we did physical exercise the next morning we threw ourselves through the assault course with violent determination, toughening ourselves up, welcoming the cuts and bruises and aching muscles.

Kolya was right about the belts. At the end of our first month of training we were put on to a plane at Vilnius airport. We were not told our destination, but the long flight took us south-east, across the vast plains of Russia to central Asia. When dawn broke it illuminated, thousands of metres below us, barren scrubland, stretching to the horizon. As the sun climbed higher and its rosy flush spilt across the earth, the foothills of a distant mountain range bubbled up darkly from the plain. A city was spread out below us, dissected by a sinuously curving river, still shrouded in the grey light of early dawn. Only the upper tips of the acres of high-rise apartment blocks were caught by the sun, reaching like bloodied fingers for the underbelly of the plane. We landed in Tashkent in the early hours of morning.

At the airport a row of KamaZ trucks were waiting for us, their tarpaulins flapping and billowing in a strong breeze. We jumped up into the trucks, tired and bleary eyed, and gazed out in amazement as we bumped through the huge city; streets lined with poplars, monumental tower blocks the like of which I had never seen in my life. Fountains glittered in the morning sunlight; the squares seemed wider than the small town I had been raised in.

The trucks took us to a large base outside the city, which, in contrast to its barren surroundings, was lined with trees beneath which stretched tidy green lawns. Large portraits of politburo members hung at regular intervals down the long avenue that ran from the main gates of the compound to the large concrete barracks and parade ground.

Training began in earnest almost immediately. Equipped with backpacks, filled with soft sand till they weighed thirty kilos, and wearing eighteen-kilogram bulletproof vests, we were marched up mountains. Boots slipping on the dusty scree, my hands were soon covered in a thousand small cuts and bruises mottled my body. My muscles ached, my feet were blistered, and my lungs burnt in the hot dry air. Though it was late autumn, it was still hot in the daytime. In the evening, as soon as the sun dropped, the temperature plummeted.

One morning, Oleg Ivanovich, our company commander, drove us into the desert. The low, stony scrub stretched away into the distance, disappearing into the early morning haze some kilometres away, with barely a ripple in the earth. He ordered the driver to stop when the desert surrounded us on all sides and no evidence of civilisation was to be seen. Ivanovich nodded at a pile of shovels in the back of the KamaZ.

'You drive exactly one kilometre up the road,' he said, jerking his chin ahead now, to where the road shimmered into liquid on the horizon. 'Then you pull off and take these shovels and dig a hole deep enough so that I cannot see a fucking trace of this ugly truck. Is that understood?'

Quick nervous glances flicked between us. Kolya looked as though he was about to protest but as he opened his mouth Yuri, a pale young Uzbeki conscript, broke in.

'Yes, sir,' he said.

Ivanovich glared around at us. 'Good,' he said, and a thin sarcastic smile twisted his lips. He reached beneath a seat and pulled out a bottle of vodka. From the back

45

of the truck he took a stool and wandered away from the road.

'What the fuck?' Kolya said, making sure Ivanovich was well out of earshot. He turned on the young Uzbeki boy. 'You stupid little fucker. If you're so keen, you can go dig the hole yourself.'

'Leave him alone, Kolya,' I said. 'It's not his fault Ivanovich is such an arsehole.'

'I was just keeping you out of trouble,' Yuri protested. 'If you go shooting your mouth off, he'll be on your back again.'

'I don't need your help,' Kolya snarled.

We drove a kilometre down the road and the driver pulled off into the low scrub. We took the shovels from the back of the truck and Yuri measured a large rectangle in the firm, dry earth. He subdivided the rectangle and apportioned each of us an area to dig. Kolya glowered at him. The earth was cracked and hard. The shovel bounced from the dusty surface, jarring my arm. Using the edge, it was possible to lever up small clods, which we tossed over our shoulders. Beneath the baked surface the earth was less resistant. We worked hard, dispensing with our jackets, feeling the sun beat heavily on our backs, charring the skin on our necks. We worked until every muscle strained and it seemed impossible to continue gripping the shovel, the finger muscles cramping, raw blisters rising and tearing, until our hands were pink with blood and split flesh. We dug down into the parched Uzbeki earth, and felt it rise around us like a grave, dug until all we desired was to lie on the cool earth and give ourselves to eternal rest.

When we had dug so deep the sinking sun could no longer torture us, there was a cry. We stopped and clambered out on to the sloping mounds of earth, lay on our backs and gazed into the cool blue sky. We heard the engine of the KamaZ fire, but did not look up. Yuri trotted away across the sand, turned one hundred metres away and waved the driver on. The truck rolled down the slope into the hole and we lay and waited on Yuri's verdict.

'I ain't moving. I don't give a shit, I'm not digging any more,' Kolya said.

Yuri stood by the road, shimmering in the light of the sun, which was setting. We watched him. He did not call or indicate whether he could see the top of the truck, which was close to the edge of the hole, but came trotting slowly back across the sand towards us. We sat up and watched him approach. His pace slowed as he came close and he slouched wearily across the last twenty metres of sand, his shoulders drooping.

'It's fine,' he said. 'You can't see anything.'

Kolya stood up. His face was set like concrete and his eyes flickered with fury. He slipped down the slope to where Yuri was standing, and grabbed the young Uzbeki's dirty vest.

'You fucker!' Kolya spat.

'What?'

'Why didn't you just call from over there?'

'What do you mean?'

Kolya pushed Yuri back. Yuri looked at him, fearfully.

'You know what I mean, you little arsehole.'

He jabbed Yuri hard with his fist. Yuri stumbled, raising his arms to defend himself. We watched in silence from the low mound of earth. No one had the energy to move and intervene. As Yuri fell to the ground Kolya kicked him viciously. Yuri screeched, a shrill, fearful protest.

47

At that moment the figure of Oleg Ivanovich staggered into view, black against the setting sun. He approached slowly, weaving from side to side, stumbling occasionally in the brush. His face, we could see when he drew closer, was scarlet. He stopped when he was close to us and gazed around with an irritated but bewildered look on his face.

'Where's the fucking truck?' he yelled, gaping distractedly from one face to another. 'What the fuck have you done with it?'

'He's sunburnt,' someone whispered.

'And pissed.'

'He must have fallen asleep in the sun.'

'He's probably got sunstroke.'

Ivanovich staggered forward towards Kolya, who was still standing over the cowering figure of the Uzbeki conscript. He raised a finger and stabbed it against Kolya's chest.

'Where's the truck?' he snarled, and bent over and vomited on Kolya's boots. He straightened up, but his eyeballs were floating loosely around the whites of his small eyes and a few moments later his legs gave way and he crumpled to the ground with a thud. We gathered around his supine figure, a silent, bemused crowd.

'Is he dead?' Yuri whispered, his voice shaking.

'Don't be so stupid.'

'Better get him back to base as quick as we can.'

We loaded Ivanovich on to the back of the KamaZ and drove back to base. The sun had already set and it was dark by the time we dragged his unconscious body into the medical wing.

Word of our posting came through at the end of our period of training. All of us had heard whispered stories about Afghanistan. For the first years of the conflict the reality of the situation was kept secret by the government. Even when the zinc coffins began coming home on the planes they called black tulips, the silence was maintained. There was no suggestion on the gravestones of those first young men that they had died in battle. But as the years passed and conscripts returned to their homes after service, rumours fluttered like dark angels from ear to ear, with stories told in hushed voices of soldiers flayed, of limbs chopped from bodies, of coffins filled with earth because there was no body left to fill the uniform of dead sons sent home.

In the faces of some the panic was visible – tight, pale lips and eyes that flickered rapidly from one object to the next, as if searching for something. Others disguised their fear with coarse jokes and laughter that was a little too loud.

I received a letter from Liuba the week before we left. 'We all miss you,' it read, 'please take care of Kolya for me, I don't know what I will do if anything happens to him.' I sat on my bunk and felt dark, lonely arms enfold me. There was nobody, I thought, who would miss me if I returned home in a zinc coffin. Nevertheless, I took a pen and wrote, 'My dear Liuba, I miss you and your laughter. Kolya is with me still and we have been posted together to Afghanistan. Do not worry about us, we are strong. I will look after Kolya and bring him home to you.'

The political instruction we received increased as the day of our departure drew nearer. Grigov, our Political Officer, harangued us in hour-long sermons about our 'International Duty', about the need to secure the Union's southern border, the need to defend the peace in the territory of our friends, to defend the citizens of Afghanistan against the bandits and counter-revolutionaries funded and armed by America, to build houses and hospitals, schools and roads, to build mosques and sink wells to provide clean water supplies for our friends across the border. To continue, in other words, the brave and noble work of the soldiers who had gone before us, who had begun the struggle to bring peace and revolution to Afghanistan.

'In the *kishlaks*, the villages, they had no clean water. We have dug them wells,' Grigov told us. His uniform was the neatest I had ever seen; everything about Grigov seemed well cut, neatly tailored, smart. A little thrill passed down my spine as I listened to him. The idea of giving myself wholly to some greater enterprise was exhilarating. 'Before, the girls in Afghanistan were allowed no education,' Grigov continued, extolling the benefits of our international aid, 'but in the spirit of the revolution they are now allowed to go to school. The women in the villages are given medical care by our army doctors. It is your patriotic duty to build the way forward for our comrades in Afghanistan.'

For the first time in my life, I felt I belonged. I was needed. I had my part to play in rebuilding Afghanistan. It did not matter that I was an orphan, or that I had not succeeded at school. In my bunk at night I lay in the darkness and thought of Grigov's words. I imagined sinking wells in remote villages, building schools, bringing food and medical aid to those in need. The images of the propaganda films we had been shown flickered through my head: Afghani farmers waving from the fields as the Soviet army passed; children running, grinning joyfully, to gather the sweets thrown by a soldier; young girls in smart blue uniforms bent studiously over their books in recently built classrooms. My International Duty. I whispered the words to myself, thrilled by their sound. My International Duty.

Chapter 7

Wandering out from the apartment blocks on to Freedom Boulevard, I flagged down a taxi. The driver was an elderly Russian, smoking a cigarette that smelt so bad I was compelled to wind down the window a little. He seemed almost asleep as he steered the old Mercedes out into the fast-moving traffic heading towards the Old Town.

A thin light illuminated the crack beneath Tanya's door. Pressing the buzzer, I glanced guiltily at my watch. It was just after midnight. I heard the soft fall of bare feet on the parquet. I pressed my face close to the door.

'It's Antanas,' I called quietly.

The lock turned and I heard the bolts being drawn back. When Tanya opened the door I could see she had been in bed; she was wearing a nightdress and her hair was rumpled. Her expression betrayed both concern and delight.

'Is everything OK?' she asked.

She stood back, allowing me to enter, and took my jacket.

'I'm sorry,' I said, 'to disturb you so late.'

We walked through to the sitting room, which was illuminated by the small lamp that had been on the last time I had visited Vassily at home. A cushion and sheet lay crumpled on the sofa.

'I couldn't sleep in the bed,' Tanya explained. 'It seemed too big.'

She rested her head against my shoulder and for some moments we stood in the doorway, silently, gazing into the room, empty without his bulky presence, his laughter and stories.

When finally Tanya spoke she said, 'Shall we have a glass of brandy?'

The bottle was beside the sofa. Tanya fetched another glass from the kitchen and poured two generous measures. Sitting beside her I felt the warmth of her legs as she curled them up between us. She pulled the band out from her hair and ran her fingers through it, loosening it.

'The place seems so empty without him,' she said. 'I am so glad you came.' She paused then, seemingly struck by a thought. 'But what about Daiva? Will she not . . .'

'We had an argument,' I said.

'Oh, Antanas.'

Tanya held my fingers between her own, caressing them softly. When I drained my glass, she reached down, picked up the bottle and refilled it.

'Why did you argue?' she asked.

I shook my head. 'Everything. Nothing,' I said. 'The same things as always.' I found I was reluctant to mention what had happened. 'My drinking. She can't stand it any more. I can't either.'

'You're pale and your hands are shaking,' Tanya said, squeezing my fingers. 'What's wrong?'

I tried to speak, but the words caught in my throat. I felt the darkness bloom, felt its black petals uncurl, its gloomy scent fan out through my body, coiling around me like a snake, tightening around my chest.

'I don't know,' I began.

Tanya moved closer and rested her head against my shoulder. Her hand lay on my arm. I stood up and went

53

over to my jacket, which Tanya had hung on a peg in the hallway. I took the note Vassily had written just hours before he died and gave it to Tanya. She read it silently. When she had finished, she looked up, her brow creased in a frown.

'What is this about?' she said. 'Why did he need you to forgive him?'

'I've no idea,' I said, walking over to the window. 'I was hoping you would be able to explain a little more.'

Tanya shook her head. 'I know nothing,' she said.

'Did he not say anything more in the hospital?'

'No.' She thought. 'He was very agitated. He made me promise to make you find Kolya. That's it.'

Opening the window, I gazed down into the street, remembering how I had stood in this very place just a couple of days before, with Vassily behind me in the chair.

'The other evening,' I said, 'when I was here, Vassily insisted on telling me one of his tales. There was a jewel he discovered while we were in Afghanistan – a bracelet. It was a valuable one. Something happened – he did not explain – but when he got back after the war, for some reason he was consumed with guilt. He buried the bracelet.' I shook my head, unwilling, still, to be drawn into this story.

Tanya looked perplexed. 'I don't understand.'

'Neither do I,' I said. 'He wants me to find Kolya to hear all about what happened, as if I don't know enough already. As if it hasn't haunted me too over the years.' I paused, my mind snagging on the memories, fluttering already, darkly, at the back of my mind. 'I told Vassily,' I continued, 'I wanted nothing to do with this. I have tried so hard to forget those years. I don't know why he wants me to remember now.'

Closing the window, I came back over to her. She took my hand.

'I don't understand why he didn't tell me any of this if it has been eating away at him all these years,' Tanya said quietly, more to herself than me. 'There were never secrets between us, there was never anything that was not said.' She paused. 'Vassily never held anything back, he told me everything. You know him, you know what he was like.' She looked up at me. 'He was unable to keep a secret, he was incapable of lying. Words just bubbled up out of him. That was the way he was.'

I nodded.

'Why don't I know, then?' she said again. 'Why did he say nothing to me if it caused him so much pain?'

'I think there were things Vassily didn't say for my sake,' I said. 'When he took me from the hospital I tried so hard to forget those years. At first it was easy. The medication I was given at the hospital closed my mind down, cauterised it. But as the years passed the dreams began to return. I have them still. There are times I am afraid to sleep.'

'What do you dream?'

'Of fire. Of a girl. Faces. Fear. Anger. Of unspeakable things.'

'What is it you are afraid of?'

'I don't know. There was a time I thought it had gone – the fear, the dreams. For months, years even, they disappeared, and I thought I had finally beaten them. When Daiva became pregnant it was as if I myself had been impregnated with a seed of light. It grew inside me, filling me with hope. But they have come back. I'm afraid of them. I drink, because the drink holds back the darkness. But the drinking isn't helping me; it's driving Daiva away, it's ruining every good thing I have.'

Tanya reached up and touched me. She pulled me close and we embraced. I looped my arms around her and felt the warm give of her body, like a ship drawing up against the harbour wall, the gentle thud as it impacts and is drawn tight, fast, by the ropes that are flung out, curling through the cold air, to waiting hands.

'What are you going to do?' Tanya asked a little later.

'I don't know,' I confessed. 'Vassily wanted me to find Kolya. Said Kolya would tell me whatever it was he had not been able to and in return I would give Kolya directions to find the bracelet. I told him I had no interest in hearing Kolya's stories, but he got angry, said it was important.' I shook my head. 'Kolya wrote Vassily a begging letter, saying he needed money for hospital treatment. For drugs, more likely!'

'What could it be that Vassily kept so secret?'

I shrugged.

'How would you find Kolya? Is he here in Vilnius?'

'Vassily gave me Kolya's letter. It seems he is back in the city.'

'What did you do with it?'

'I threw it away,' I said. 'I want nothing to do with it.'

We sat then, together, for some time in silence, each pondering the events that had unfurled over the last few days.

'I feel betrayed in some way,' Tanya said. 'As though I've just discovered there was more to him than I knew. As though he hid a part of himself from me.'

*

When I returned to our apartment the next day Daiva was in the hallway, taking her coat from a hook. 'We need to talk,' she said, when I opened the door. I paused on the threshold. She stood in the shadows, making it hard to see the expression on her face: to judge whether her eyes were red-rimmed with tears again. Perhaps it would have been better if I had turned then and gone back out, but I could not think of anywhere I might go.

I shrugged off my own coat and hung it on a peg. She stood, arms folded, against the wall.

'I'll just change,' I said, indicating my crumpled clothes, wanting to avoid the conversation for a few more moments. She nodded. The baby was not in the bedroom, her cot was empty, and I could hear no sound from the sitting room. I opened the cupboard to get some dry clothes and noticed that the small pile of baby clothes was gone.

'Where's Laura?' I asked, once I had changed.

'I've taken her to my mother's,' Daiva said.

We stood in the kitchen in silence, looking out from the window down at the street below, dark already though it was only late afternoon. Daiva filled the kettle and put it on the hob.

'I'll make you a drink,' she said. Her voice was soft and there was concern there, but not a bridge. I nodded and sat down at the table. I fiddled with some of my daughter's toys while she boiled the water and made the coffee.

'I can't go on like this,' she said suddenly, her back to me, pouring the steaming water into the cups.

I did not reply. She turned and put the coffee before me. The steam curled up and dissolved in the gloom. She sat lightly in a chair on the other side of the table, her hands folded in her lap. Her legs were close enough for me to reach out and touch. I could, I knew, get up and go round to her, put my arms around her, and perhaps it would have worked. Perhaps, after all, there was still a path by which I could have gone back to her, a bridge that remained standing while all the rest smouldered.

I spooned sugar into my coffee and stirred it slowly, deliberately, not raising my eyes from the cup. I sipped it, but it was too hot and it scalded my lips. She raised her hands to her face and for a moment I was afraid she was going to start crying again. I looked up sharply. She rubbed her hands across her eyes and looked at me.

Her hair fell around her face. I noticed she had made herself up. Her eyes were not red-rimmed, they were lined with mascara. Her cheeks were flushed a little, and she was wearing lipstick. She looked more beautiful than I remembered seeing her in months.

'I'm going,' she said. 'I'm leaving.'

'Yes,' I said a little too quickly. I looked back at the steam. Put my fingers into it, feeling the drops condensing warmly on my skin. Maybe I should have said something more. A thick pain had gripped my chest and a sense of sorrow overwhelmed me. I said nothing. I did not know what to say, did not know any more which words would take me to her, which words I could use that had not already been used, that might open up some line of communication rather than lead back into the same argument.

I should, I knew, explain that it was not Tanya but the past which was pulling me away from her. I should tell Daiva that, after protecting me for so many years, her cool indifference to my past was failing me now.

That the ghost of a love was seducing me once more from the grave. But I could not explain because I did not want to face up to the pain myself. Did not want to remember. Because I struggled still against the dark hole opening up beneath me.

It had, anyway, been to Tanya that I had always turned with my fears. As the years had passed, especially after Daiva became pregnant, the natural closeness between Tanya and me had became more of a strain for Daiva. Occasionally her cool pride broke and she would fly at me in fury. Though it was Tanya who had introduced us, Daiva rarely saw or spoke to her or Vassily now.

I exhaled slowly, wearily. The chances were, in any case, that my drinking had gone on too long for Daiva to want to start building bridges back across to me. There had been too many arguments, too many of her friends alienated by my behaviour, too many scenes. She needed those bridges down, I suspected. I had hurt her too much. Let her down too often. Promised too much, time and again, but changed nothing.

She got up and put her cup by the sink. For some moments she stood above me in the gloom, perhaps waiting for me to reach out and stop her. Perhaps giving me one last chance to say those words I could not find. Then she sighed and turned away. I heard her putting on her coat and rummaging in the bottom of the cupboard for her handbag. She opened the door and for a few seconds she paused again, or perhaps she was just checking she had all she needed. The door closed and I heard the click of her heels on the stairs.

In the cupboard above the sink there was a bottle of her brandy. The bottle Daiva kept there in case friends came around, which they never did any more. Taking the bottle and a glass, I went to the balcony and poured myself a drink. It was a few minutes before she emerged. There was a taxi waiting which she must have ordered before I came home. She stepped into it and it drew away slowly, jolting in the deep potholes. I watched until it turned into the thick flow of traffic on Freedom Boulevard.

Lying on the sofa, I drank some more of the brandy. Daiva had forgotten to take Laura's teddy bear, I noticed, the one I had bought her some weeks before. I picked it up and fondled it. When I lay down, though, it was of Vassily that I thought. He lay silent now. His stories had been stilled. Vassily had rebuilt me, had enabled me to forget, to find new purpose in life. But now he was gone.

Chapter 8

When I awoke the next morning, Laura's teddy bear was clasped tight in my hand, while beside me, on the floor, the bottle of brandy lay on its side, empty. With my ear pressed painfully to the floor, I could hear the sound of the couple in the apartment below shuffling through their morning routines – the run of water, a man's cough followed by the trumpeting of his nose, the sharp bark of his wife calling him and his responding grunt; the sound of their feet moving slowly across the floorboards, unhurried, following their accustomed patterns, patterns that had taken them through thirty years of marriage, the birth and rearing of children, the loss of their eldest boy in Afghanistan, communism, revolution, jobs and unemployment.

I rolled on to my back and felt a paralysingly sharp pain shoot down my spine. My arm was numb and my fingers cold and lifeless. I flexed them, working some blood back into circulation. Beneath me I heard the sound of a chair being pulled out from the table and its creak as my neighbour sat down to his breakfast.

My own apartment was eerily silent. Laura always woke early. It was the first sound of the day, her small cry, followed by the sound of Daiva turning in her sleep, waking slowly. Laura would stand at the bars of her cot and call to us. Daiva's voice would be thick and rough with sleep, and the bed would dip as she levered herself up. They would wander out to the kitchen, leaving the door open so I could hear them talk as Daiva lit the hob and warmed some milk. Later she would drop Laura on the bed beside me, and put a cup of coffee on the small table beside me, and I would sit up then and watch as my daughter played.

Once the feeling returned to my left side, and the pain had receded from my neck, I raised myself into a sitting position. The curtains were not drawn and a tentative early morning glow lightened the room. Far away, in the distance, the clouds had broken up a little and there was a glimmer of bright sky. My head throbbed and the clothes I was still dressed in felt soiled. I stripped them off, letting them drop on to the sofa.

The water in the shower was hot and beat against my skin. For a long time I stood there, allowing it to wash over me, warm me, ease the muscles knotted in my shoulders. I held my face up to the surging jets and closed my eyes.

The moment I turned off the shower tap, the telephone rang. Its shrill tone echoed in the empty apartment, jangling, insistent. The sudden burst of noise made my pulse race. I stood riveted in the bathtub, the water trickling around my feet, listening to the sound. Looking down at my hands, I noticed they were shaking.

Reproving myself, I stepped out of the bath. Taking a towel from the hot-water pipe, I rubbed myself down quickly. It would be Daiva, I thought, and a sudden small bubble of hope rose from deep within me and burst through the surface of my consciousness. I opened the door and hurried across the hallway to the telephone, my bare feet leaving damp prints on the wooden tiles. As I put my hand on the heavy black receiver it fell silent. I knew, even before I had put it to my ear, that I had missed her.

I dropped the receiver back on to its cradle and squatted by the small table, chin resting on my knees, watching the telephone, willing it to ring again. I sat until the water dried on my skin, and a draught from beneath the door had chilled my feet. The telephone remained stubbornly silent.

It had been early February, seven years before, when the snow lay thick upon the city, that Daiva had first come to see me in the workshop Vassily and I owned. I took off my mask and unplugged the lathe.

'Were you looking for Vassily?' I asked.

'No,' she said, avoiding my gaze. 'I was looking for you.'

'Perhaps we can go out for a little lunch, then,' I suggested. 'I know a place not far from here.'

'Fine.'

The café was busy. As we sat by the window, our knees touched beneath the table and I felt the warmth of her legs against my own. Her blonde hair fell across her face as she looked down the menu and she twisted it between her thin fingers. Her nails were painted a deep pink. Her features were finely shaped, delicate. She smiled nervously when she looked up, catching me examining her.

'The *chanahi* is good,' I said.

The clay pots of *chanahi* were still sizzling when the waiter placed them before us. When we opened the lids the aroma was released in a spicy cloud – stewed mutton, potatoes, onion and tomatoes. For some moments we ate in silence. I noticed the smoothness of her skin, the cherry-red fullness of her lips and the deep shadow at the base of her throat.

'Shouldn't you be at university?' I asked to break the silence.

'Yes,' she said, not looking up. She scraped her fork against the clay pot, lifting off the crisp potato baked to the inside of the rim.

'You decided to take the day off?'

'Yes.'

For a few moments longer I examined her, unsure of her feelings. When we left the café it was snowing; tiny, powdery, paper-light flakes that danced on the breeze. Blue sky edged the broken clouds and the sun glittered on the rooftops. A network of narrow paths had been trodden in the snow between the low trees. The fine snow fell around her, glistening in a stray beam of sunlight, so that she was encircled by a halo of golden flakes. She turned on the track in front of me, frozen clouds of breath suspended in the sun. I stopped a few paces from her and gazed at her. She looked like an angel.

I came to her and she did not move away. Her breath was warm against my skin. Her eyes closed as she sank against me. Her lips and tongue tasted of the spices of the *chanahi*. Sharp. Rich.

We hurried through the snow, slipping down a steep bank on to the street, tumbling and falling in the thick snow, not letting go of each other. My icy fingers fumbled with the lock on the back door of the workshop. Inside, I pulled a rolled-up mattress from the cupboard and took a couple of blankets and laid them on top of the large tiled stove. Daiva laughed, opening the door of the stove to check it was not burning too high.

She gasped when my fingers worked through her clothes to find her skin, rough with goose bumps.

'You're freezing!'

She slipped her hand beneath my jumper, her icy fingers dancing across my stomach, making me shiver, so that I shouted too, bellowed into the air, shaking the dust-laden cobwebs on the ceiling above us. She looked fragile in the wan light reflected off the snow outside the window, inverting the shadows on her body.

The heat rose from the stove beneath us, warming us, relaxing muscles tautened by the cold. I felt her hands, the tickle of her lips gliding across my chest, the soft brush of her hair against my throat.

'At first – when you came to Vilnius – you didn't like me,' she said later.

She hitched herself up, cradling her chin in the palm of her hand, and traced lines across my face with the tip of a finger. I closed my eyes and pictured her as I had first seen her, in Tanya's apartment, the evening Vassily and I had arrived in the city.

'You were pretty sharp with me,' I said. 'I think I was scared of you.'

'Was I sharp with you?'

She leant down and brushed my skin with her lips. I pulled her close, letting her weight press me down into the thin, warm mattress.

'I was nervous,' she said. 'I thought you would laugh at me. I felt like a young girl with you, as if I knew nothing.'

'I like that,' I told her, 'that you ask nothing. I feel I can forget with you.'

The draught from beneath the door began to chill me and I got up from beside the telephone.

Once I had dressed, I searched through the cupboards

to find some breakfast. Daiva had bought food, presumably for me to survive on, as her departure seemed to have been planned further ahead than I realised. Opening the wardrobe in the bedroom, earlier I had found that she had taken a suitcase and many of her clothes. I sliced some smoked sausage and cut a thick slice of bread, boiled the kettle and made a strong coffee. On the window sill was an old radio and I turned it on, tuning it to the Polish station.

Before leaving the apartment, I stopped by the telephone. I picked up the receiver, and was about to dial Daiva's mother's number, but hesitated. Though it seemed the most likely place for Daiva to have gone, there was still a possibility she hadn't, and then I would be forced to explain myself to her mother. And anyway, I thought, what was I going to say? What was there left to say that had not already been said? I replaced the receiver, pulled on my jacket and left the apartment.

The workshop was on the edge of the Old Town. Mainly we sold the jewellery we produced in the cramped room behind the shopfront. Several other craftsmen sold their goods through us too. The door was locked when I got there and already, after an absence of only a few days, the place looked dusty and neglected. I shut the door behind me, keeping the 'closed' sign in place in the window. The shop felt cold and damp. I switched on the light and lit a small paraffin heater in the back to take the chill from the air.

The workshop was strewn with work. Pulling my chair close to the heater, holding out my hands to the blue flames to warm them, I recalled the promise Vassily had made, soon after he had taken me from the hospital to Tanya's village.

'I will teach you how to work amber,' he said. 'We will be jewellers, the two of us, craftsmen of the highest order, the best on the Baltic coast. I will teach you all you need to know. We will make jewels and forget about the past.'

A neighbour in the village, a stooped elderly man with wild silver hair, had machinery for working amber. The workshop was in the basement of his house. Its tiled floor and cabinets were white with dust from the worked amber. Even the cobwebs were heavily sugared with it. The walls were lined with templates and everywhere there were tubs full of amber chips, some buttery yellow, others chalk white, whilst others were rich shades of orange or red. A pot of small black amber beads was like a tub of caviar. Held up to the sun, they were blood red. Heated, the small oxygen bubbles at their heart exploded, giving the pieces a crazed look.

In a crudely built outhouse were the machines for polishing and firing the amber. A barrel filled with cubes of oak turned for two days, smoothing and polishing the surface of the ancient resin.

As I was remembering, the telephone on the shelf above the heater sprang abruptly into life, rattling harshly, causing my heart to flutter in panic. For a couple of seconds I sat and watched as it rang on the shelf, then I snatched it up and held the receiver to my ear. My heart was beating rapidly, and crazily, for a moment, it was Vassily's voice I was expecting to hear, longing to hear.

'*Da?*' I said into the echoing silence. 'Who is there?'

The telephone hissed and crackled but nobody answered.

'Who is it?' I called.

Faintly, I thought, I could hear the sound of breathing,

but it might have been only the wind, or the sound of cavernous space that occasionally opens up between one telephone and another.

I waited a moment longer then replaced the receiver. Sitting down again, I lit a cigarette. When I had stubbed it out in the overflowing saucer, I got up and went back over to the telephone. I dialled the number for Vassily's apartment and listened as it rang and rang.

When it became clear than Tanya was not home, I turned on my desk lamp and pushed aside the piles of invoices and orders strewn across it. Beneath the sheets were some pieces of amber I had been working a few days before. I picked up one of the small tear-shaped pieces and held it up to the lamp, examining the way the light entered it and hung suspended in its heart.

'You know where amber comes from?' Vassily said, one evening, in the village. We were beside the pond, close to Tanya's grandparents' cottage. Vassily had given Tanya a necklace he had fashioned. Each piece of amber had been shaped and smoothly polished and strung on to a silk thread. In the centre of the string of beads was a larger piece, a translucent, golden tear.

'Many years ago, when the forest grew thick here, when this land was under the care of other gods, when the spirits lived in the trees and Perkunas, the God of Thunder, ruled in heaven, the most beautiful of the goddesses was a young mermaid called Jurate.'

Vassily's face reflected the glow of the sun, which was setting across the village. On the opposite side of the pond a heron rooted among the reeds.

'Jurate was the most beautiful mermaid,' he continued. 'Her hair was golden and her eyes blue, bluer than the sky on midsummer's morning. She lived not far from here, just off the coast, beneath the waves in a palace built of amber.

'In a small village like this one, there lived a young fisherman called Kastytis. Kastytis would take his boat and fish in the waters of the beautiful Jurate's kingdom. Jurate sent her mermaids to warn him away, but Kastytis paid no attention to the messengers of the goddess beneath the waves. He continued to sail out and cast his nets on the water above her palace.

'One morning Jurate herself rose to the surface to confront the fisherman. But when she approached him in his boat, she instantly fell in love. She took the young fisherman with her, beneath the waves, to her amber palace, and there they lived.'

Vassily stubbed out his cigarette in the dirt. Clumsily the heron took to the air, its wings beating over our heads, up across the trees towards the seashore.

'And they lived happily ever after?' Tanya asked.

She was sitting by him and with a small pang of jealousy I noticed their closeness. Vassily shook his head. He took another cigarette and Tanya lit it for him. The flare of the match illuminated their faces in a warm, bright glow. The sun had settled behind the trees and the air was pink and blue and cool.

'Jurate, you see, was already promised to another,' Vassily continued. 'Long before, Perkunas had promised the young goddess to the god of the waters. Perkunas was furious when he discovered that Jurate was in love with a mortal. He cast a bolt of lightning down from his heavenly throne, shattering the goddess's palace of amber. Jurate was imprisoned within the rubble of her ruined palace for all eternity.

'When the winds are high and the waves break heavily upon the shore, the sea throws up fragments of her palace. And sometimes, too, it throws up these.' He touched the tear-shaped amber drop on the necklace that lay at Tanya's throat. 'The tears of Jurate, a prisoner still, crying beneath the waves for her lost love, Kastytis.'

Before I turned off the desk lamp, I glanced around to see whether there was anything needing my urgent attention. There were bills that needed settling, but I was in no mood to deal with them. I gathered them together and pushed them into a leather briefcase to take with me. Switching off the lamp, I turned to the heater. As I extinguished the flame and bent to check it, I noticed a shadow flit across the door. Straightening up, I turned to call that the shop was closed. A dark shape stood outside, face pressed to the dirty glass, peering through.

'We're closed,' I shouted.

The figure did not move. Irritated, I took the key from the desk and shuffled over. As I approached, the figure stepped back, away from the glass. It was an old lock, and the key fitted awkwardly, so that I had to jiggle it to get it to turn. It undid with a solid clunk. The door flew open, catching my wrist, twisting it painfully. Astonished, I stepped back as the figure moved forward rapidly, entering the shop, pushing the door closed.

'*Zdrastvuy*, Antoshka,' the man said. 'It has been a long time.'

'Kirov.'

The lean figure nodded and grinned humourlessly, turning the key in the lock.

'Don't want any of your customers disturbing us, now, do we?' he said.

'I thought you were in prison . . .' I stammered.

Kirov laughed. He threw back his closely shaved head, his mouth opening to reveal gold teeth that glinted dully.

'I would have come to see you at home,' he said, 'but when I telephoned this morning you were not in.'

I was about to explain I had been in the shower, but stopped myself. In his presence the familiar feelings flooded back; feelings I thought I had left behind, that the years and the haloperidol and vodka had scratched from the surface of my memory. The stink of thorn-bush. The scent of wood smoke. Oil. Sweat. Fear. Dust billowing up from the wheels of the APC. For a moment I was back there, in Afghanistan. I stood rooted to the spot, unable to speak, unable to move. It was as if he had leapt from my dreams; my nightmares.

'What do you want, Kirov?' I asked, finally.

'To renew old acquaintance.' He chuckled, wandering over to my desk. He placed the door key on the table and picked up one of the tear-shaped amber beads, examining it closely. 'In these times of mourning it is important we all pull together, no?' He grinned again, dropping the amber on to the table.

'He always was fascinated by amber,' Kirov continued, settling himself in Vassily's chair. He waved his hand, indicating I should sit. Reluctantly I did so, opposite him. 'Never understood it myself,' he said, 'not unless it was worth something. Very few of the stones and jewellery we smuggled out of Afghanistan were worth much. There was just the one, really. Just the one.'

His fingers formed a tight steeple, the tips resting against his lips. He gazed over them, his piercing grey eyes settling on me, examining me.

'You would know all about that one, wouldn't you,' he said.

71

I shook my head. 'No, Kirov, I know nothing.'

'Oh, come now, Antoshka, he told you nothing? You know nothing of the bracelet?'

Again I shook my head.

'We got it in Ghazis,' he said, gazing at me, openly examining the effect of his words. He laughed as if this were funny, but as he chuckled his eyes continued to stare at me stonily.

'Vassily told me nothing,' I said. 'You really are talking to the wrong person.'

'You think you owe him something? I know, you're an honourable man, Antanas. The question is, was he?'

'What do you mean?' I said.

Kirov eased himself forward in Vassily's chair. A sly grin crept across his face.

'Vassily. Was he an honourable man? Was he worthy of your gratitude, your respect?'

'I don't know what you're talking about,' I said.

I got up and took the key from my desk, indicating to Kirov I considered our conversation ended. Kirov, however, did not move. He watched me closely. With deliberate care he slid a packet of cigarettes from his pocket and extracted one. Slouching back into the chair, raising his feet and resting them on the edge of the desk, he lit the cigarette and blew a cloud of thin blue smoke into the air above his head.

'No, you don't,' he said at last. 'You have no idea what I am talking about, do you? How much did our friend Vassily . . .' He paused mid-sentence, took another drag on his cigarette and tapped the ash from it on to the floor. 'How much did he tell you? About what happened there, in Afghanistan?'

'We didn't talk about it.'

Kirov laughed. 'I'll bet he didn't.'

'I said "we" didn't talk about it,' I corrected him pointedly.

Kirov rose from his seat suddenly. He stepped over to me, raised a finger and prodded my chest.

'There are things you should know,' he whispered. 'There are things he should have told you. The kind of things a friend would have told you. You think he was being considerate of your feelings, stepping around the past, keeping it from you? You think it was for your sake he did not say anything? You're mistaken, Antanas. You're very mistaken. There are some stories Vassily should have told you. There are some confessions he should have made.'

He drew steadily closer, until I could feel his hot breath against my face. His eyes had narrowed and his lips were trembling. With a shudder I recalled the almost sexual thrill he had taken from killing in Afghanistan. Recalled the way he would lick his lips before we went on a raid, the way they would tremble like this as he tested the blade of his knife against the soft pad of his thumb, drawing a little blood, sucking it up, savouring it on his tongue.

I recalled the evening when, drunk, he had grabbed me in the heavy darkness by the latrines, the blade of his knife cold and sharp against my throat.

'I've seen you watching me,' he whispered, his breath hot in my ear. 'In the showers.'

I had heard of his reputation. I tried to pull away, but he pressed the blade deeper so that it bit into the soft flesh of my throat. I felt his hand reaching, searching. A torch beam startled him and I was able to slip out of his grip.

'I'll get you,' he whispered.

'Wouldn't you like to know what Vassily did?' Kirov

taunted me. 'Wouldn't you like me to tell you?'

I stepped away from him and stumbled against a worktop. As I steadied myself, my hand came down on a pair of shears we used for cutting metal. My fingers curled around them, behind my back, opening the blades. Kirov advanced on me. His eyes glittered maliciously. A sudden image of him bent over a body flashed through my mind, the knife bloodied in his hands as he slit around the ear of the dead Afghani. Taking the lobe, he lifted it with the care of a chef and eased it away from the side of the skull as his knife sawed at the gristle.

'It's not a pretty story.' Kirov grinned. 'But then that's why I like it so much.'

I whipped the shears from behind me and flicked the blades threateningly in his face. He stepped back, startled. Not giving him a chance to recover, I thrust them at him again, forcing him to take several paces backwards and stumble on the bags of unworked amber.

'I want you out of here,' I said, my voice trembling. 'I want you out and I don't want to see you back.'

'Now, Antanas . . .'

'Get the fuck out of my shop.'

I stabbed the shears forcefully towards him, and he had to step back again. This time he tripped and sprawled on the floor, in the soft pale dust of the amber.

'I want you out, Kirov,' I breathed, standing above him, ready with the shears to slash him if necessary.

He got to his feet, dusting himself off as he rose. For a moment I thought he was going to lunge forward and fight, but he grinned and backed away. When I unlocked the door and opened it, he lingered a moment longer.

'That bracelet, Antanas, it belongs to me,' Kirov said.

'I paid for it with all those years rotting in a cell. Kolya has it, *da*? You know where he is? Is he here in Vilnius? I will get it – and him for what he did to me. While I was in prison, he thought he was safe, but now . . .'

'I've not seen him, Kirov.'

Kirov nodded and grinned, as if he did not care whether or not this was the truth.

'I'll find him,' he muttered. 'You just stay out of it. If you don't . . .' He smiled. 'I know where Tanya lives. She's all on her own now . . .'

When he left I locked the door immediately. Taking the key from the lock, I drew the blinds down over the windows. Without turning on the lamp, I slumped into my chair by the desk and waited until I had stopped shaking.

Chapter 9

Kabul. February. The sky had cleared and the temperature had risen a few degrees. The mountains that ringed the city were thick with snow. Kabul was fragrant with the scent of wood fires, the air blue with smoke and sharp, bitter cold. The plane left Tashkent on the first. Our last days in Uzbekistan were an unbearable strain and Andrei Konstantinovich, a plump, red-faced conscript from Estonia, blew a hole in his hand while on sentry duty.

'Don't fucking think you'll get out of it like that, you fat little bastard,' Oleg Ivanovich screamed, as the young boy lay moaning in the medical wing, three of his fingers missing. 'I'll get you sent to the worst fucking hellhole you have ever seen. You'll wish it was your stupid fucking pimple of a head you had blown off!'

Kabul glittered faintly in the darkness below us. As the plane dipped down towards the earth, helicopters rose to escort us. Flares arced across the sky from the choppers, illuminating the night with their brilliant colours. We pressed our faces to the window and watched the spectacle like children on New Year's Eve. Kolya whooped.

'The flares are for our protection,' the pilot explained. 'The muj have ground-to-air heat-seeking missiles. The heat from the flares deflects them.'

We gazed down then into the dark creases of the hills, as if we might see, huddled in the shadows of night, small, fierce bands of insurgents. The hills were black, though, revealing nothing of the danger that might be lurking in them. The airfield, as we swooped down towards it, was dotted with hundreds of small fires, which glittered so that it seemed, for a moment, as if the plane had been upturned and beneath us stretched a starry expanse of sky. As we drew closer, we could see, huddled around these fires, the tents of the *dembels* – soldiers who had served their two years and were waiting for their flight home.

A large crowd of them gathered around the plane as it drew to a stop at the end of the runway. They surrounded us, staggering drunkenly, laughing and calling.

'You don't stand a chance . . .'

'You won't survive . . .'

'Better to kill yourselves now. You don't want to know what they will do to you . . .'

We stumbled through the crowd to the trucks awaiting us, to take us through the town to our base. The moon hung heavily over the city, as though it were closer to the earth here than it had been back home. The streets were deserted, only soldiers visible at the corner checkpoints, waving us through peremptorily.

'Curfew,' the driver explained.

In the centre of our barracks, on the edge of the city, a large eucalyptus spread its bare branches across a well-trimmed lawn. The dusty parade ground glimmered in the moonlight. I took a deep breath of the sharp night air and stood for a few moments gazing over the rooftops towards the mountains. They shone milky blue against the pitch darkness of the sky.

*

The rhythm of life soon established itself. Six a.m. reveille. Physical training. Breakfast. Line-up. Political studies. Weapons-cleaning. Lunch. Duties. Dinner. Lights out. Reveille had to be perfect; three seconds and one hundred and eighty men had to get out of bed and fall in. After forty-five seconds we had to be in full uniform. One person failed and we all did it again. And again. And again until we were perfect.

We soon learnt, too, the immutable hierarchy of the army in Afghanistan. The lowest level of this hierarchy was the new recruit, fresh in the country. After six months of service you became a 'granddad' and nearing the end of service a *dembel*.

The new recruit was nothing, an object, a punch bag or slave for the granddads. Their word was the word of God.

'What's your name?' Kozlov, a granddad from Moscow, asked as I waited outside the stinking latrines on the first day. Behind him stood another granddad. Kozlov eyed the packet of cigarettes I held.

I told him my name.

Kozlov held out his hand. For a moment I did not grasp his meaning.

'Give me the cigarettes,' he said then, as if to an idiot.

Instinctively I slipped them into the pocket of my jacket. They were my last pack of More cigarettes.

'How long have you been here?' Kozlov asked.

'What's it to you?' I said. I glanced at Kolya, who stood beside me. There were two of them and two of us, I figured.

Kozlov laughed. His face twisted into a sneer. He was not much bigger than me, but his body was lean and taut, his skin tough and tanned. He grabbed the front of my jacket and swung my back against the concrete wall of the latrines.

'Nobody taught you no fucking manners, you little shit?'

'I think this kid needs teaching a few lessons in respect,' the granddad behind Kozlov chipped in.

'Lick my boots clean, you little shit.'

I stared at him, watching the curve of his smile, believing even then, perhaps, that it was a joke. I didn't see the first punch coming. His knuckles ground into my kidneys. I gasped and fell to my knees. Kolya stepped forward but the other granddad grabbed him and threw him aside.

'Lick my boots, shitface, lick them until they shine,' Kozlov snarled. He hit me hard. My head snapped back and cracked against the concrete wall. Out of the corner of my eye I saw Kolya scrabble away from the boot of Kozlov's friend. Kozlov karate-chopped the base of my neck and I crashed to the earth by his shoe. He thrust his foot against my face, splitting my lip. As I struggled away, his other boot came down heavily on the back of my neck.

'Lick them, or I'll break your fucking neck,' he hissed.

I licked them. I felt the thick dust furring my tongue, the sand gritty on my teeth. Kozlov kept the pressure hard against the back of my neck so that I could barely move and had to stick my tongue out to reach the toe of his boot.

'Lick it well, make it shine, or I'll squash your backbone and cripple you for life. You think anybody is going to give a fuck? Do you think anybody will listen to you? Do you want me to tell you what would happen if you reported this? Let me tell you. The senior officer would come and ask why you hadn't been trained properly, then you would get a proper fucking beating for having reported your seniors. Do you understand?'

I heard the shuffle of feet on the gravel as the latrine door opened. The pressure on the back of my neck lessened so that I was able to swivel my head free and roll away. I looked up to see a large form blocking the light of the sun above me.

'Enjoying yourself, Kozlov?' a voice asked.

'Just teaching the kid a few rules,' Kozlov said. He bent over and pulled the packet of cigarettes from my pocket. When he had gone, the large shape bent down and lifted me up.

'You OK?'

I nodded.

'Vassily,' he said, holding out a large hand. His grip was crushing. 'From Novgorod. I heard you speaking Lithuanian to another of the recruits.'

'You've been to Lithuania?'

He nodded. 'Yes. It's not so far from Novgorod.'

I leant back against the latrine wall. My kidneys throbbed painfully and I found it hard to straighten up. Vassily took out a packet of cigarettes and offered me one.

'You're lucky that was Kozlov,' he said, holding out a red plastic lighter. 'He's been here only six months and is still flexing his muscles. Believe what he said, nobody would give a fuck if he broke your neck. You want to go home, you better learn some rules.'

For the next few days, when I pissed blood flecked my urine. I stumbled through physical training, assault courses, hand-to-hand combat using shovels, sticks, knives, breaking bricks with our fists, martial arts. When we were not fighting we were washing the clothes of the granddads, starching them, sewing gleaming new white patches of cloth on their collars, making them drinks; 'Everything but holding their dicks when they piss,' as Kolya put it.

Twice a week a convoy left the base to pick up supplies from Kabul. Kolya and I were picked for duty on the convoy's armed escort. Vassily was chosen too. After loading sacks of potatoes and boxes of tinned milk on to the back of the KamaZ, Vassily suggested he introduce us to the city. Shouldering our Kalashnikovs, we followed him, leaving the truck in the compound.

The streets were cluttered with wooden carts loaded high with boxes of firewood so large and heavy it did not seem possible that the small mules could pull them, or that they would fit down the narrow lanes. The dusty roads were heavy with traffic. Camels, mules, Toyotas, Mercedes, Zhigulis, Volgas imported from Russia. A brightly painted bus – yellow and red with orange flowers and geometrical patterns, a riot of colours and rattles and grunts, bags and suitcases piled high on its roof, belching acrid fumes into the street. Pipes poked from buildings, pouring sewerage into the gutters.

Around us rose the mountains, blue and misty, faintly visible through the thick clouds of wood smoke hanging over the streets. Turbanned men wandered around indolently, while women flitted along in small groups shrouded in chadors – blue, green, faded and tatty or stiff and neatly embroidered. There was something spectral about the way they passed noiselessly down the street.

'Don't stare at the women,' Vassily said, nudging me. 'Not unless you want your balls cut off, or a knife in your gut.'

Nervously my eyes flicked away from them. I glanced around to see whether any of the Afghan men had noticed I had been watching. As we approached them, the men parted to let us through. They kept their faces down, avoiding any form of eye contact, staring grimly at the ground.

'Let's get a little drink,' Vassily said with a grin.

He pushed through a heavy beaded curtain into a small café. We followed him in. The café was a large room opening off the street. A thick, oily cloud of aromatic smoke hung beneath the high ceiling. Vassily breathed in deeply, savouring the scent. He tapped the side of his nose and grinned. The room was subdivided into smaller rooms by means of chequered curtains. Pulling stools to one of the high tables, we settled down. A young Afghan boy in a dirty brown chemise wandered across, an insolent grin on his face. Vassily rubbed his knuckles playfully on the boy's head, ruffling his hair. The boy pulled away, protesting.

'Give us a bottle of water,' Vassily told the boy. 'Some of your special water.'

The boy turned lazily and wandered back across to a door by which stood a cooker that looked as if it had been cobbled together from the scraps of many other machines. He returned after a couple of minutes with an unlabelled litre bottle of clear liquid and three greasy glasses.

'How do you know that isn't poisoned?' Kolya said, pointing at the bottle. 'I've heard they do that.'

Vassily shook his head. 'Here no,' he said. 'They're not stupid. They wouldn't dare sell anything that is poisoned for two very good reasons. One – they wouldn't have any more business and they need the money.' He rubbed his thick fingers together. 'Two –

we would shell their fucking arses off if they tried.'

The vodka was strong. We downed a couple of glasses quickly. Vassily slipped a thin cigarette case from his coat pocket. The case was inlaid with amber. He opened it carefully and offered each of us a hand-rolled cigarette. Closing the case, he tapped the amber lid with the tip of his finger.

'Smell,' he said. 'The finest-quality hashish to be had.' He grinned.

The smoke burnt its way to my lungs. Beads of sweat jumped out on my forehead. With the vodka and the hashish, it felt as though my whole insides were on fire. I felt both nauseous and weightless, as though I had been pumped full of helium. The smoke stung my eyes. Vassily's large red face wobbled before me. Through eyes filled with tears I saw him laughing. He reached across the table and clapped a hand on my shoulder. Kolya, I noticed, was looking green. His face was set, his lips thin and his eyes screwed up as he concentrated.

We stumbled back, bolt upright, stifling laughter, conscious, despite our state, of the danger. Picking up the truck from the compound on the edge of the city, we drove out through the streets lined with low mud-brick buildings. The walls of the houses were dry and crumbling, and in places riddled with bullet holes. There were small shops that seemed abandoned and a Soviet hospital which could have been built no more than ten years before whose walls were already cracked, with large chunks of plaster falling away.

Turning into a narrow street that ran between two rows of high buildings, Vassily stepped hard on the brakes. Ahead of us a commotion blocked the street. A small crowd milled around a KamaZ. The door of the truck was open. Children skipped in the dust.

'Trouble ahead,' Vassily muttered under his breath. His right hand felt for his Kalashnikov.

'What is it?' I asked.

He shook his head and edged the truck cautiously down the street, his gun across his lap. The group of Afghans milling around the KamaZ turned towards us and even at a distance of fifty metres it was possible to see the anger on their faces. A stone ricocheted off the windscreen. I gripped my own gun tightly. An acute rush of fear and adrenalin cleared the fug of vodka and hashish that had clouded my brain.

'Let's back out of here,' Kolya suggested, his voice strained.

'And leave the guys in that truck?'

'There are only the three of us.'

A group of children ran along beside us, their small, dark faces smeared with dirt, their tatty shirts flapping. Gleefully they shouted, jumping up and down, picking handfuls of dust from the street and throwing it at the truck.

'*Shuravi – Shuravi – marg – marg – marg!*' they shouted.

A young girl stood in the shadows by the wall. She was dressed in a green shalwar-kameez; her eyes were large and as green as her dress, her hair dusty red. In her small hands she clutched a ribbon. *Marg, marg, marg*, she mouthed with the other children, an excited little smile curving her pretty lips, dimpling her soft, full cheeks.

'What are they saying?' Kolya asked.

'What are they saying?' repeated Vassily, glancing across at Kolya. 'They are singing, "Death to the Soviets – death – death – death".'

A cold shiver ran down my spine. I glanced across

at the beautiful young child standing in the shadows. She waved the ribbon before her; the sunlight caught the silky golden cloth and it shone gaily. *Marg, marg, marg*, she sang. For a moment, as we passed, our eyes met. She was, I realised, the first Afghan that had met my eyes in the week I had been there. She drew the ribbon to her face and stroked it against her cheek.

'*Allah akbar! Allah akbar! Shuravi marg!*' The voices of men joined those of the children. The crowd that had been milling around the stationary KamaZ advanced down the narrow lane towards us.

'Radio for back-up,' Vassily snapped at Kolya. '*Davai! Antanas, let's go.*' He opened the door of the truck and jumped down into the road, bringing his Kalashnikov up into a firing position. I opened my door and rolled out into the dust, clutching my gun tightly. The children scattered with loud screams full of fear and anger. I heard the stutter of Vassily's gun. As I drew myself up to face the angry crowd of young men, I felt a sharp pain as something cracked against the back of my head. I swivelled round. The pack of children fled. The small girl remained alone by the wall, the ribbon hanging loosely from her plump hands. In her beautiful green eyes I saw that she was paralysed with fear.

The metallic chatter of Vassily's gun reverberated around my head. The narrow street echoed with shouts and gunfire and then the clatter of a helicopter. The Mi-24 hovered menacingly above the rooftops, blocking out the sunlight. Blue-pink streaks plumed from the shuddering, dark angel that had come to our rescue.

The angry crowd melted away into the shadows and dark passageways, leaving one figure writhing in the dust. The helicopter rose noisily into the sky, swooping away across the rooftops of the city. Vassily walked

85

forwards to the supine figure. As he drew close the man sat up suddenly and the polished blade of a knife glinted in the sunlight.

'Vassily!' I called.

There was a short burst of gunfire and the figure danced backwards and crumpled to the ground.

We edged forwards, Kolya keeping the truck close on our heels. Vassily's eyes swivelled nervously from wall to wall, seeking out the small windows, the rooftops or narrow passageways from which a sniper might pick us off. From the opposite side of the stationary KamaZ, an APC trundled slowly towards us. Kozlov sat on top of the APC, his gun resting across his knees. He grinned when he saw us.

'You three, huh?' he said, jumping down. 'Playing heroes or just trying to die as quickly as possible?'

The windscreen of the KamaZ was shattered, and the headlights broken. The dented driver's door had been forced open. We peered in. The driver lay slumped across the steering wheel. Kozlov pulled him back. His face was a bloody pulp. I stared at the glistening fatty tissue.

'Fuck!' Vassily muttered behind me.

'He ran into some local kid,' Kozlov said. 'He radioed in for help, but as you can see he was too late.'

'The child?' I said.

Kozlov shot a glance at me.

'Was it . . . ?'

'Dead? Let's hope so. One less *sobaka* to worry about.'

I glanced down the street to where the young girl had been standing. She had gone. I wandered back, looking around warily. In the dust where she had been standing was the short length of gold ribbon. I bent down and picked it up. It felt soft and smooth between my fingers. I stroked it against the skin of my cheek. The fine cloth snagged on the coarse bristles that sprouted unevenly across my jaw.

'Antanas, comrade,' a voice called. I looked up. From the truck Vassily was waving for me to join him. 'Come on, my friend, let's go.'

Chapter 10

As the afternoon gave way to evening and the light began to fade, I remained at my desk, staring blankly out through the dirty glass door into the street. Around me rose the spectral *kishlak* Ghazis. The village lay east of Jalalabad, towards the border with Pakistan. An old stone bridge spanned a lively river, which plummeted from the mountains through ash and juniper woods and into the walnut orchard in the low winding foothills around the village. The marketplace was crowded. It was hot and noisy.

'It was in Ghazis,' Vassily had said, 'in the Hindu Kush. You remember it?'

I remembered Ghazis. There are some places that sear themselves on to the skin of your being, that mark you so indelibly no amount of drugs or alcohol or work or love will wash their shadow away.

I stood up. In a cupboard beneath the sink there was a bottle of vodka. We kept it there for when we stayed late. Sometimes, when we had finished the day's work and settled at the desk, paperwork strewn between us, untouched, unread, bills unpaid, Vassily would begin one of his tales, a snippet of information he had learnt and was eager to share, which would develop into a story. On these occasions we would get out the bottle and a couple of glasses and drink and talk until the telephone rang and Daiva demanded to know whether I would be coming home that evening.

The bottle was three-quarters full. Setting it on the desk, I rinsed a glass under the tap by the lathe. Choking smoke burnt the back of my throat and the flames crackled in my ears as they rushed along the dry wood, shrivelling the grass. Ghazis. Unscrewing the top of the bottle, I poured a generous measure into the glass. I raised it to my lips. The smoke plumed from the hilltop, like a volcano. From nowhere, then, the pitiful cry of a child arrested me, catching all at once the hate, the raging anger from my heart. The glass hesitated against my lip. I stopped, the dust rising in swirls around me, the smoke, forced down by the wind, curling into the trees. I looked back up towards the barely visible village, the sun behind it dark and brooding. Lowering the glass to the table, I rolled up my shirtsleeve and examined the crinkled skin.

A soft knock at the door startled me. Pulling down my sleeve awkwardly, I twisted around, half expecting to see Kirov's face once more. But it was Tanya who stood in the doorway, the light of a street lamp illuminating her from behind. I unlocked the door and let her in.

'You're all in darkness,' she said. 'I didn't think you were here.'

I looked around. A buttery slab of light from the street fell through the glass in the door, faintly illuminating a patch of floor. The rest of the shop had dissolved into the evening gloom.

Tanya took off her coat and shook it, before hanging it over the back of a chair. She relit the paraffin heater and turned on my desk lamp.

'Are you OK?' she asked, noticing the opened bottle, the glass on the table and my shirtsleeve, hanging loosely around my wrist.

'Kirov was here,' I said.

'Kirov?'

'Vassily never spoke of him?'

She thought for a moment, then shook her head. 'Not that I can remember.'

'We served together in Afghanistan. Vassily told me he was in prison.'

A look of concern crossed Tanya's face. 'Did he hurt you?' she said. 'What happened?'

'No, he didn't hurt me,' I reassured her. 'He wanted to know about the bracelet.'

Tanya pulled the two chairs close to the heater and drew me down next to her. I held my fingers up before the flames. They were, I noticed, shaking.

'I can't stop them,' I said to Tanya, ruefully. 'Every time I look at them, they're trembling like leaves on the trees.'

She took my hands in hers and held them tight, massaging them gently with the tips of her fingers.

'Tell me about Kirov,' she said. 'Tell me what he said.'

For a moment I weighed in my mind whether I should tell her of the veiled threat he had made against her. I decided not to.

'He is under the impression,' I said, 'that I am after this bracelet. He was warning me off, I think. He is after Kolya.'

Tanya shook her head, a bewildered frown creasing her forehead.

'Kirov was taunting me,' I added. 'He suggested Vassily was not the friend I thought he was, that he was not as honourable as I believed.'

'Its not true, Antanas,' Tanya said. 'You know Vassily has been a good friend to you.'

'Of course, Tanya,' I reassured her. 'He rescued me. He nursed me back to health. If it was not for him I would not have survived, I wouldn't have found the strength to carry on.'

Tanya stared into the flickering jets of flame for a few moments, silent. They were changing slowly from blue to orange as the heater warmed up.

'Do you know where Kolya is?' she asked finally.

'No.' I shrugged. 'Not unless it said on the letter.'

'Does this Kirov know where he is?'

I shrugged again. 'I don't know what Kirov knows.'

'Would he harm Kolya?'

If I paused before I answered, it was not because I had any doubts about whether Kirov would be prepared to kill to get what he wanted.

'We were on a patrol, once, in the mountains,' I said to Tanya, 'when we got cut off. Snipers had opened up on us from behind the walls of a ruined village, driving us farther up the mountain. Darkness fell, trapping us at the top of a ravine. The temperature dropped well below zero and we were hopelessly equipped. We sat huddled up in a crater, fearing that at any moment the muj would discover us and if they didn't the cold would kill us before the night was out.

'There was an Uzbeki boy, Yuri. He decided he was going to make a break for it. If he had been seen or captured he would have drawn attention to the rest of us. We tried to stop him but he would not listen. As he climbed out of the crater, Kirov caught him. Covering the boy's mouth with one hand he slit his throat. He held the boy tight as he jerked about, blood squirting out across the rock, pooling at our feet. Not one of us said a word. Kirov held him until he was dead, then pushed him into the corner. We sat through the night with his body there, waiting until first light when some back-up finally arrived.'

Tanya shuddered.

'Kirov will kill without compunction,' I said, realising, as I said the words, their significance.

'What are we going to do?' Tanya said, after a while.

'I told Vassily I was not interested in hearing about how he got the bracelet.'

'But don't you want to know what Kolya has to say?'

'I've spent eight years trying to forget about it all.'

'Much good that has done you,' Tanya said. 'Still you dream, you wake in the night trembling, shouting. Your drinking is pulling apart your relationship with Daiva. Perhaps it's time you faced up to things.'

I stood up and walked over to the door. The wind gusted, rattling the glass in the window. Sullen clouds darkened the sky, bearing night prematurely.

'You think I should try to find him?' I said.

She got up and walked over to me. I felt her standing close behind me. She rested her head between my shoulder blades.

'Yes,' she said. 'Vassily wanted you to. I think you should, for him. He made me promise to make you. It was important to him and it's important that you stop burying your experiences, it isn't helping you. And so what if Kolya just wants to sell the bracelet to buy drugs? What is that to you?'

Not answering, I stared out into the street.

'You have no idea where to start looking for him?' Tanya asked.

'No,' I said, 'I haven't seen him. Not since Afghanistan.' I turned from the doorway. 'The letter,' I said, 'if only I had not thrown away the letter.' I had a sudden vision of it, snagged in the branches of the birch tree by the banks of the Vilnia.

'What?' said Tanya, seeing me hesitate as I crossed the room.

'The letter,' I said. 'I was in the Uzupis Café. I screwed it into a ball and tossed it out towards the river. It caught in the twigs. Do you think it's possible . . . it's still there?'

Tanya looked dubious. 'I don't think there is much hope.'

Tanya's apartment was warm and inviting after the icy wind. It was less than a kilometre from the shop, but in the time it took us to walk that short distance we were chilled to the bone. Tanya's teeth chattered as I closed the door behind us.

'I'm going to take a hot shower to warm up,' she said.

She disappeared into the bathroom. In the sitting room I turned on the standard lamp. The sofa was still made up as a bed. Clogging the surface of the low table were empty cups, sticky glasses and overflowing ashtrays. The air was thick with the smell of stale cigarette smoke and brandy. Clothes littered the floor.

Finding a clean glass, I poured myself a drink from the half-empty brandy bottle and drank it quickly. I poured a second and relaxed with that. Glancing at my watch, I noticed it was late. Instinctively I felt a spasm of guilt. I almost rose, before I remembered than Daiva had gone, that she would not be waiting for me. That the apartment would be empty. I sank back into the sagging armchair and drained the second glass. Remorsefully I considered how many times I had made her wait. How many times I had not been able to face going back to the apartment and had continued drinking with Vassily instead.

Hopelessly, and though I knew better, I got up and went over to the telephone. Dialling the number for our apartment, I listened as it rang.

After a minute I replaced the receiver and stood by the table, my mind skimming back across the last couple of years, recalling the number of times I had failed to come home to her, the number of times I had shamed her in front of her colleagues with my drunken sarcasm so that she had stopped inviting them to our apartment.

Hearing footsteps behind me, I turned. Tanya was dressed in a white cotton dressing gown; her hair was wet and dangled around her face in loose dark curls. She smiled hesitantly and my heart lurched. Zena, I thought, and trembled at how much she looked like that other beautiful young woman in that other world, that other time.

'I'm sorry about the mess,' Tanya said, looking at the detritus of her life scattered untidily about the room. 'I just can't seem to . . .'

Her explanation faded away when she saw how I was looking at her. When I reached out for her, she did not step away. I pulled her close. She rested her head against my chest. My lips grazed her hair, which was damp and smelt fresh and clean. I felt that if I reached down and touched her she would not stop me, that she needed closeness, the physical touch of another human, the comfort of skin against skin. I longed to, but didn't.

In the bedroom, in the pale light that filtered through half-drawn curtains, I undressed quickly and slipped in between the clean sheets. We lay close; I could hear her breathing, could feel the heat from her hand by my own, could smell her soap-scented body. With every part of my body I could sense her.

'Tanya,' I said, to remind myself who it was by my side.

She turned over and I felt her breath on my skin, could see her face milky cool in the light of the moon.

'Yes?' she whispered.

I reached out and ran a finger gently across her cheek.

'I feel confused,' I confessed. 'Confused and afraid.'

Mistaking my meaning, she sighed and nodded. 'Yes,' she said. 'Me too.'

I withdrew my hand and we lay close but not touching. After some minutes she turned from me and later I heard the catch in her breath and a slow exhalation and knew she was sleeping. My mind spun. The image of a girl played across the ceiling above me. As much as I tried to banish it, she returned. Screaming. Her face distorted by fear. Screaming.

Leaving Tanya, I went back to the sitting room and poured myself another two drinks. When I went back to bed, I lay and watched the wind-tousled shadows of the trees dancing on the ceiling and thought of Daiva and Laura and where they were and wondered whether Laura had noticed my absence. I recalled the soft sound of her breathing as I lay in bed. The moments when, waking in the night, I would lift my ear from the pillow and hold my breath to listen for some sound of her, straining, unable to relax back into sleep before I heard the low sigh, or a faint rustling as she moved in the crib.

Spring had come suddenly, the year I met Daiva. Buttery yellow petals broke through the melting snow and the clouds flew higher, large billowing cumuli, which sparkled in the sunlight. Sharp showers sluiced away the last of the grey packs of ice, and children reappeared in the streets, shouting and laughing and running after a winter of incarceration.

In the early summer, Daiva and I had taken the trolley bus to the edge of the city and wandered in the forest, down to the river, where we lay in the deep grass at the edge of the water, watching the heron poking around the fields and the trout lolling lazily in the warm shallows.

I clung to our desire; found peace in the act of love. There no thought was required. I abandoned myself to the cool smoothness of her skin, the feel of her ribs, the arch of her belly, the sharp, hot exhalation of her breath.

As the months unfolded, the tightness of my chest loosened and the crushing weight lifted from me. I no longer jumped at the sudden crackle of static on the telephone line. I no longer woke in the night, with a scream on my lips, upright and soaked with fear. That other life – that life I slewed off, like a snake its skin, as Vassily put it – no longer haunted me with its dark emptiness.

I awoke in Tanya's bed the next morning just after dawn, and, unable to return to sleep, got up and made myself coffee. The sky was bright and cloudless, and over the tops of neighbouring buildings I could see the trees in Kalnu Park tossing in a strong breeze. I felt curiously calm after the events of the previous couple of days, as though, having slipped down a crevice, my fall had finally been broken and I was left on a ledge, regarding my position.

Sipping the coffee, I thought of Vassily, of the years we had spent together and all that he had done for me. I thought of Kolya, too, the young boy I had grown up with in the children's home, his bright face, his laughter. Of how he had blushed in shame when Liuba had declared her affection for him.

Tanya was sleeping still when, just before eight o'clock, I took her coffee. Sitting beside her, I brushed her dark hair from her face. She stirred and looked up and smiled sadly.

'I was dreaming,' she said.

'I'm sorry.'

'No,' she said, shifting, running a hand through her hair, taking the mug of coffee from me, 'there's no need. I've been living in a dream since he died, before that even, since the time we finally admitted to ourselves he was ill, the evening he came home and told me it had been diagnosed as malignant. It's been unreal since then, a waiting, not daring to hope, not daring to think.'

'I have not thought for years,' I told her. 'I have existed. Each day a conscious act of will, to live without thinking. If I tried hard enough it almost worked. Daiva, the baby, the work with Vassily. It was enough. What cause was there to think of anything else, to remember that there had been anything else? But perhaps you were right, yesterday evening, maybe it's time I faced up to it.'

'So what are you going to do?' she asked.

'I think I should find Kolya.'

Tanya nodded and reached out to take my hand. 'But how will you find him?' she asked.

'I don't know,' I confessed. 'I really don't know.'

*

The café on the bank of the Vilnia was closed. Scaling the high wall, I peered over into the beer garden. The chairs were upturned on the wooden tables and the glass doors closed and curtained. Squinting into the early sun, sharp and bright after the rain, I scanned the trees down by the water. Against the brilliant shimmer on the surface of the river it was impossible to see whether the letter was there still, balled in the mesh of twigs. For some moments I considered climbing over the wall to go and see, but the street was busy and I had no desire to involve the police in my search.

Disappointed, I wandered back across the bridge into the Old Town, heading along Bernadinu in the direction of the university. A large crowd of students congregated in the courtyard of the university, smoking and talking and laughing. Often Vassily would visit his old friend Gintaras Zinotis, a professor in the Department of Archaeology at the university. Zinotis knew everything there was to know about ancient jewellery and was an expert on the history of amber. He had served in Afghanistan in the very early eighties. Though he looked every centimetre the university professor, it was possible to see beneath the worn jacket and the spectacles, beneath the slight paunch and his pipe, the lean figure of the soldier he had once been. Zinotis belonged, I knew, to the Afghan Vets organisation, and it was possible, I considered, that through his contacts he might have heard something about Kolya, or would be able to direct me to somebody who might know where he was.

His small office was at the end of a long corridor. I had been to the university on only one previous occasion when Vassily had asked me to pick up a book the professor had promised to loan him on the jewellery of the Kushan Empire. Now I knocked on the door and waited, feeling out of place among the young students, folders tucked beneath their arms, waiting for their lectures.

When the door did not open, I knocked again, loath to be disappointed for the second time that morning. A creased face appeared at the door, staring furiously over the top of half-moon spectacles.

'Yes?' Zinotis said irritably. He looked me up and down and, realising at once I was not one of his students, his frown eased a little. 'Who are you looking for?' he added a little more pleasantly.

'Professor Zinotis?' I asked, though I recognised him immediately.

'Yes?'

'My name is Antanas, I am a friend and colleague of the jeweller Vassily. We have met once before.'

The professor opened the door a little wider. He took off his glasses and polished them absently on the sleeve of his pullover.

'I heard the news,' he said. 'I'm very sorry.'

I nodded. Zinotis stepped to one side and indicated I should enter his office. The room was small and oppressive. Books lined every wall and were piled in high, unstable heaps on the floor and desk. On the sill, beneath the small, dusty window, were various lumps of amber, some of them worked, displaying their inclusions, organisms trapped when the resin was still liquid, while others were dull, raw, milky pieces. There were two chairs in the room, one by his desk and a second by the wall, beneath a particularly wobbly-looking pile of volumes.

'Please sit down,' Zinotis said, offering me his chair. 'I would offer you a drink, but I'm afraid I don't have a bottle. Always when Vassily came he would bring one with him, but it has been a long while since he was last here.'

Zinotis perched himself on the edge of the desk, shifting a pile of folders aside.

'What can I do for you?'

'Vassily, I know, often came to talk to you about jewellery,' I said, not sure how to raise the topic or how much I should say.

Zinotis laughed. 'Vassily and I always talked about ancient jewellery. He had a fascination with the history of amber and its spread around the ancient world. He had some wonderful stories about its origins.'

I nodded and paused. Zinotis raised his eyebrows, waiting.

'I'm looking for somebody,' I said, 'and I thought there was the smallest chance you might be able to help me.'

'I can try.' He smiled, a little bemused.

'Kolya. Kolya Antonenko,' I said. 'He served with Vassily and me in Afghanistan. Perhaps you have heard something about him through the veterans organisation?'

'Kolya Antonenko?' Zinotis played with his half-moon spectacles. He thought hard, then blew out his cheeks. 'No,' he said, 'I don't think so.'

'Have you any idea who might be·able to help me find him?'

Zinotis twisted the spectacles between his fingers. His watery blue eyes examined me.

'It's important, is it?' he asked.

I hesitated a moment, considering what I should tell him.

'Before Vassily died,' I said, 'I went to visit him. He was sick, but very lucid. He told me about a jewel. He wanted Kolya to have it.'

Zinotis followed my words with evident interest. When I paused he urged me to continue.

'Did he describe the jewel?' he asked.

'You know what he was like with his tales,' I said. 'Perhaps this was no more than one of those. He said it was a bracelet. A filigree gold band which held an oval piece of amber. The amber was a large piece, I believe, and without flaws, but what interested him were the inclusions in it. There were two beetles, perfectly preserved, copulating.'

'This bracelet,' Zinotis clarified, 'it is something Vassily had? He gave it to you?'

I hesitated again. 'No,' I said, 'not exactly, but he wanted Kolya to have it.'

At that moment there was a knock on the door. Zinotis stood up. He looked across at the door and seemed to consider whether he should answer it. After glancing at me, he stepped over to it and, opening it, poked his head into the corridor. When, a few moments later, he closed the door and turned back to me he was once more polishing his spectacles on the sleeve of his pullover.

'I don't know,' he said, shaking his head. He paused and fitted the spectacles back on to his nose and gazed at me through them, as if weighing me up. 'I can certainly ask around. This bracelet, though . . . would be very interesting to see, if you were able to bring it to me. It might be worth quite something, if it's as good an example as you suggest.'

'I'm not interested in the jewel,' I said. 'Vassily wanted me to find Kolya. There is something he wanted me to hear from Kolya, something about the bracelet. I don't know, it makes little sense to me.'

Zinotis continued to stare at me. His gaze was at

once penetrating and absent. 'Kolya Antonenko,' he said, turning the name on his tongue. 'Maybe I did meet him, with Vassily, now that you mention it – years ago. I will have to make some enquiries.'

I stood up, a little disappointed that he knew no more.

'I'm sorry to have taken up your time,' I said, holding out my hand.

'Not at all,' Zinotis replied. 'You must pass on my deepest sympathy to Tanya. He was a great companion, he will be missed by many people.'

Despondently, I retraced my route back towards the bridge over the Vilnia. It was mid-morning and the traffic was a little quieter. The Uzupis Café had just opened when I reached it. A young woman was unfolding the glass double doors and securing them with bricks. Inside, the staff were wiping tables and arranging chairs. I ordered a coffee and took it out to the decked area at the back of the café. Glancing down towards the river, I saw the letter immediately, suspended in the tangle of twigs and branches where I had thrown it.

The land sloped steeply from the back of the café to the bank of the river. I slipped down the grass and, holding the wiry trunk of a young birch, hung out over the water to retrieve the ball of paper. It was damp. Delicately I eased it from its resting place without ripping it.

As I clambered back up to the café platform, I noticed the waiter leaning against the door jamb watching me.

'Just doing my bit to keep the city tidy,' I said, taking my place back at the table where I had left my coffee.

He raised his eyebrows and turned back inside.

With care I straightened out the envelope, smoothing it gently with the palm of my hand. Untucking the flap, I pulled out the single sheet inside the envelope. The letter was relatively dry. Kolya's spidery handwriting ran down the page, a little faded but quite visible. My heart was pumping hard, I noticed, and my fingers trembled as I held down the corners of the page while I read.

Vassily,
Forgive me for writing to you when I promised I would leave you alone. You are my last hope, and I don't believe you will, after all, turn your back on me.

When we spoke a few years ago, things got heated. We both said things that should not have been said. We were all to blame over the bracelet. The years have flown, and yet it seems only yesterday we were in that shit-hole of a country. Not a day goes by when I do not think about it, nor a night in which those years and what happened don't revisit me and terrify me once more.

But now I am in desperate need of your help, my old comrade. I am ill. I have returned to Vilnius to get treatment at the clinic, but it is expensive. I need money. I need my share from the bracelet – after all, I have suffered too.

Kolya

On the back of the letter, when I turned it over, I found some scribbled instructions in Vassily's hand.

Chapter 11

At the end of our first week in Kabul, junior officers flew in from around the country to take their pick of the new recruits. A tanned, wiry officer with blue eyes that seemed barely able to open in the startling sunshine chose a small group of us to replace the *dembels* from his platoon stationed near Jalalabad, east of Kabul, towards the border with Pakistan. Kolya and Vassily were posted with me. A small helicopter was waiting at the airport to transport us across the mountains. We were each issued a parachute as we climbed into the belly of the chopper. The helicopter was already piled high with goods. A *dembel* held out a packet of cigarettes.

'Have a smoke,' he said with a laugh. 'It's going to be your last.'

As the helicopter rose into the clear sky, we watched Kabul drop away behind us. Every few minutes flares whistled out from the sides of the helicopter.

'The muj have got better equipment than we have,' the blue-eyed officer said. 'They've got Stinger missiles. The CIA are funding the insurgents, channelling arms through from Pakistan.'

Deep mountain fissures ran between Kabul and Jalalabad. The rocks erupted from the earth as sharp as knives, baking in the intense heat. Gorges dropped away, hundreds of metres deep, so that they seemed like narrow channels into the very heart of the earth.

The sides of the mountains were clothed with ragged skirts of thorny bushes. Occasionally, in valleys, on the banks of bubbling torrents, there were willows and poplars and mulberry trees. On the plains, beside pock-marked roads, lay ruined villages, their dry mud bricks crumbling back into the ground they were raised from.

I gazed down at the passing scenery in wonder. Camels slumped sullenly beside a dusty track. On a plain by the river lean goats flocked around a large vaulted black tent and small children shouted and danced, arms flapping as we passed. Villages rose from the parched earth with narrow streets running between high-walled compounds. From the outside these family enclosures, with only small wooden doors opening out on to the world, looked barren and dusty, but inside were pleasant courtyards with flowers and vegetable patches shaded by large trees. All this was roofed by the sky, a tautly stretched cerulean awning, punctured by the towering peaks of the mountains.

As we flew east towards Jalalabad the day grew warmer, the vegetation more lush and the air heavier. Jalalabad was a large town, green and hot and lively. We were overwhelmed by the sudden sweet scent of ripe fruit, the startling blaze of colour and the frenzy of noise – donkeys, cars, parrots, stalls, monkeys, turbaned men, the blare of Hindi film classics; the dust rising in choking clouds, cars rattling and jolting along streets that were barely passable.

Our base was twenty kilometres out of Jalalabad, but the road was so poor it took almost an hour to get there. Around the base on every side rose mountains capped with snow, which glittered dazzlingly in the sun. A river ran close to the base, sucking noisily at the pebbles and rocks as it passed. Beyond the river grew a small wood of poplar and willow, skirting the lower slopes of the rising foothills. Two walls of fencing topped by barbed wire encircled the base, ten metres apart. Between them the ground was mined. The base was rudimentary; the officers had constructed basic huts for themselves but the rest of the soldiers still lived in large tents that billowed in the breeze.

Our first task was to construct huts for the grand-dads, who spent most of the day lounging in their tents, nursing bottles of vodka and smoking. Hardly a single granddad was dressed in uniform; they slopped around in vests and sports trousers with slippers on their feet.

To build the huts we dug holes in the earth and filled them with clay and water. We worked the clay all day and then put it into ammunition boxes and left it to set. These rudimentary bricks we bound with wet clay. The huts we built were small and dark. At first we fitted glass into the windows, but at the end of the first week there was an attack and the exploding rockets shattered the windows, so we made do with polythene.

A granddad took us in the KamaZ with an accompanying APC to a deserted village a few kilometres down the road to get wood for the roofs.

'When we first set up camp here,' the granddad explained, 'we got fired on from this village. One of our soldiers got hit in the stomach. We rounded up all the men and interrogated them, but how the fuck were we going to find out who it was? There were fifty of them. Some were little kids and then there were the grizzled old granddaddies with their long white beards and their big fucking turbans. We took one of the men, an ugly fucking git, and shot him to teach them a lesson. The next thing we know the whole

106

fucking village has uprooted and headed off for the mountains.'

The village was at the top of a slight incline surrounded by irrigated fields. The road ran at the foot of the rise, a track leading from it, winding into the centre of the village. The high walls had begun to crumble. Between each of the compounds ran narrow, rutted lanes. We let in a couple of dogs to check there were no mines or booby-traps. In the centre of each courtyard was a well, and around it several complexes of rooms, with beaten-earth floors and sun-dried brick walls painted with lively patterns.

The purpose of the APC soon became clear. Systematically the driver set about destroying one of the compounds. From the dusty rubble we pulled what wood we could find and loaded it on to the back of the KamaZ. It was only once the huts for the officers and granddads had been finished that we were able to construct shelters for ourselves.

Of the thirty-five soldiers stationed on our base, twenty of us were new recruits, and we were from all parts of the Soviet Union, as was general policy. New recruits were not allowed to drink alcohol. Though, technically, we got a small allowance of vodka per week, this was taken by the granddads.

'What are you fucking looking at?' one granddad barked in my ear, catching me eyeing a bottle on his desk. 'Do you understand you are not even allowed to look at vodka, you little shit? Get your little beady eyes off it.'

I lowered my eyes to the floor, as he had indicated, and apologised, but my contrition was not enough to divert a beating. In fact the beatings came so often that it was strange to collapse on to my bunk at the end of the day without some bruise or tender flesh to nurse.

'I can't sleep unless I've had a beating,' Vassily chuckled, one night.

In our bunks, Vassily regaled us with tales he had heard and laughed at the indolent brutality of the granddads.

'Did you hear about the recruit stationed not far from here?' he said, one night. 'His base was at the top of a mountain to the north of Jalalabad. One night one of the granddads sent him out to get some milk. The boy was scared – who knows what band of rebels he might have stumbled across in the darkness? But as he was working his way down the mountainside he was attacked by a snake.'

'A snake?' We sat up in our bunks, watching Vassily in the dim light of the oily candles.

'The snake wound around him and began to crush the life out of him, so he could hardly breathe. It held him in its grip like that for half the night, and then as first light was dawning it let him go. He struggled free and made his way back to his base at the top of the mountain, only to find that while he had been gone the mujahidin had raided the base and killed the whole lot of them.'

One weekend, when the granddads were particularly drunk, we slipped off base and drove into Jalalabad to buy alcohol. Discarding our uniforms, we took our Kalashnikovs and stuffed a couple of grenades into each pocket. Vassily took a KamaZ and Kolya and I jumped into the back. At the last moment we were joined by another recruit, a lean, dark-haired Russian called Kirov. New recruits guarded the gates and we bullied and bribed our way through with little difficulty.

The market in Jalalabad was a riot of noise and colour. We slipped through the streets, attempting to remain inconspicuous, glancing nervously over our shoulders. The crowds milled and jostled around us and forced us forwards, towards the heart of the market. The street was lined with stalls piled high with fruit and vegetables – bananas, nuts, oranges, tangerines, pinky-yellow carrots, delicious-smelling bread piled high like pancakes at home. Other tables displayed hats, sheepskin coats, ox hides, TVs, digital watches, videos, tea and coffee sets from China and India. Vassily was drawn to the stalls at the side of the market selling trinkets and jewellery fashioned from local stones.

'Look at this,' he said, picking up a necklace fashioned from amethyst. 'Look, comrade, my friend, how beautiful. You know, the word amethyst comes from the Greek for "not drunken". The ancients used to believe amethysts prevented drunkenness; they made their cups from it. And lapis lazuli, look, my friend.' He picked up some of the beautiful blue stone. 'As clear and beautiful as the Afghan sky.' He held it up as if to compare and, in fact, the two did glow with a similar brilliant luminescence. 'This is one of the ways they are financing their insurgents, their arms deals. They smuggle it over the mountains into Pakistan.'

'You seem to know a lot about these things,' I said.

'I'm a jeweller,' he explained. 'It is my job to know about jewels.'

We slipped into a small store at the side of the market where Vassily knew vodka could be purchased illicitly. Being a driver, he had accompanied older soldiers into Jalalabad on previous occasions. A small, wizened man with a straggling white beard stood in a dark doorway at the back of the store, wrapped tightly in the cloth the Afghans employed universally. The cloth served as a turban, a wrap and something to spread beneath them when they sat. By the side of the man stood a small boy, who stared at us frankly.

'Drink?' Vassily said, tilting back his head and miming emptying a bottle into his mouth.

'What you got?' the old man asked in broken Russian.

Vassily indicated Kirov, who was carrying a plastic bottle of fuel, which we had drained from the KamaZ. Kirov placed the bottle on to a scarred wooden desk beside the man.

'Phh!' The old man waved his hand dismissively. 'You drink that.'

'What's the matter with this?' Vassily demanded. 'Last week you take it.'

'Last week you was with different men,' said the shopkeeper. 'I know them . . .' He waved his hands indolently in the air. 'Years.'

'How much?' said Vassily.

'What you got?'

'You've seen.'

'What else?'

He wafted his thin, strong hands towards us. Kirov slipped a grenade from his pocket and laid it beside the bottle of fuel. Vassily glanced at him and then at the grenade. For a moment I thought he was going to snatch it up, but he didn't. The old man smiled thinly and nodded his head. He nudged the boy, who slipped through the door behind them and returned a few moments later with a jar of clear liquid. Vassily unscrewed the top and smelt it. He took a small sip, then nodded.

'Good.'

The old man nodded but did not smile again. We made our way quickly back to the KamaZ, which we had left some streets away. Kolya, whom we had left to guard the truck, was in the back, his gun resting across his chest. He sat up with a start as we jumped in beneath the canvas.

'It's only us,' I said.

He set the gun down. 'Well?'

Vassily held up the bottle. A broad grin broke across Kolya's large, square face. He reached for the bottle and kissed it.

'So what are we waiting for? Crack it open.'

We passed the bottle around between us and Vassily took a packet of cigarettes from his pocket and handed them out.

'Where did you get these?' I asked, surprised.

'Ah!' He tapped the side of his nose.

The alcohol burnt our bellies, unpicked our cares. Three of us settled back against the side of the truck, while Kirov sat with his legs dangling from the back, his gun across his lap, keeping watch.

'I was in Lithuania,' Vassily said. 'Once, on my way to Kaliningrad.'

'What were you doing in that shit-hole?' Kolya asked.

'Amber.'

'You are interested in amber?' I asked.

'You know where amber comes from?'

'From beneath the sea,' I said.

'But originally? Let me tell you the tale of the origin of amber.'

'Oi!' Kolya protested, but Vassily ignored him.

'Phaeton wanted more than anything to drive the chariot of the sun across the sky like his father the sun god. But his father wouldn't let him; wild horses pulled the chariot and only Phoebus was strong enough to control them. But Phaeton would not let his father alone. Finally he gave in.'

Vassily paused as the jar of vodka came round to him. He took a large slug of the spirit and grimaced. 'Fucking appalling,' he said, wiping his lips on the back of his sleeve. He passed it on to me.

'Phaeton was so happy. He raced across the sky, showing the world how great he was. But suddenly the horses bolted. He lost control. The chariot swooped down close to the earth, setting it ablaze. Whole forests burst into flame, mountains exploded, fertile planes became parched deserts. He swooped down so low over Africa that all the people were scorched black.

'Zeus struck Phaeton dead with a bolt of lightning, to save the earth, and his body fell into a river, which bubbled and simmered from his heat. Phaeton had three sisters. The three beautiful young women went in search of their brother. When they found the river in which he had fallen they stood by it and wept. Day and night, week after week, they stood and wept beside the river, until their bodies wasted away. Their feet rooted themselves in the earth and their waving arms grew leaves. The trunks of their bodies became thick with bark. They became poplars wailing in the evening breeze. Long after they had been turned into trees they continued to cry and their tears turned into amber, which rolled down the smooth bark of their bellies and dropped into the river.'

Over the following week the sporadic gunfire coming from the woods, across the river, became more sustained. The night was disturbed by the shudder of incoming rockets. The mud-brick buildings we had built shook and dust billowed around the small space, coating us thickly. The rolling explosions from the two howitzers that opened up from within our compound made sleep impossible.

At daybreak, after one particularly heavy night, the CO informed us of a plan to strike back at the *dukhs* – the insurgents. Information from Military Intelligence suggested that the *dukhs* were sheltering in a village ten kilometres away, on the other side of the river. The sappers headed out first, checking the road through the forest for mines. We followed, two APCs, the mobile command centre and a BMP bringing up the rear, its caterpillar tracks tearing up the rough surface of the road.

We advanced slowly, the road winding through the trees, climbing steadily. Deep gullies dropped away at our side, and along their bottoms fierce streams crashed down from the mountains.

'We should burn these fucking trees down,' said Sasha Goryachev, another new recruit, his face drawn tight with nerves. He was sitting on top of the APC beside me, stiffly upright in his bulletproof vest, his ammunition belt slung across his belly. Dust billowed up from the road, thickly caking our clothes and faces. The muj loved the trees. Green meant snipers – trees meant hidden *dukhs* just waiting to spring their ambush. Whole forests had been felled by our troops across the country. Deserts were safer than jungles.

I cradled my gun across my lap; my eyes flicked from tree to tree, searching in the darkness for a glint of the enemy. My pulse raced and I felt a strange mixture of exhilaration and numbing fear. I glanced over at Kolya, who was sitting next to Vassily on the

APC in front. He raised his thumb and grinned. We perched lightly on the tops of the APCs in case of mines. If you were stuck inside when a mine exploded you had no chance.

The village was just above the tree line, its baked walls rising above the verdant treetops. It was situated on a rocky outcrop, which was riddled with dark holes. The village slumbered silently beneath the hot sun, its walls shimmering in the haze of heat bouncing up off the rock. We paused while a small group of granddads headed for higher ground to get a clearer view of the village. They returned after an hour not having seen movement within the walls.

As the armoured cars moved in, we sheltered behind them, covered, in case any hidden snipers should try to pick us off. The streets between the high walls were too narrow for the vehicles and the commander split the platoon into small groups to comb through the enclosures. I followed Chistyakov, Sasha and two grand-dads down towards a small wooden door at the end of the street, attempting to imitate the feline movements of the granddads, who slipped among the shadows with none of the shivering fear the new recruits were showing.

The door was locked. A shiny new metal padlock glittered in the afternoon sunlight.

'They've fucked off,' Pavlov, one of the granddads, said. He kicked the door hard, shattering the wood. Through the hole he tossed a grenade and we fell back quickly. The explosion ripped the wooden gate from its hinges, tossing it high in the air into a neighbouring enclosure. The mud-brick wall around the gateway billowed out and crumpled into dust. We darted forward across the rubble into the courtyard of the house.

'Watch for trip wires, watch for booby-traps,' Pavlov

called across his shoulder. Our eyes scanned the ground as we ran forwards.

The village was empty. Each house had been padlocked and deserted. We sacked the rooms, scattering the contents of the house in search of anything worth stealing. In a storeroom there were some sacks of rice, which we loaded on to one of the vehicles, but there was little else of any value.

'They've fucked off down the *kirizes*,' Pavlov commented, referring to the irrigation channels that honeycombed the country, running beside roads, under fields and villages.

'Fall back,' the commander instructed.

We took up our places on the personnel carriers while the BMP opened fire on the houses with one of its heavy guns. The dust rose in choking clouds, forming a dark pillar above the village. I felt oddly disappointed. My pulse still raced, my heart hammered and the adrenalin continued to surge through my veins. I wanted to run and fight, to burn the energy that bubbled up within me. I noticed my hands were shaking; yet now I felt not a trace of fear.

At that moment Pavlov, who had been sitting beside me, jumped forward off the APC. His knees crumpled as he hit the ground and he stumbled forwards. I laughed. I was about to jeer at him when I noticed that the back of his skull was missing. For some moments I stared at his figure sprawled awkwardly in the dust, trying to grasp what I saw. As I hesitated another figure toppled forward off the APC, crunching into the dust beside Pavlov. He twisted slightly, squirmed as though he were trying to burrow into the dust, then lay still, his hand reaching out and gently touching Pavlov's.

'We're under fire,' a voice shouted.

'*Dukhs!*'

I glanced around desperately. It was unclear from which side the shots had come. I slithered down off the back of the APC, and crouched in close against the shuddering warmth of its metal side.

'There,' somebody was calling. 'From over there.'

I glanced across at the second APC. Kolya and Vassily crouched in the dust, staring out at the trees on the other side of the vehicle, their guns raised. I felt a sudden rush of adrenalin and, swinging myself around to the front of the APC, emptied a magazine in the direction of the thick undergrowth. The air rattled with the noise of sub-machine-gun fire. I heard the rapid thwack of bullets bruising the metal above me, and then their shrill whistle as they passed above my head. I dodged back behind the APC. Glancing up at the BMP, I noticed its gun dancing back and forth, bewildered, unable to fix upon a target. The ground shook under the impact of a rocket launched from the thick cover of the forest. The metal jerked behind my back and a rush of hot air and dust billowed out from beneath the APC.

The BMP finally decided upon its target and fired. The trees burst into flames. The roar of heavy gunfire grew deafening. So deafening I did not hear the rapid rattle of bullets on the side of the APC above my head. It was the startled look of the commander, who half turned before he fell, and the dancing trail of dust that raced past my feet which alerted me to the fact that we were coming under fire from behind. I became aware at that moment that the APC was moving. As the BMP gun continued to pound the forest, we jumped into the APCs, dragging inert bodies from the dust, holding them tight against us as we squeezed inside.

The APCs raced down the rough track shuddering and jolting. The bullets sang against the metal skin around us. I curled myself over the body I was clutching and buried my head into its chest.

Chapter 12

I folded the letter carefully and put it in the pocket of my jacket. Finishing the coffee, I left the café, ignoring the looks of the waiting staff, and walked up towards the workshop. The letter was addressed from the Santariskes Clinic on the northern edge of Vilnius. Kolya's message disturbed me. Santariskes Clinic had specialised units for dealing with tuberculosis and Aids, among other things.

The letter had been posted a couple of months previously, and though it was quite possible Kolya was no longer there, it seemed the best place to start looking for him. I had not seen him since returning to Lithuania. Though we had grown up together and had both been posted to Jalalabad, our friendship had become more strained as the months passed in Afghanistan. As Kolya's problems became worse, he became more unpredictable, irritable and often violent in his treatment of new recruits.

The workshop, when I arrived, seemed colder and more uninviting than ever. It had normally been Vassily who arrived first in the morning. When I got in he would have the paraffin heater burning and would already be working at the lathe, or at his work table, fitting the amber to golden rings, stringing them on silken threads, bagging them up to send on to Riga where the Japanese dealers would buy them for the market in the Far East.

The letters I had collected from the post office, en route from the Uzupis Café to the workshop, included a fair number of new orders and enquiries concerning work ordered some time ago. I dropped the letters on the desk and switched on the light above my lathe.

Vassily had taught me the basics of the trade in Tanya's village as soon as I began to recover my strength and the shaking of my hands had subsided.

'Come,' he said one morning, 'I will teach you to work amber.'

Sitting me down by the machine, he turned on the tap. The lathe whirred and the water trickled down across the spinning wheel. Taking a piece of amber, he showed me how to clip it on. Gently I pressed it up against the wheel. A light hung low over the machine. The waste water dripped away into a sink, pooling beneath a surface yellow with scum. The diamond skimmed away the skin from my fingers and dark drops of blood stained the dusty white surface of the work table.

'When you pick it from the beach,' Vassily said, taking a piece of unworked amber and showing it to me, 'look, it could just be a pebble, it's nothing special. It's blank. To reveal the beauty inside it, its warmth and light, and the inclusions in the heart of it, it must be worked with love and care.

'Some people can work amber, others can't,' he continued. 'Amber is like that. Immediately I can tell who will be good and who isn't. The amber you work is warm, Antanas, comrade, it has energy.'

When the amber crumbled on the lathe as I tried to cut it, I would curse and leap up, my fingers bloodied. Vassily laughed. 'It is an important fact,' he would tell me, 'the age of the amber. It needs to be, you see, about fifty million years old. Less and it is no use.' He took the crumbled amber from the lathe and rolled the chips in his fingers. 'Twenty million years, thirty million years, it is too young, the quality is not good enough, it will just crumble when you try to work it. As you see.' He threw the chips into the fire.

'And how do you tell?' I asked, running my fingers under the tap. 'How can you tell which are the older pieces, the better pieces?'

He laughed again. 'You work it and if it crumbles then you know. Don't worry,' he added, pointing at my fingers, 'amber is a natural antiseptic, you won't get an infection.'

I worked hard at the lathe for a couple of hours, transforming the light, dull lumps of amber into gleaming drops of fire, dropping the finished pieces into plastic butter tubs. I was taking a break, sitting at my desk sorting through the orders that had arrived in the post, when the telephone rang. After a moment's hesitation I picked up the receiver. It was Tanya. Her voice sounded brittle and tense, as though at any moment she might break down and cry.

'Can you come over?'

'I was hoping to,' I said. 'Are you feeling OK?'

'Come over,' she said, and put down the receiver.

Turning off the lathe and the light, I took a few of the letters to deal with later and locked up the shop. I was concerned by the tone of Tanya's voice. Though she had been upset, she had not sounded so on edge before. As I wandered distractedly down the road, I dropped one of the letters as I was pushing it into my pocket. The envelope fluttered to the ground and I had to lunge and grab it before it landed in a puddle created by a blocked drain.

As I straightened up, out of the corner of my eye I saw a rapid movement, a dark shape flitting from one shadow to another. I turned. The street was busy and, glancing around, I could see nothing out of the ordinary. The fear of shadows, of sudden movements glimpsed out of the corner of the eye, was the shared inheritance of all Afghan veterans. Like beaten dogs we flinched at every sound, shied from every flicker. Stilling my heart, I walked on.

When I got to Tanya's apartment block, I was about to push open the door when I heard a shout from behind me. Tanya stood in the doorway of the beer hall on the opposite side of the road. Tucking a scarf around her throat, she came over.

'I couldn't sit in there on my own,' she said, looping her arm through mine, pressing her cheek against my shoulder.

'A bad day?'

She grimaced. 'Come upstairs and see.'

'What do you mean?'

She did not reply, but took my arm and pushed me through into the dingy stairwell. She led the way up the stairs, taking them two at a time. She paused before fitting her key into the lock and indicated that I should look. Leaning close to the door, I noticed that the wood was scuffed around the area of the lock, and there were sharp splinters in the jamb. The lock itself was gleaming steel. New.

'You had a break-in?' I asked.

In answer, she slid the key into the new lock and turned it. Holding the door open, she indicated for me to enter first. A little apprehensively I crossed the threshold into the apartment. There was little evidence in the small hallway of any signs of a disturbance. Tanya's handbag sat on a table by the door, the pictures were undisturbed and the wooden floor shone in the shaft of light falling from the kitchen window.

'I had just managed to clean up the apartment, after feeling so ashamed when you were here,' Tanya said.

Puzzled, I slipped off my shoes and stepped across the hallway to the sitting room. Pushing open the door, I stopped abruptly. The room was strewn with books and papers. Stepping forwards, the better to see the confusion, I trod painfully on the sharp debris carpeting the floor.

'What happened?' I asked.

Tanya stood behind me in the doorway, looking over my shoulder.

'As far as I can see,' she said, 'they have taken nothing of any value.'

I gazed around the room. Books had been pulled off shelves and tossed on to the floor, on to the sofa, the armchair. The standard lamp had been knocked off balance by the weight of a tome on St Petersburg; a flying volume of Pushkin had shattered the vase on a small table by the wall. Folders of papers had been scattered and now lay like chilly drifts of snow across hillocks of Russian literature, mounds of books on jewellery, knolls of poetry. Pieces of amber, Tanya's jewellery, fragments of vase and broken glass gravelled the floor.

'Who did this?' I gasped.

'Somebody was looking for something specific, I think,' Tanya said. 'I was at work when the police telephoned to tell me a neighbour had reported a disturbance in my apartment. Mrs Gaskiene was worried I had gone mad in my grief. She came to knock on the door, only to find it gaping open and this mess in the front room.'

As I bent to pick up an amber necklace that lay on the carpet by my feet, I sensed immediately that this had been the work of Kirov.

'What do you think they were looking for?' I asked Tanya, not voicing my fear. I recalled the comment he had made in the workshop. *I know where Tanya lives. She's all on her own now*. Was this a warning? I wondered. Or was he looking for the bracelet, or evidence of Kolya's whereabouts?

'No jewellery seems to be missing,' Tanya said, bending down beside me, taking the necklace from my fingers. 'Vassily made this for me,' she added. 'You remember?'

'Yes,' I said, the memory of that moment flooding back as I fingered the beads of the necklace. 'Just before you left the village to come to Vilnius.'

We were in the kitchen, in her grandparents' home, around the large old table. It was late evening and the room was dark and warm, the door of the tiled stove open in the corner, providing us with light and heat. Tanya had told us she would have to return to the capital to continue with her studies. Vassily attempted to convince her to stay, but, though she seemed genuinely sad to be leaving, she was determined to go back to university.

'I will bribe you to stay,' he said.

'There is nothing you could offer,' Tanya shot back.

Vassily laughed. From his pocket he pulled out a necklace. Each of the amber beads on the silk string was a different shade. Translucent yellow, the shade of sunshine, to currant black. He held it up. 'Women are not able to turn from the power of finely made jewellery. When they see a piece of jewellery they love, there is nothing they will not do to get hold of it. It has always been so, since the beginning of time. You know the story of Freyja?'

Tanya laughed. 'No,' she mocked, 'but I'm sure you will tell us.'

'She was the goddess of love,' he said with relish, smacking his lips. 'She was beautiful, the most beautiful woman in the ancient world. Not only was she the goddess of love, she was the goddess of the sexual act; she loved beauty and sensuality. But she was also goddess of the dead and was mistress of a secret magical science that could read the fates of men and brought fecundity and birth. She was married to Od, god of fury, and was happy.

'One day, while she was wandering along the border of her kingdom, her eyes fell upon the most beautiful necklace she had ever seen.

'Her kingdom bordered that of the Black Dwarfs. As she peered through the trees and the thick undergrowth she caught sight of the gleam of gorgeous stones. Four dwarfs were crafting a beautiful necklace, which caught the sun whenever they held it up. Entranced, Freyja could not stop herself from slipping into the glade where the dwarfs were working and going to admire the necklace.

'"How much does it cost?" she asked them. "Tell me, I will pay whatever sum you ask for."

'The dwarfs shook their heads. "This," they told her, "is the Brisingamen. There is no price you could pay." But Freyja begged them. It was the most beautiful jewel she had ever seen and she could not imagine living without it.

'You see,' he said, 'you have to know the power a piece of jewellery can have on you. You have to know the pull some stones have.' He paused a moment longer. 'Freyja would have paid anything to have that necklace. The four dwarfs huddled together and discussed the price for which they would be willing to sell the Brisingamen. Finally they decided. "We will sell you the necklace," they said to her, "but there is only one price we will accept."

'"What is it? Just name it," said Freyja.

'"You must make love with each one of us," the dwarfs said. And such was the power the beautiful necklace had on her, Freyja agreed to the price instantly and with joy. Betraying her husband, she slept with each dwarf for a day and a night, pleasuring them with whatever sensual delights they wished for. And on the fourth day she left with the necklace strung around her neck, radiating beauty.

'But she had betrayed her husband,' Vassily said, quietly emphatic. 'And when you betray somebody you are sure to be found out sooner or later.

'Freyja had been seen,' he continued. 'The odious Loki had seen everything. He went to her husband and told him all he knew. Od would not believe that snivelling spirit of evil. He demanded Loki prove his tale to be true.

'But how could Loki prove his tale?' Vassily drained his glass of vodka and poured a new one. 'Freyja had hidden the jewel.' He paused again for effect, looking around at each one of us sitting around the table. 'Loki turned himself into a mosquito. He flew into Freyja's chambers and bit her as she slept. The bite irritated her and she scratched and tossed and turned in her sleep. Loki grabbed the necklace from beneath her pillow and took it straight to Od.

'Od flew into a rage. He threw the necklace aside and the next day he disappeared. When Freyja woke the next morning, she discovered that both her necklace and her husband had gone. Ever since that day she has wandered the earth looking for her husband, weeping continously. The tears that fall upon the rocks, seeping into the seams, turn into gold. Those tears that fall upon the sea turn into beads of amber.'

'Seven years ago,' Tanya said. 'It seems a lifetime.'

She put the necklace on the low table and picked up some more of the scattered fragments of jewellery and amber pieces.

'There wasn't much money here,' she continued. 'You know what Vassily was like – as soon as it came in it went out, he had no desire to hoard it beneath the mattress and anybody who knew him would have known that.' She paused, surveying the mess of papers and books. 'It seems,' she said, 'that they were after some of his papers or his books. It doesn't make any sense to me.'

'I think it could have been Kirov,' I said quietly.

'Kirov? Why?'

I shrugged. 'He may have thought there would be something here that would reveal where Kolya is. Where the bracelet is.'

Tanya shivered.

'What scares me,' she said, 'is that I have no idea what is going on. It is like standing on the edge of an abyss in the darkness. This great hole has opened up before me and I don't know how to deal with it. Vassily and I told each other everything. We had no secrets, we would never lie to each other, that was what we said again and again.'

She stood up and kicked out at an upturned book.

'Fuck him!' she cried. 'How could he die and leave this mess? Why did he not let me know what was going on, Antanas? Why did he lie to me?'

She kicked another volume, sending it ricocheting across the small room. I stood up and took hold of her arms.

'How could he have done this to me, Antanas?' she said bitterly.

'Calm down,' I said. 'I know as little as you.'

'I'm sorry,' she said, red eyed.

I tried to draw her down on to the sofa, to calm her.

'You must find Kolya,' she said. 'He is the only one who can explain what this is all about.'

'I'm worried,' I said. 'The more we get involved in this, the more dangerous it is for you.'

'Why should it be dangerous for me?'

I shrugged. 'Who knows what Kirov will do.'

'I'm becoming more frightened of the shadows,' Tanya said, 'the empty spaces, the not knowing.'

She went into the kitchen to make some coffee, and I turned my attention to the mess. I gathered the books and replaced them on their shelves, collected the scattered sheets of paper, stacking them on the sofa to sort later into their appropriate files. Tanya reappeared with coffee, put it down and began to sweep up the splinters of glass and broken fragments of vase and cups. We had more or less finished when I noticed, behind us, the shadow of a figure standing in the doorway.

Hearing feet on the tiles behind her, Tanya started and spun round, her face ashen.

'The door was open,' Zinotis said. 'I knocked but nobody answered.'

'This is Professor Zinotis,' I explained to Tanya, my

own heart beating rapidly from his sudden appearance. 'A friend of Vassily's.'

'I'm sorry,' Tanya said, 'I'm a little on edge today.' She held out her hand and Zinotis took it and shook it warmly. 'Vassily has mentioned you,' she added. 'It's strange we never actually met when he was alive.' Her lips tightened as she said this, and I was afraid she would break down again, but she didn't. She offered him a seat, taking from it a pile of the papers we had collected together. He declined the coffee she offered him, but took out an old pipe.

'Would you mind?' he asked.

'Not at all,' Tanya said.

It was obvious Zinotis had not been expecting me to be there. For some moments he seemed at a loss as to what to say. He covered this with the careful packing of his pipe. He lit it and exhaled the rich, spicy smoke.

'I came over to offer my condolences,' he said.

Tanya smiled and thanked him.

'We spent many afternoons together,' Zinotis added. 'Swapping stories about various jewels, legends.' Turning to me, he said, 'I've been giving some thought to what we talked about this morning.'

'Have you had any ideas?'

'I thought perhaps Tanya would know something,' he said, 'but I suppose you have already discussed that yourself.' He smiled apologetically.

'I'm bewildered by the whole thing,' Tanya said. 'Do you know anything about this bracelet? Or what it is Vassily wanted Kolya to tell Antanas?'

Zinotis sucked on his pipe thoughtfully. His shoulders lifted slightly in a shrug.

'No,' he said. 'Little more than what Antanas told me earlier.' He paused and gazed out of the window.

'Vassily was involved in smuggling jewellery while he was in Afghanistan,' he continued after a few moments. 'The bracelet is presumably something they brought back from there.'

Tanya sat up. 'He told you this?'

'He talked about it a little,' Zinotis said.

Tanya turned to me. 'Did you know about this?'

I nodded. 'A little,' I conceded. 'It was not something I wanted to get involved in.'

Tanya shook her head. 'He said nothing about it to me,' she murmured, more to herself than Zinotis or me.

'He got the piece in a village called Ghazis,' I told Zinotis, 'over in the east of Afghanistan.'

Zinotis raised his eyebrows and nodded. He brought the pipe to his mouth but, discovering it had gone out, took out a packet of tobacco and began to refill it. 'By all accounts,' he said, 'there were a lot of jewels and artefacts swimming around in Afghanistan. Like those from Bagram, the summer capital of the Kushan Empire, which was on the Silk Route that connected Rome with India and China. Alexander the Great founded a city there. In 1936 an archaeological excavation in Bagram uncovered one of the greatest finds of the century. The coins and jewellery dug up were on display in the Kabul Museum.'

'*Were* on display?'

'The museum was plundered after the Soviet army withdrew. Little remains of the collection.'

'You're suggesting Vassily bought something stolen from there?'

'I'm not suggesting anything,' Zinotis said, shaking his head. 'I was just speculating. During the period of our occupation the museum was well guarded.

Unfortunately the American-backed rebels were not quite so concerned about the cultural heritage of the country they were liberating. However, even though the collection was guarded well when our troops were there, the fact is pieces did go missing. There was a trade in artefacts.'

'But would they have had amber in Afghanistan?' I asked. 'I mean in the time of Alexander the Great or during the period of the Kushan Empire?'

'You would be amazed,' Zinotis said. 'Amber from our coast has been traded since the dawn of time. Despite the fact that this was one of the remotest parts of Europe, pagan until the fourteenth century, merchants ferried our amber across the world thousands of years ago. Pieces were found in the tomb of Tutankhamun, who lived in Egypt almost one and a half thousand years before the birth of Christ. The Phoenicians transported it around the coast into the Mediterranean. The Greeks were fascinated by it.'

I smiled. 'You remind me of Vassily, a walking encyclopaedia of amber.'

Zinotis laughed. 'What a store of information he had! We spent hours swapping stories over drinks.'

Having tamped down the tobacco in his pipe, he took out a match and attempted to light it. For some moments he sucked at it, then lit another match and tried again. The fragrant aroma of the tobacco filled the room. Thick smoke plumed up around his head, shrouding his pinched face for a moment.

'The Chinese were fascinated by amber too,' he continued. 'They believed it was the soul of a tiger which had died and passed into the earth, giving it magical properties. The Tibetans call it perfumed crystal. There are many routes it could have taken to get to Afghanistan.'

He paused again, sucking pensively on his battered old pipe, his eyes casting around the room, tidy now, though the books and papers were disordered.

'But the important thing is to find Kolya, yes?' he said. 'Vassily wanted him to have the bracelet.'

I nodded.

'Still,' he continued, 'smuggled jewellery needs a seller.' He smiled. 'You might have need of me. I know a little about the market. If you hear anything about Kolya . . .'

He levered himself up from the armchair.

'Thank you for your help,' Tanya said.

'What do you think?' she said later, when Zinotis had left.

'I don't know,' I said. 'It's true Vassily was dealing in artefacts. It wasn't something I paid much attention to when we were out there. I just considered it to be part of his love of jewellery.'

Tanya sighed.

'Will you stay?' she asked later, when darkness had fallen.

'Yes,' I said, looking over at her curled in the armchair, the dim light of the standard lamp casting shadows over her small, pretty face, and thinking of my own empty apartment. 'Maybe it's better I stay with you tonight.'

Chapter 13

'Memory is a funny thing,' I said as we lay enveloped by the thick darkness and stillness of the night. 'I remember the scent of oranges. I can still remember the way it used to smell in spring.'

'Vassily would say that,' Tanya said. 'You should smell the spring in Jalalabad, he would say to me, when the snow melts on the mountains, when the trees blossom.'

'I remember the smell of charred flesh, too, the smell of bombs and dust and sweat and fear.'

Tanya reached out, under the sheet, and took my hand in hers, caressing my fingers gently with her thumb.

There had been orange blossom on the trees at the time of that first raid. We had regrouped at the foot of the mountains. The pine and spruce growing higher up had given way to ash and oak. An orange grove rambled across a low hill. The trees were decked with blossom. When we scrambled out of the APCs we were greeted with the scent of narcissi, which grew in profusion on the grassy banks of the road, scarlet and yellow.

I sat in the dust, still cradling the lifeless body of Pavlov, gazing out across the orchard as we waited for the medical choppers to arrive to take the dead and injured to Jalalabad. In the centre of the orchard, on the brow of the hill, stood a small cottage only partly visible between the trunks of the orange trees and their blossoming branches.

Vassily squatted down beside me and followed my gaze out over the hill towards the cottage.

'What a beautiful place,' I said.

Vassily nodded and placed a hand on my knee. 'Beautiful and terrible.'

He lifted the shattered body of Pavlov and laid him in line with the other corpses at the side of the road. There were five. Taking out a rag he used for testing the oil in the KamaZ, Vassily wiped the blood from my face. We stood in silence over the bodies of our friends for some time.

'I remember the scent of narcissi,' I told Tanya, drawing closer to her in the darkness.

When the Mi-8s arrived we loaded the bodies into their trembling, swollen bellies. Vassily picked a handful of the brilliant yellow narcissi from the side of the road and laid them on the chests of the soldiers in their body bags. The helicopters shuddered and rose with a roar.

We watched as they soared sinisterly over the orange grove, black against the bloody sun. Beneath them the pale blossom shivered and fell like snow upon the cooling earth. Vassily laid his hand on my shoulder.

'Death will not go hungry tonight.'

It was while we were away on that first raid that Kirov met Hashim. I pictured the Afghani merchant, his thin straggly beard, dirty shalwar-kameez and dark turban, his uneven smile and the way he used to cough up phlegm and spit it on to the floor in large dark pools, stained with *naswar*, tobacco mixed with opium.

In the short time Kirov had been in Afghanistan he had already learnt how to abuse the system. Following the incident in Jalalabad, when he had paid for vodka with a grenade, he had begun buying all kinds of privileges with stolen goods and services. Rumour had it that his mafia connections in his home town of Kaliningrad would have bought him a 'white ticket' out of national service if he had not been implicated in the violent rape of a teenage girl, which made a two-year break in central Asia seem sensible, until things quietened down.

When Kirov went to pick up some goods from Jalalabad one day, he met a merchant who told him he had something that might interest Kirov. Hashim had various things at the back of his store – jewellery, Western cigarettes, Russian vodka, tape players and televisions from Japan.

It was late when we arrived back at the base after the raid. Kirov was lying back on his crudely made bunk, smoking Marlboro cigarettes and listening to a Western cassette – Kim Wilde, on a new Japanese tape player.

'What the fuck?' Kolya muttered.

Kirov sat up with a sly grin and proffered the packet of cigarettes. We each took one and stood around the tape player, gazing at it in wonder.

'How many *cheki* did it cost?' Kolya wanted to know.

Kirov shrugged. He pulled a bottle of Stolichnaya from beneath his blanket and waved it before our eyes.

'Get some glasses,' he said.

'Stolichnaya!'

'Where the fuck?'

'Shhh! If the rest hear they'll all want some.'

'Turn off the light.'

The glasses clinked in the darkness. We sat beneath the small window, listening to music playing softly on the tape player, smoking the beautiful, smooth Marlboro cigarettes and drinking Stolichnaya, which tasted as sweet as milk after the spirits we had been making for ourselves.

'Maybe we died too,' Kolya said, his voice weary, but cheerful. I could see his wide grin in the faint light from the window. 'Maybe we were killed and are in heaven, like the muj think.'

'Don't they get whores too?' asked Vassily.

'Where did you get all this stuff?' I asked Kirov.

'A trader in Jalalabad,' he answered.

The next time the convoy drove into Jalalabad for supplies, we went to Hashim's small store near the hospital. It was then we discovered the prices we could get for things. Anything. The wing mirrors from the KamaZ, spare wheels, ammunition, uniforms, medical supplies. We could get a hundred thousand *afoshki* for a Kalashnikov. Bulgarian biscuits from the army store would fetch a good price, as would sweets, canned milk.

With the *afoshki* we earned selling equipment we had stolen from the base, we were able to buy products from the West coming through from Pakistan. Cigarettes, good vodka, cassette players, video players and presents we could take home when our service was over. We sold our boots, which we rarely wore owing to their extreme unsuitability for the terrain we were in, and our flak jackets, sleeping bags and uniforms, which were all so uncomfortable in the hot climate that they were never used either. They did not fetch much money, but it was often enough for us to buy better equipment, which the mujahidin were smuggling into the country. The only time we were required to wear uniforms was when senior officers visited from Kabul or Jalalabad, which was rare. Generally full uniform was only insisted on for the newest recruits.

It was the jewellery which caught Vassily's eye. He lingered over the huge lumps of lapis lazuli, the beryl and the gold and silver, some of which was obviously antique.

'Where did you get this stuff?' he asked. 'Is there more?'

'This?' Hashim said. 'This is just shit. If you want some real pieces, then I can get you some that would interest you.'

'What kind of pieces do you have?'

Hashim waved his hand above his head, as though rare, precious pieces of jewellery were so common in Afghanistan he could just pluck them from the air.

'Many pieces. Not far from here was once an ancient and important Buddhist site. There are many pieces of jewellery and other things you might be interested in. You're interested in Buddhist icons? No? There are many more things that will interest you. But . . .' He rubbed his thumb and index finger together, '. . . they cost.'

'You find me something interesting and I will find the way to pay you,' Vassily said.

I fell asleep with Tanya's fingers curled in my own, the warmth of her body close to me. In the darkness, a vision of the waves of pale blossom rolled over me. I was walking beneath the trees, reaching up, plucking a sprig from a low branch, examining the delicate petals, marvelling at the careful colouring of each miniature canvas. A child laughed. The blossom slipped from my fingers and fluttered to the ground. The earth was dark, rich. I bent to retrieve the pale petals. My fingers loosened the earth, searching delicately.

'Leave it,' somebody said. 'Wait for the sappers.'

I inched forwards across the ground, eyes straining for evidence of the buried mines. I stiffened. A child was crying. My fingers reached out again to loosen the earth.

'Leave it,' a voice said.

A child was crying, a pitiful ululation, a desperate, heart-rending sob.

'Just wait for the fucking sappers.'

The earth was stippled. Tiny plumes of dirt rose before me. Little pillars of dust. The dull thwack of bullets entering a tree trunk.

'Sniper!'

'Find cover!'

I lay still, lips pressed tight against the hot earth, ears pricked like a dog's, heart thudding in the dry soil, a searing pain slitting my skull in two. I rolled, was trapped. Could not move.

I gasped, my mouth gaping, drawing in air, as though surfacing from beneath the waves. My eyes opened wide, straining against the darkness. My hands flayed, pulling at the sheet wound tight around me, balled in my fists, suffocating me. I sat up, struggling to catch my breath, placing myself slowly, feeling the edge of the bed, the tight knot of sheets, the worn carpet beneath me. Tanya still asleep. I buried my head in my knees, pressing my eyes shut.

When the panic had receded and my pulse calmed, and I had unwound the sheets from around my body, I sat on the edge of the bed. My head throbbed and, lifting a hand and touching it gingerly, I discovered I was bleeding. I had banged it against the corner of the side table, falling from the bed.

I got up, pulled on Vassily's old dressing gown and slipped out of the bedroom, pulling the door quietly closed behind me. There was a half-drunk bottle of brandy on one of the bookshelves in the sitting room. I took a glass and poured myself a large one. Turning on the standard lamp, I settled in the armchair. By its arm there was a pile of photo albums Tanya had not tidied away. Many of the photographs had fallen from the pages when they had been pulled from the shelf and she had put them by the chair, planning to sort them out.

Flicking through the albums, I looked at my friend, young, full of life. I came across a photograph I had taken the summer after we moved to Vilnius. Vassily stood on the beach dressed in a pair of shorts, clasping Tanya to him. Sea water was still streaming from his hair and beard so that he looked like Neptune risen from beneath the waves, and Tanya was screaming, pulling away from him, her dark hair swinging out against the shimmering light bouncing from the surface of the sea. I picked the photograph up, examining closely the two bright, happy faces.

'Amberella, Amberella,' Vassily was shouting. I could hear his voice, remember its exact cadence, remember the way they had fallen, struggling, to the sand the moment after this picture had been taken, Tanya laughing and screaming and shouting for help. It was the summer after Tanya had introduced me to her university room-mate Daiva. She was standing behind me, watching the two of them. Slipping her arms around me, she rested her chin on my shoulder. It was a moment of pure joy.

'Amberella was a beautiful young girl who lived here in the village,' Vassily had told us the evening before.

It was late June and we had borrowed a car and driven to the coast to visit Tanya's grandparents. We took a bottle and settled on the beach, watching the sun set, listening to the wash of the waves on the sand. It was a sultry evening but later we built a small fire, for its light, not warmth.

'Her father was a fisherman and they lived in a small hut,' Vassily continued. 'Though their house was the smallest and meanest in the village, Amberella was the prettiest girl for miles around and her father and mother adored her.

'Each morning she would run out to this beach and take an early morning swim in the sea. One morning, as she was swimming, the current caught her and she was dragged down beneath the waves, down into the depths of the sea. The prince of the sea had seen the beautiful young woman bathing in his waters and fallen in love with her. It was he that had reached out and drawn her down to his palace in the rocks, far below the surface. Amberella was his prisoner. The sea prince kept her as his princess, in his fabulous palace built with bricks of amber.

'Poor Amberella was heartbroken. She wept and begged the prince to return her to her parents, who she knew would be stricken with grief at losing their only daughter. The prince was angry that Amberella wept and begged him daily to let her go. Finally, however, moved by her pleas, he harnessed his frothing white horses and rose with her to the surface of the sea in a raging storm.

'Amberella's father was in his fishing boat when his daughter rose from beneath the sea in the prince's chariot, with a crown of amber on her head and amber beads laced about her neck. As she plunged once more beneath the tossing waves she pulled the amber beads from her neck and threw them to her father. And that was the last he saw of her.

'When the storms rage and the waves crash upon the beach, still Amberella tosses her amber beads from the window of her palace beneath the sea, hoping they will wash up on the shore to show her parents that she loves them and thinks of them always.'

Putting the photo album aside, I stood up. A photograph spiralled to the floor from my lap. Bending down, I picked it up to slip back into the album.

It was a black-and-white photograph and the quality of the image was very poor. It was of a group of uniformed men, arms draped around each other's shoulders, caps awry, Kalashnikovs held casually in hands, grins on most faces. Behind the group was a large tree, a eucalyptus.

I recognised the group immediately and found myself at the back beside Vassily. My eyes scanned down to the foreground of the photograph. Chistyakov knelt at the front, his legs and knees indiscernible, fading into the poorly developed edge of the photograph, as though when the photograph had been taken his very existence was already draining away.

I turned the photograph over. On the back, in pencil, somebody had scrawled 'Jalalabad 1988'.

'June,' I said, and poured myself another brandy.

Chapter 14

The morning after the photograph was taken, two helicopters were scrambled from the base to deal with sniper fire coming from a village on to the road to Jalalabad. Chistyakov joined the small group of granddads boarding the Mi-24s.

'Have a last cigarette, before you go,' Kirov said, proffering his packet of Marlboros.

'Don't say "last"!' Chistyakov snapped. 'What's the matter with you?'

Kirov grinned maliciously. Superstitiously we never used the word 'last'. As the helicopters disappeared into the distance, I joined the supply trucks' military escort heading into Jalalabad. The wind was gathering force and raising dust in dark swollen clouds, which rolled across the plains and hung above the city like a thick autumnal mist, blurring the sun. The dust stuck to our slick, sweaty bodies. Each movement we made grated; our tongues were thickly furred with the fine Afghani soil, our hair stiff and white. The Afghans pulled their shawls tightly around themselves, covering their faces. The whole city seemed to be shrouded under a suffocating, billowing grey burqa.

We were returning to base slowly, an APC before and behind the supply trucks, when a call came through that the two helicopters that had gone on the morning raid had been brought down by the mujahidin, and that Chistyakov was missing.

We were met by a couple of BMPs just outside the village. One of the granddads who had been on the morning raid came over to parley with us.

'I thought the muj brought your two helicopters down,' Lieutenant Zhuralev said.

'Did they fuck!' the granddad spat. 'The pilot crashed. We landed just outside the village. It was quiet, so we were going in to take a look around. The wind got up, blowing like hell, so we could barely see a fucking thing. We should have pulled out then. As we got close to the village the *dukhs* opened fire. Not from the village but from some *kirize* behind us. As we were retreating, one of the pilots panicked – he started to take off. What with the wind and dust storm he comes down in some trees. In the confusion we lost some of our boys. Chistyakov is unaccounted for; we think the muj must have taken him.'

As we wound slowly down the rutted lane to the village, which was situated on an incline, the wind began to drop. The sun appeared, bloody and heavy, sagging towards the hazy horizon. The fields and trees were white with dust. As the late rays of sun caught them they shone scarlet. We were a kilometre from the village when Kolya, sitting beside me, spotted the dark shape in the dirt a little way off the road.

'There,' he called.

I jumped from the back of the APC and made my way towards it.

'Stop!' Lieutenant Zhuralev called. I turned to him. He was perched on top of the leading APC. 'Mines,' he called irritably. 'Do you want to get blown to pieces?'

A couple of sappers jumped down with their dog and began a careful reconnaissance of the area.

The body, when I got to it, was sheathed in gritty dust. It was, in fact, just the torso of a body. For some moments it was hard to recognise what I was looking at. It looked like the carcass of a sheep or a goat. The arms had been hacked clumsily from the body. The bones glistened where they poked from the flesh. The head had been hacked away too, leaving folds of flesh. The legs were gone, and the genitals.

The torso had been peeled. The skin hung off in folds of fatty flesh, tarred now with dust. I stopped a couple of paces from it. Despite the sticky heat I felt my spine turn to ice. I placed my gun on the ground beside me.

'Is it him?' a voice called from behind me.

I did not answer. No air was able to work its way up or down my throat. I felt my jaw clenched tight, so tight it hurt.

'Is it Chistyakov?'

I turned to the APC, which had pulled carefully from the track, staying within the parameters of the area checked by the sappers.

'How the fuck would I know?' I shouted, the words tearing at my throat, the exertion causing tears to spring to my eyes. I turned back to the torso.

'Fuck,' I heard Kolya whisper behind me, from the top of the APC. 'Fuck, fuck, fuck.'

The sweet stink of raw flesh drifted backwards and forwards with the eddying wind. I looked down the valley towards the mountains, towards the rise of trees, dark already, slipping quietly, unobtrusively into the oncoming night, as if guiltily sidling away from the event, wanting nothing to do with it.

I felt a surge of blinding rage swell in my chest. It caught as it rose to my throat. I turned quickly from the torso to face Sasha, who was vomiting by the side of the APC.

It was too late to launch a raid on the village that evening. We returned to the base and passed the night in silence; even the granddads were subdued. When the pre-dawn light seeped over the peaks of the mountains, we stubbed out our cigarettes and readied ourselves for the raid. I moved in a hashish dream, following my hands and feet through the necessary actions. I held the rage tight in my chest, feeding off it, not sure even against whom I raged.

The choppers rose into the cool air, turned and swooped away across the trees, down the river towards the village. The moon was up still, its large, pale face mournful and tired. As the sun edged its way up the mountains from China, across Pakistan, the western sky remained dark. White clouds plumed from the wheels of the APCs on the road beneath us. I thrust a magazine into my Kalashnikov, heard it click into place and kissed it. 'For Chistyakov.' The metal was cool beneath my lips.

I gazed down at the country below us, pale beneath the light of the moon and the dying night. The river glittered. The forest was dark. The village rose up before us on the swell of a hill, still slumbering. Behind us, a dark eagle, flew another chopper.

There was no pause above the huddled streets. No time for thought. As we drew close, the helicopter banked sharply and dived down towards its target. Dawn was shattered with the whistle of rockets. Blue-pink flames sprayed from our guns. There was a heavy thud and a dark column of debris erupted from the village. A second rose beside it. The other chopper moved in behind us and a moment later the village was transformed into a bubbling cauldron of mud and dirt and rags and spokes of wood. I felt the hairs on the back of my neck rise. My heart pounded. I heard a whoop beside me. Kolya gripped my shoulder. His eyes were large, his pupils dilated.

The helicopter descended. As it rocked against the earth we leapt from its belly. My feet did not feel the ground beneath them. I flew across the churned earth. Kolya let off a round and I heard the bullets thud against the crumbling walls of the village. Wooden beams pierced the broken walls, like ribs from the carcass of a long-dead animal.

As I leapt across the walls, my eyes flicked from the dark corners to the smouldering mounds of rubble, searching for signs of life that needed to be extinguished. The only movement was the slide of clay as the walls crumbled around us. The village was deserted. The air was heavy with the scent of explosives, with the acrid smoke from burning wood, with dust churned from the earth. The rotors of the helicopters throbbed, the fire crackled, and our feet crunched in the rubble. From the far side of the village there rose a pitiful wailing. We scrambled towards the sound.

Beneath the rubble we found a dog, its body twisted and crushed, its fur matted with blood and dust. Kolya raised his gun and shot it. Its small body jerked against the earth and fell silent suddenly, mid-wail.

Tethered at the foot of the hill there were goats and a couple of camels and an ass. They gazed up towards the village as if astounded by the sudden destruction of their home. A granddad who had joined us by the dog raised his gun and fired. The ass dropped to its knees and keeled over on to its side. Another granddad cheered. He fired himself, but his shot went wide and the first soldier jeered at him.

I turned away from the small group gathered at the edge of the village. As I wandered back across the flattened walls and charred spine of the settlement, I heard the crack of their rifles and the frightened moan of the animals tethered below them. In the corner of what had been a house, I stooped and brushed away the dirt. On the packed earth floor was a child's kite, broken-backed and ragged. From its tail hung a pink ribbon.

The sun rose above the jagged ridge of mountains and caressed the earth with its light. The heavy throb of the blades of the helicopters had ceased and from the trees behind the village I heard the call of a bird. I took the ribbon from the bottom of the kite and felt its synthetic smoothness between my cold fingers. Behind me the flattened village sighed and creaked as it settled once more into the dirt from which it had been raised.

Before we left, fuel was siphoned from the tank of one of the choppers and poured over the animals. Lieutenant Zhuralev tossed the burning stub of his cigarette on to the mound of corpses. As we rose into the air and circled the shattered village, the smoke curled into the pale morning sky.

Snowcapped mountains glittered in the rising sun. The river twisted and turned and rushed, white-backed, across its rocky bed. Cranes broke from the reeds as we passed, startled by the pulse of our rotors. The higher slopes of the mountains were dark with fir and cedar. Beneath them, across the foothills, the sun caught the leaves of the ash and alder and walnut trees. The sky was brilliantly clear. Deep blue. The colour of the

Virgin's gown in an icon in a church I had seen once as a child. Pure blue. What a beautiful country, I thought.

Chapter 15

Zinotis's thick old volume on the *Jewellery of the Kushan Empire*, which I had borrowed for Vassily some years before, was at the bottom of a pile of books in the back room of the workshop. My eyes fell on it almost as soon as I stepped into the room. I had returned to get some cash from the safe hidden beneath the floorboards. It was very doubtful I would get any information out of the Santariskes Clinic if Kolya was not there. It was hard enough to get information from doctors about yourself, never mind about other patients. A few dollars might extract an address from one of the badly paid orderlies.

Distracted, I pulled the book from the pile and took it over to my work table. The volume was pale with the dust of the worked amber. I opened it, cracking the dry old spine as I did so. I flicked over the pages, examining the dark photographs of jewellery from a long-extinguished civilisation.

Standing the volume by my chair, I lifted the thin carpet in the corner of the room and pulled open the small hatch in the floorboards. A metal safe was bolted to the concrete in the hole beneath the floor. Taking out the key, I unlocked it and drew from the safe a plastic bag. Wound tightly inside the bag was a roll of dollar bills. Extracting two fifties, I stuffed them in my pocket and replaced the bag in the safe, shutting and locking it, and smoothing down the carpet above the hatch. An orderly in the hospital earned around one hundred dollars a month. Fifty dollars ought to be enough to buy an address. Taking the volume on the *Jewellery of the Kushan Empire*, I locked up the workshop and took the trolley bus to my apartment.

Approaching my block, I glanced up over the trees, and searched among the hundreds of windows for my own. The cool light of the weak sun, veiled by clouds, reflected from the window, open slightly to let in a breath of air. Having mounted the stairs, I paused for a few moments outside the door of the apartment, listening. The idea of going into its silent emptiness sent a shiver down my spine.

Suddenly, crushingly, I missed my little daughter's face, the soft sound of her breathing in the night, the tight clench of her small hand on my finger. I missed Daiva, the sweetness of her scent, the gentleness of her touch, the light ring of her laughter, which I had not heard in months.

I turned the key in the lock, quickly opened the door and stumbled inside. The apartment was cold and felt forsaken. I unscrewed the top of a bottle of vodka, and raised it to my lips, not bothering with a glass. The liquid was cool on my tongue and then the heat flared up from my stomach, burning its way to the back of my throat. I took another gulp and felt the pain in my chest receding, the tightness of my skull loosen.

I lay back on the sofa and closed my eyes. My breathing came more easily now and the pain had gone. I listened to the hiss of tyres on the road eight storeys below, the low throb of engines, the calls of children playing outside, a broken melody being picked slowly from a piano in the apartment above.

I thought back to the late October days of two years

before. After some years together, in an attempt to solve some of the problems and tensions in our relationship, Daiva and I had married in the autumn. Vassily and Tanya witnessed our wedding. October had faded in a pale blue haze of bonfires that hung in the still air, in soft reds and the rich yellow of the leaves of the oaks and maple twisting to the earth in slow, dancing loops, crinkling under foot.

On the first of December Daiva woke early and ran to the bathroom. From beneath the sheets I could hear her vomiting. I pulled on a dressing gown and hurried to her. Her face was a pale shade of green. Carrying her back to bed, I tucked her beneath the sheets. When I returned from the kitchen with coffee and a glass of water, she was retching again, into the bin beside the bed.

'I think I'm pregnant,' she said, falling back against the pillows.

I lifted the covers and undid the buttons of her night-dress. Her body was warm. I ran my fingers down her chest to her belly. There was no sign anything had changed, no evidence of the miracle at that moment occurring in her body. I laid my head on her stomach and listened to the low gurgles of her digestive system, trying to imagine what was happening inside there.

'What do you think?' she said, her voice laced with concern.

'What do I think? Daiva, it's wonderful.'

'You don't worry it is all too soon?'

I lifted myself up so my chin was resting on her soft belly and gazed into her sleepy face.

'No,' I said. And truly I felt that. The past dropped away from me, the need for a past, a history. Everything lay in the future, in the slow growth of the seed within her womb, the development of its limbs, the swell of her belly – life, new life, gestating within her. All concern suddenly lay in the months and years ahead, not in the years that had gone.

By the time the worst of the winter was over, the swell of Daiva's belly was noticeable. Her whole body seemed to blossom, like a bud on the first spring flowers, defiant of the frost, shooting up from the dark, cold earth, at first a bulging, tight calyx, then growing, swelling, the leaves stretching stickily around the maturing petals.

And as she grew and we felt the first tentative kicks against the inside of her womb, the stretch of the baby's limbs, and as the days grew longer and brighter and the maples and birch budded beneath our windows, I allowed myself to believe I could hold back the darkness, that the fear would not return. When an engine misfired, when the telephone crackled suddenly and sharply, when a child screamed as I stood in the queue in the store and the cold prickling sweat jumped out on my forehead and my heart raced, I would stand aside, hidden in the shadows, and take a quick mouthful of the spirit in the small metal flask Daiva had given me for Christmas. Just one mouthful, to feel its heat burn its way up from my stomach, blistering my fear. Just one mouthful and then I would step back into the queue and make believe nothing had happened.

Daiva gave birth in the late summer. On each of the five days they kept her in the maternity ward, I went and stood beneath the window. Each time I came, she held the small parcel of blankets up for me to see. On the fifth day she stood in the hospital entrance, the plaster crumbling from the walls around her.

When I approached, she held out the bundle. I felt

the light weight of the baby in my arms. Still so small. I kissed the little bulge of her cheek and her eyes flicked open and looked up at me. Her eyes were dark and honest, they examined me, her brow furrowing seriously. Her lips opened and she uttered a little growl and struggled beneath the tightly wrapped blankets. My heart leapt.

'She's saying hello,' Daiva whispered, close beside me.

We drove back to the apartment and lay on the bed, the three of us, as the sun sank slowly behind the apartment blocks. Carefully I unwrapped Laura, allowing her to roll and flex her arms and legs. She squealed with pleasure. I gave her my thumb and her tiny fingers wrapped themselves around it, gripping it with a surprising strength. After a while she began to cry and Daiva fed her. I watched as the feverish sucking gave way to a soft pull at the nipple, a thin blue trail of milk dribbling from her full lips. Her eyes flickered and closed. Daiva's eyes closed, too.

A little later, levering myself up from the sofa, I changed my clothes, transferring the fifty-dollar bills to the wallet in my new jacket. To get to Santariskes Clinic required taking a trolley bus into the centre of the Old Town and another back out to the outskirts of the city. I had contemplated telephoning the hospital, but realised I would get nowhere without the crisp American bills. Before I left the apartment, I telephoned Tanya to check she was OK. The telephone rang and rang but there was no answer.

I walked quickly to the trolley-bus stop, glancing over my shoulder, nervous of being watched, not relaxing until I had boarded the number 16 into the Old Town, certain I had not been followed.

Santariskes Clinic is spread over a large area with many different buildings. After only a moment's hesitation, stepping down from the trolley bus, I turned to my left and entered the main reception area of the hospital. A middle-aged woman sat behind a desk, reading.

'I'm looking for a friend,' I said, approaching her.

'What ward?' she asked, not looking up from her book.

'That's what I don't know,' I said, forcing a jovial smile on to my face.

She glanced up, an irritated crease furrowing her brow.

'What is your friend in for?' she asked, not attempting to hide her frustration.

'I'm not sure,' I confessed. I smiled again, hoping futilely to find a chink in her steely demeanour.

For a moment she looked at me as if I were a cretin.

'So how am I supposed to help you?' she barked, openly aggressive now.

I sighed. I had little energy to go wandering around the many buildings of the hospital, hoping someone might have heard of, or remember, Kolya.

'It's like this,' I said. 'A friend of mine wrote me a letter. I haven't seen him for some time. The address on it was Santariskes Clinic – he was here, but I don't know if he still is.' I began to remove the letter Kolya had sent Vassily from my leather case, but already I saw her eyes sliding from me, the features of her face stiffening as she turned her attention away.

'Please,' I said.

I opened my wallet and slipped out one of the fifty-dollar bills. I let her see it. 'I really need to find this friend,' I said. 'I would be most grateful if you were able to help me.'

When she looked at me again, her eyes were full of contempt. She snapped shut the book on the counter in front of her. It was, I noticed, a cheap Western romance translated into Russian.

'What are you wasting my time for?' she said. Her eyes darted to the fifty-dollar bill half concealed in my fist. 'Go and take your American money to the whores at the Hotel Lietuva.'

Her voice began to rise and I glanced around nervously. A few heads had turned in the large, under-lit reception hall.

'Kolya Antonenko,' I continued. I folded the letter, revealing only the address at the top, and pushed it across the scarred wooden counter towards her. 'Perhaps he is still here. It is vitally important I find him . . .' I hesitated for a moment, considering what story would convince her. 'A very good friend has died,' I tried, pinning my hope on this truth, 'a comrade from Afghanistan. We all fought together. The funeral is in a couple of days.'

The receptionist exhaled slowly, releasing her breath through clenched teeth, so that it hissed like a tyre deflating. She looked at me frankly, aggressively, then turned on her heel and disappeared into the office behind her. I looked after her, unsure whether she had been convinced or not. For some minutes I stood there, by the counter. I could hear her voice, muttering angrily, as she moved about the office, whether to somebody else or herself, I could not tell. I was about to turn and go when she reappeared. She glanced at me as if amazed and irritated to still see me standing there.

Pushing a pad across the counter, she picked up her romance again.

'Name,' she said.

I paused, unsure whether she wanted my name or Kolya's. She was engrossed once more in her book and did not look as if she wanted to be disturbed. I wrote Kolya's name neatly in Russian and Lithuanian characters on the paper and pushed it back across to her. She did not look up or take the paper.

There was a low bench against the wall on the opposite side of the reception hall and I wandered across to it and slumped down. Vassily's funeral was indeed in two days' time, Tanya had told me. I thought of him, asleep in the morgue. Soon he would be interred in the dark earth. Vassily, who had nursed me back to life, who had given me the means by which to survive, who had rebuilt my past and given me a reason to look to the future.

I glanced across at the receptionist. A nurse had stopped by the counter and the two were talking animatedly. I stood up and wandered across to the doors, looking out across the large tarmacked parking area towards the trees.

Ghazis, I thought, recalling Vassily's words. *It was in Ghazis in the Hindu Kush. You remember it? Yes. Of course you do.* I hitched up my sleeve, slightly, almost unconsciously, and stroked the tender skin, the raw pink flesh. Flickering in the thick glass of the hospital reception hall window I saw the dance of flames, the dark swirl of smoke. Ghazis. *There are things he should have told you*, Kirov said, *the kind of things a friend would have told you.* What is there I need to know? I thought. I knew too much already, more than I ever needed to know, more than I could bear to know. And there was no honour in knowing those things.

A tap on my shoulder startled me. I spun around.

The receptionist stood beside me. She was looking at me with concern.

'Are you OK?' she asked.

I wiped the perspiration from my forehead and pulled down my sleeve, struggling, with trembling fingers, to button the cuff.

'Here,' she said, pushing a slip of paper at me.

I took it. For a moment I gazed at her, dislocated. She turned and marched back towards her desk. Looking down at the slip of paper, I noticed it had an address on it. Kolya's address.

'Thank you,' I said. '*Spasiba.*'

I hurried after her. '*Spasiba,*' I said again. She had taken up her novel again. I slipped the fifty-dollar bill across the counter. '*Ochin spasiba.*'

She looked up and shoved the money back at me roughly.

Chapter 16

By the end of July we had been in Afghanistan for six months. The *dembels* left and we graduated to veteran status. We were the granddads. A group of new recruits arrived on the base, straight from Moscow and Moldavia and Tallinn. We threw a large party, extracting money from the recruits to buy rice and meat for the *sashlik*, for vodka and Bulgarian biscuits. The departing *dembels* organised our initiation. Twenty strokes of the buckle end of a belt across the backside. Not a murmur of complaint; we stood up and shook their hands. They slapped our backs. We were one of them now.

One of our first jobs with the new recruits was to escort the Agitprop Brigade on an excursion to a village. The propaganda detachment consisted of an APC and a truck with a large red cross painted on its side. Their vehicles were flanked by a couple of our APCs, a BMP and a fuel truck. Lieutenant Zhuralev complained loudly as we pulled off the main road and headed down a winding track towards the village.

'It's madness,' he said. 'What's the fucking point in playing doctors and nurses out here? I don't see why I should risk my men just so that these fucking villagers can show off their sores and diseases and load up with grain that would be better off in our bellies.'

A large crowd milled around the village. We sat on the APCs, guns at the ready, eyes vigilantly scanning the area. A loudspeaker was set up beside the Agitprop's APC and began blaring out Soviet patriotic music. A couple of doctors set up a table and a long line of villagers snaked up to it.

'Crowd control,' Zhuralev barked at me, pushing me forwards towards the doctors. 'Keep the locals in order.'

I strolled over to the flimsy wooden desk erected by the doctors. There were two of them. One was a tall, thin Ukrainian, the other, from Siberia, was small and dark with watery eyes. They had a nurse with them who spoke the local language and was acting as an interpreter. A young man from the village barged his way forwards towards the doctors at the desk. When I shoved him back and told him to wait he said something to me rapidly and pointed to his stomach. He was thin and stooped, with a long dark beard. I waved him back, and when he continued to press forwards, I put my hand on his chest and stopped him roughly.

'Get back and stop pushing,' I shouted.

The nurse turned, hearing me. Approaching quickly, she pulled me away from the stooped villager impatiently. She spoke to the man in a quiet, calm voice. He explained his problem to her, his voice rising, his bony hands gesticulating. He pointed at me and the young nurse glanced over her shoulder.

'Tell him to wait his turn,' I said, pressing forwards towards the man, whose long dirty fingers had taken hold of the nurse's faded green shirt.

The nurse's eyes flashed angrily. She called for one of the doctors, indicating for him to come over.

'His wife is giving birth; she is in the village.'

Nodding, the doctor went to fetch some equipment. The nurse turned to me. 'You come with us,' she said. 'We need some security.' She turned and followed the young man down a narrow lane into the village. I glanced over towards Lieutenant Zhuralev, but his back was turned. Nervously I followed the nurse's receding figure, concerned about walking into a trap. The doctor from Siberia caught up with me and grinned.

'One more *sobaka* to welcome into the world,' he said, a little breathlessly, as he hurried forwards with his bag. 'As if there aren't too many already. In a few years' time he'll be throwing stones at us when we go past.'

There was a small group waiting outside the house when we arrived. The nurse took the clean cloths and the medical bag the doctor had brought with him.

'You stay here,' she said, pointing to a spot outside the door. I glanced at her furiously. 'Unless, that is, you want one of these men to blow your brains out.' Her small hand swept around, indicating the crowd of men who had gathered near the door. They gazed at me sullenly, their beards straggling over long soiled shirts. The nurse ducked in through the doorway. I raised my gun apprehensively.

'Give a yell if you need some help,' the doctor shouted after her. He grinned and pulled a packet of cigarettes from his pocket. Knocking the packet against the palm of his hand, he flicked a cigarette towards me. Nodding to the stooped young father-to-be he offered him one too. The young man smiled shyly and took one of the Russian cigarettes. The jangle of patriotic music drifted across the mud-brick walls from the Agitprop APC. From inside the building came the sound of a woman shouting. I could not tell whether they were cries of pain or anger.

'You think she's OK in there on her own?' I said.

The doctor grinned. 'Zena? Sure she is OK. What do

you think they're going to do, shoot her when she has delivered the baby? That isn't how it works, you know that: they're all nice and friendly when we're here. We'll give them some sacks of rice, medicate their problems, hand out a few leaflets and everybody will grin and say what a great thing the revolution is. And then when we've gone, the men will be off to the mountains to join their mates, bombing our bases and laying mines and sniping at us.'

The nurse appeared twenty minutes later, wiping her hands on a cloth, the medical bag tucked beneath her arm.

'They're both fine,' she said.

She had a dirty stain on the front of her shirt, which she dabbed at with the cloth. As we paused in the courtyard while she spoke to the stooped young man, I watched her. She had a good body, barely disguised by the unflattering khaki uniform. When we walked back up towards the marketplace, she stumbled in a rut in the dusty road, and I felt the weight of her body press against my own. A rush of excitement surged through me. Glancing up, she must have noticed the expression on my face. She shook my hand from her arm aggressively.

'You speak the local language?' I said, to hide my embarrassment.

'I speak Pashtu, Dari and Russian,' she said, matter-of-factly, as if anybody might.

'How did you learn?'

'Pashtu from my mother and Dari at school.'

'You're one of them?'

'Don't look so shocked, I'm not going to shoot you.'

'No, it's just that . . . it's unusual.'

'It's a long story,' she said, waving her hand

impatiently. A bead of perspiration ran from her hair-line and clung to her forehead.

'You work in Jalalabad?'

She nodded. 'Mainly at the hospital in Jalalabad, but I like to come out with the brigade, and they find me useful.'

Turning the corner, we left the village. The crowd was clearing away from the APCs, bustling back into the narrow lanes and sheltered courtyards, uninterested in the propaganda leaflets that a member of the Agitprop Brigade was distributing. The doctor had packed away the flimsy table. Lieutenant Zhuralev, seeing me, beckoned me over angrily.

'Where the fuck have you been?' he shouted, above the noise of the local songs blaring from the loudspeaker. He turned on a soldier from the Agitprop Brigade who was leaning up against the side of his APC, smoking a cigarette. 'Turn that irritating music off.'

Before I went over to him, I stopped the nurse. She looked at me questioningly, the beads of perspiration rolling down her forehead and settling in her eyebrows.

'Maybe I could see you, when I get a day free in Jalalabad?' I said.

She looked at me and narrowed her eyes suspiciously. 'I'm not a whore.'

Before I could say anything more, she turned away and marched quickly over to the other two doctors. Faintly, above the noise, I heard the sound of their laughter.

'What the fuck have you been up to?' Zhuralev demanded again when I reached the APC.

'Escorting the doctors, sir.'

'Well, next time, get fucking permission.'

Vassily was on the back of the APC. He grinned as he pulled me up.

Chapter 17

The address the receptionist had given me was on Warsaw Street in the Rasa district, just behind the railway station. On the trolley bus home I stared at the slip of paper. I had not, I remembered with regret, asked the receptionist whether she knew what Kolya was being treated for. The chances were, however, that she would not have told me.

My first memory of Kolya was of when we were six years old. He was sitting in the brightly painted, metal-framed playhouse in the garden of the children's home. Ponia Marija pushed me through the door and pointed towards the sunlit lawn.

'Go play, Antanelis,' she whispered in my ear. Her voice tickled. I could not remember anybody whispering to me before. I brushed my ear and stepped out into the garden, leaving Ponia Marija to speak to the woman who had brought me to the children's home.

Shrinking back into the shadows, I watched as the children dashed past, screaming and shouting. A small girl paused, staring at me curiously, before she was tugged away by another child. I wandered across the grass towards the fence. Beyond the garden the land sloped away towards a copse of trees and a large lake. Looking out over it, I wondered whether my house lay that way.

'Hey!' a voice called from behind me.

A square-faced boy with small dark eyes was hanging out of the playhouse on the grass.

'I'm a cosmonaut,' the boy shouted, ducking back into the shade of the hut.

I trotted over to the playhouse and stood by it, gazing in at the boy.

'I'm a cosmonaut,' he repeated.

I climbed in beside him and sat on the hard wooden bench.

'Five!' he shouted.

I joined in, pressed close to his side, feeling the warmth of his leg against my own.

'Let's be soldiers,' he said after a while, bored with counting from five to blast-off.

'I'm not here long,' I told him. 'Just until my mama comes out of hospital.'

He gazed at me for a moment. 'Let's play soldiers,' he said.

The centre of the Old Town was crowded with people finishing work and the trolley bus I caught was packed tightly. I jumped off a few stops before my apartment and walked slowly up the hill, enjoying the late afternoon sunshine. The clouds that had hung over the city for the past week had broken up; they sailed like the high snowcapped mountains around Jalalabad, far above us.

As I approached my apartment block, the door of a car opened, narrowly missing my leg. I jumped back against the wall, stumbling in my panic.

'Are you OK?' Zinotis said, stepping out of the car.

I nodded, shakily.

'I gave you a shock.' He smiled.

'I thought you were somebody else,' I said.

'Oh?'

'It's nothing.' I waved my hand, self-consciously. 'Come up for coffee. I found that book Vassily borrowed from you some while ago.'

He looked perplexed for a moment, then seemed to remember.

'Ah!' He grinned.

As I boiled some water, Zinotis leafed through the volume on jewellery from the Kushan Empire.

'I just happened to be passing,' he called through from the front room, 'and I thought I would pop in to tell you some interesting things I discovered a little earlier.'

When I entered the room with the coffee, he was putting on his half-moon spectacles to inspect a picture.

'I was talking to a colleague,' he said, not looking up from the book, 'from the Department of Antiquities. I told him about the bracelet and he said he thought he knew what it was I was referring to.'

I sipped my coffee and watched him. He took off his glasses and slid them back into the breast pocket of his jacket.

'He was convinced the bracelet you described was one which was fashioned first for the Emperor Nero. The Romans were obsessed with amber – northern gold, they called it. A Roman soldier was sent north to get some and came back with such an immense quantity that the nets at Nero's games in the Colosseum were decorated with it, as was the armour and swords of the gladiators. Pliny writes about it.

'Pliny also mentions a jewel Nero wore in his *Historia Naturalis*. He refers to it in terms of the inclusions, which were of scientific interest to him.'

He fished inside his jacket and pulled out a folded sheet of paper.

'Legend has it,' he continued, opening out the paper, a photocopy, and looking at it absently, 'that the bracelet was later presented by an Egyptian princess to Tamerlane, the great warrior king born in Samarkand, who went on to build a bloody empire stretching from Delhi to Baghdad.

'It was one of those artefacts I told you about before, unearthed in Bagram by a British adventurer and displayed in the Kabul Museum. It was stolen from the collection in the mid-eighties.'

Leaning over, he handed me the piece of paper.

'What is it?' I asked.

'I copied it a couple of hours ago in the library. It's a newspaper article. My colleague mentioned he thought he had seen it at one point and I was able to trace it.'

I took the paper from him and glanced at it. Faded, barely distinguishable, it showed a photograph of a bracelet. The filigree band was intricate and thick, as was the clasp that held the large oval piece of amber. The amber was spherical, beautifully translucent. The inclusions were spectacular, so perfectly centred, so clear, it seemed as if they had been especially arranged for display.

'Ancient amulet stolen from Kabul collection,' the caption ran beneath the photograph.

'You know,' he said, when I had finished reading, 'this bracelet would be worth a lot of money on the black market.'

I nodded. 'Are you sure this is the one?'

'It fits,' Zinotis said. 'The description he gave you . . . Afghanistan . . .'

He rubbed his chin furiously. 'Of course, it would

be necessary to examine it to make sure it was not a fake.'

'But surely,' I said, 'it's not possible to fake the inclusions in the amber?'

'Of course you can,' Zinotis said. 'There have been some very clever examples.'

For a few moments we both lapsed into silence, each preoccupied by our thoughts.

'If you have this bracelet,' Zinotis said, 'I would be very keen to have a look at it.'

'I don't have the bracelet,' I told him. 'I'm not interested in it.'

He looked up, questioningly. 'Oh?'

'It's Kolya I need to find.'

Zinotis smiled. 'Of course,' he muttered. 'So you said yesterday morning.'

He gazed at me for a few moments, as if he was trying to judge what my real interest was. I realised how strange my behaviour must seem to him.

'But when you find him,' Zinotis continued, leaning forwards, interrupting my thoughts, 'you will have to give him the bracelet. Would he know what to do with it? Would he know somebody who could sell it for him?'

'I don't know anything about that.'

'He could get into trouble, of course, selling stolen goods.' He smiled. 'It would be worth a lot, though, on the black market.' His smile turned into a roguish grin. 'If you can't find Kolya . . .'

'I have his address,' I told him. 'If Kolya needs your help I will tell him to contact you.'

He stood up and held out his hand.

'I will help in whatever way I am able,' he said.

We shook hands and he left. For some while I did

not move as I pondered the situation. What, I wondered, did Vassily want me to know, which only Kolya could tell me? Why was he not more explicit? Why could he not tell me himself? *The price was too great*, he had said. If there was one thing I had learnt from Vassily it was that beautiful jewellery shouldn't be sullied by talk of money. As I sipped my coffee, I remembered a conversation we had had shortly after we had arrived in Vilnius and started up our business.

'We need to get our own supply of amber,' Vassily said. We were sitting in the beer hall across the street from his apartment. 'To buy our amber here in Vilnius would cost too much. If I tried to get some out of the bastard we are working for, there would be no profit in doing the work. We need to go to Kaliningrad to get some for ourselves; it is the only way.'

There was a large factory that processed amber in Ribachi, a small village in the Russian enclave of Kaliningrad. Amber was excavated from the Curonian Lagoon, then cleaned and processed at the factory.

'I know the place,' Vassily told me. 'There are people at the factory I know from the old times. You see, the thing is, comrade, you don't want to be paying too much tax to import the amber. What kind of a profit are you going to make then? What is the point in you doing the business, just to feed some greedy border guards? No, no. On one set of papers you buy a tonne of amber and then from my friend the second tonne, and that travels without papers. This way you can make a profit. It can be done.'

'Where do they get the amber from, these friends of yours?' I asked.

'They steal it from the factory.'

'A tonne of amber?'

He glanced at me to see whether I was joking. 'Are you stupid or what?' was all he would say. He slammed his empty beer glass down on the table in front of me. 'Go get me another beer.

'Listen, let me tell you,' he continued when I returned with two more litre glasses of foaming beer and a plate of fried garlic bread. 'Since you have so many scruples about stealing from those fucking bastards who think they can trawl the amber from beneath the waves and sell it at whatever cost they think fit – let me tell you about amber.

'For many centuries people have collected amber from along the Baltic shore, when the winds have risen and the stormy sea has tossed it up on to the sand. They fished for it with nets, delving into the seaweed. Some, later, would swim out into the sea, or the lagoon, with a wooden paddle, and dive for the amber beneath the water, prising it from the seabed. Can you imagine that, eh, comrade? The danger they risked to get hold of it. Later, of course, the capitalists took over and they, as always, were wanting to improve the efficiency of the business and so introduced new machines, dredgers ploughing up the whole bed of the sea, sifting out the amber.

'It used to be that the person who found the amber, it belonged to them, but that changed over time. The dukes and local lords began to control the trade; there was money in it, so of course they wanted their cut. They were the Amber Lords. What was washed up from the sea belonged to them. The Beach Masters and the Beach Riders were the only ones authorised to collect the amber. If you collected it illegally, as the poor peasants did, to earn a few roubles, you would be fined heavily if you were caught. If you were too poor for a fine, then there was always the gallows. In the old city of Königsberg there were executioners whose sole job it was to put to death the poor collectors of amber who had been picked up in the early morning by the Beach Riders.

'Listen, my little brother, my comrade,' Vassily said. He leant over the table, grabbing my arm. 'This is what we will do. We will go to Kaliningrad, I will borrow a truck, I know where I can get one, and we will bring back our own amber, good stuff, and we will make jewellery. Good jewellery, not cheap rubbish, beautiful jewels like I used to make before the war. We will open the shop and be known as the best jewellers in Vilnius. *Niet?*'

'In Vilnius? In the whole of Lithuania!'

'In the whole fucking reach of the inglorious former Soviet fucking Union.'

'And we will be rich.'

'Rich?' He put down his glass and looked at me seriously. 'No, my little friend, not rich. Fuck riches. What is money? Money is nothing. Money is shit, a pocketful of shit. Start to want it and it is like a disease, it will grab you around the throat and throttle you. It will kill you. Have you ever looked into the eyes of a rich man? They're empty. Empty, I tell you. Fuck money, money is the opposite of beauty, and, comrade, I love beauty. She is my goddess.'

'To beauty,' I said, raising my glass.

Vassily raised his own glass. The excitement had slipped from his face. His brow was furrowed and his eyes gleamed darkly. 'Once I got mixed up – thought jewellery should be prized only for its worth. I was wrong.'

*

The telephone rang loudly, suddenly, making me jump. I levered myself from the armchair and crossed over to it. Daiva spoke before I had a chance to say anything.

'It's me,' she said.

She sounded composed, but quiet. It took me a few moments to respond.

'Hello.'

Silence lapped around our words. I could hear the sound of her breathing; tense, short breaths. I imagined her lips close to the telephone, the rise and fall of her chest. The way her hair fell down across her cheek and tickled her nose.

'Where are you?' I asked.

'Are you OK?' she said, ignoring my question.

'I'm fine.'

'You found the food I left you?'

'Yes, I found it.'

I could hear the quiet murmur of a voice behind her. Perhaps it was just the television. When she spoke again her voice was strained, but she spoke clearly and loudly enough for me to understand she was on her own.

'I'm sorry, Antanas, I'm sorry, but I had to get away, just for a while. I couldn't think.'

I said nothing. She paused, as if waiting for me to respond. If I had had a drink perhaps I would have said something. Perhaps she was trying to gauge that; how much I had drunk. My silence seemed to make her more nervous, as if it were an accusation.

'Your drinking is getting worse and I don't know how to help you any more,' she said, her voice cracking with emotion. In the subtle change in her tone, I heard the first tear slip down her cheek. A wave of sorrow washed across me.

'Daiva,' I said, 'I understand.'

'You don't, Antanas, you don't understand at all. That is the problem.'

'There are lots of problems, Daiva.'

'And drinking won't solve any of them,' she shot back. It was a line she had delivered many times before, and I knew it had come out before she could stop it. She paused and drew a deep breath.

'I'm sorry.'

'It's OK.' I closed my eyes and rested my forehead against the wall. I desperately needed a drink. My mouth was so dry I found it hard to speak, and in my chest I felt the familiar heavy press of dull despair.

'I love you,' she said, quietly, almost whispering.

I squeezed my eyes shut tightly. 'Me too.'

'Then why are you so distant? What's happening to us, Antanas?'

'Daiva,' I said, 'not now, let's not argue now.'

She didn't reply. For a minute we remained like that, listening to the silence of the telephone line.

'I'll call again,' she said finally, her voice catching on the edge of her tears.

'OK,' I said.

There was another short silence, and then I heard the soft click of her receiver sliding into its cradle. For some moments I continued to stand there, my forehead pressed against the wall, the receiver to my ear, its buzz tickling me.

Chapter 18

Girls were brought to the base intermittently. Mainly they were Russian girls who worked in offices in Jalalabad – civilian employees who had volunteered, doing their International Duty alongside their brothers, or earning some hard cash, which it was impossible to do in their towns and villages back home, saving up for their weddings. Zhuralev had picked one up fresh from Kabul and installed her in his building on the base for a couple of months before she managed to escape. Bringing them to the base for parties was one of Kirov's little business ventures. He rarely took part in military duties any more, paying off the commanding officer with the profits of his drug deals and prostitution.

One evening, as I squatted outside our barrack hut, rinsing grease from plates, a shadow approached in the swelling darkness.

'Do you have a cigarette?' she asked.

I dried my hands on my shirt and took the crumpled packet from my pocket. She took one nonchalantly and waited for me to light it.

'You not enjoying the party?' I asked nervously.

She exhaled the cheap smoke slowly. 'They're all drunk.'

She had prominent, wide cheekbones and blue eyes. Leaning against the dusty wall of the hut, she was illuminated by the thin pulse of light coming from the bulb dangling just inside the door.

She made no secret of her name or background. She was, she said, Masha from Krasnoyarsk. She worked in an office, she told me; typing, mainly.

I rinsed the last of the plates and took them inside. When I came back out we stood for some time in silence, smoking, listening to the noise of the party. An argument broke out briefly, and there was the sound of a glass shattering. A young woman's voice screeched shrilly, angrily, and the argument subsided.

'I hate it here,' she said with some feeling.

'The base, you mean?'

She shook her head. 'Afghanistan. Don't you?'

I thought for a moment. 'I don't know,' I said, 'I don't really think about it. There doesn't seem to be anything else. It's not like I have any choice.'

'Do you have a girl?'

'Here?'

'Don't be silly. Back home.'

'No.'

'I can't stand the dust here. Or the noise.'

She dropped the butt of her cigarette on to the earth, and ground it into the dust with the heel of her shoe.

'I can't stand the smell. Anything. Every night I dream about the dark green of the trees of my home town and the river that runs by the foot of the garden of my mama's house. My little sister.'

She was wearing a neat cotton shirt and a little red scarf tied tight around her throat. Her hair was brushed out. She smelt fresh and perfumed.

'Well?' she said. 'Do you want it?'

I nodded mutely. She did not look at me. We walked out of the base, slipping behind the huts and disappearing into the darkness at the back of the camp, through a hole in the fencing, across the narrow, well-worn track through the minefield.

We settled beneath a tree on the edge of the field and made love mechanically. When I had given her the money she asked me for (gauchely, I had to ask how much was required) she walked back to the base on her own. I watched her recede, not having told her she was the first. When I went to sleep that night, I thought of her and decided I would call her again when next I was in Jalalabad.

A week later we once more accompanied the Agitprop Brigade on one of their visits to a village in the mountains. Zhuralev swore continually; he hated these trips.

'At best they are pointless, at worst they are a fucking security nightmare,' he commented.

The Afghani nurse, Zena, was with the brigade once more. She worked hard, examining the patients queueing in the sun, treating their diseased limbs, suppurating sores and whimpering, pale children. I repeated Zhuralev's words to her, later in the day, when she took a short break. She drank from a battered canteen in the shadow of the APC, her forehead slick with perspiration, the khaki of her shirt dark beneath her arms and down the length of her spine.

'There is no medical care in most of the villages of Afghanistan,' she said, eyeing me disdainfully. 'It is the women who suffer most. The men won't let them be treated by male doctors and will rarely allow them to go to one of the hospitals in the city if they need care.'

She emptied a small handful of water into the cupped palm of her hand and splashed it against her face, running her fingers through her thick black hair, curling it back behind her ears.

'Why do you think you're here?' she said, her eyes closed, fingers pushing the cool water into the corners of her eye sockets, flushing out the dust. 'Just to shoot the locals and destroy their villages?'

'We're here to protect the locals from the American-backed rebels,' I said, a little stiffly, discomfited to find the Political Officer's words emerging from my mouth. Annoyed at her prickliness, I was unable to stop myself. 'The American imperialists want to destabilise the country and we're here to stop them.'

Zena grunted. She opened her eyes and gazed at me for a moment. A bead of water clung to her eyelash.

'Don't deceive yourself,' she said softly. 'They don't want you here any more than they want the Americans. But as you're here, you may as well do some good.'

I flushed. Her tone embarrassed me. She held my gaze for a moment longer, then wandered back to the queueing sick.

As I watched her, a middle-aged man wandered shiftily from a doorway. He paused for a moment, glancing around at the soldiers and the rows of APCs and BMPs. He wore a dark turban, which seemed to be unravelling. When his eyes alighted on Zena, he took a step back. After a moment's hesitation he stepped forwards, determinedly, the palm of his hand beating against his forehead. Seeing him approach, I stepped forwards myself. I was about to call out to him when Zena looked up and noticed his arrival.

As their eyes met, he began to shout. At first he spoke in the local language, but after a few moments broke into heavily accented Russian.

'Russian whore . . . here uncovered . . . prostitute . . .'

For a moment Zena gazed at him, then she dropped the arm of the woman she had been examining, shooting back at him a stream of Pashtu. He stiffened visibly. The colour of his face changed as he realised Zena was a local girl. He snatched at his beard and pulled it furiously. Ducking down, he plucked a stone from the dirt, and, before I could move, lobbed it forcefully towards Zena. The line of patients scattered. The stone fell short, rolling to a stop by Zena's feet. She did not flinch. She stood with hands on hips, confronting him, willing him even, to approach her.

The turbaned man glanced around at the soldiers closing in on him. Turning, he disappeared into the shadows of a doorway, a stream of abuse drifting behind him. We laughed.

The Agitprop Brigade worked through the heat of the afternoon, until the last of the sick had been attended to, the sacks of rice had been handed out and leaflets distributed to the thinning crowd. A bowed figure approached Zena from behind, as we began the process of packing our things away. A hand reached out from beneath the large cloth wound around the figure and touched her shoulder. As she turned, he lashed out.

I heard her startled cry and looked up. Zena had bent to examine the hand of the man, but suddenly she dropped to her knees and crumpled to the earth. The figure turned and ran, the large cloth dropping away from him, revealing the man who had abused Zena earlier in the afternoon. Kolya shouted, but he did not stop. As I ran towards Zena I saw Kolya raise his gun and heard its sharp metallic retort.

When I knelt beside her, she was trembling. Lifting her, I noticed the blood flowing down her face, pooling in the socket of her eye.

'What did he do?' I said.

'I don't know,' she said, her voice no more than a whisper. 'I didn't feel anything, I didn't realise he had done anything.' Her voice shook. I pressed a cloth against the wound that tore down her face. 'But then there was blood,' she continued, 'such a lot of blood. His fingers were covered in blood and I thought the blood had come from him, that he had come to get some medical attention. I bent down to examine his hand and then I saw the blade between his thumb and finger.'

One of the doctors came over and cleaned and bandaged her wound. The razor blade had cut a thin line down her face, beginning at her scalp and finishing at her jaw.

'Let's hope the blade was clean,' the doctor commented.

When she felt a little stronger I helped her to her feet. She gazed across the market to the place where the body of her attacker lay sprawled in the dirt. She took my hand and led me across to the corpse. Kolya had hit him twice; once in the back, the other bullet catching him cleanly through the neck. The sand soaked up his blood.

'This is what a woman's body does in Afghanistan,' she said as we stood over him. Her voice was full of bitterness. 'Just the sight of her uncovered face and hair and arms. That is what we learn here from being a child. Look what happens when a woman does not obey the rules. Look and learn.'

The village marketplace was deathly quiet; apart from our convoy it was deserted. We pulled out quickly.

Chapter 19

It had already begun to grow dark when I set out, with Kolya's letter in my pocket, across the city to the Rasa district. The buildings here were dilapidated; shabby curtains pulled across dimly lit rooms, litter-strewn gutters and, in a doorway, a mangy dog that did not even stir as I passed.

Warsaw Street lay behind the railway station. I hesitated when finally I found the address given to me at the hospital. The idea of seeing Kolya after so many years troubled me. I glanced around at the run-down buildings, the conspicuous deprivation, and felt a spasm of painful shame that I had done nothing to track him down after Afghanistan, to offer him support.

I pressed the buzzer by the street door. The metal plate covering the intercom panel had been prised away from the wall by vandals and wires protruded from behind it. After a few moments a tinny woman's voice answered my call.

'I'm looking for Kolya,' I called into the twisted metal grille.

'Who is it?' the voice crackled.

'Antanas – I am an old friend of Kolya's.'

There was a short pause. The intercom hissed. It had begun to rain. Large drops splashed against the crumbling bricks, blotching them. I turned up my collar.

'He's not here,' the woman said.

'Can I come up?' I shouted.

Again she hesitated. A sharp wind drove the rain against me. The door clicked and I pulled it open and slipped inside out of the sudden downpour. The rain beat heavily against the door behind me. The stairwell was warm and dry and smelt clean. It was almost pitch black inside. I felt along the wall and pressed the light switch.

The woman was waiting by the door of her apartment when I reached the fourth floor. She showed me inside and insisted I have a cup of coffee. The apartment was neat, but barely furnished, with a few photographs displayed. After a short while she brought in the coffee and went to sit on a hard chair close to the window. Nervously, she brushed at a loose strand of hair. She was a small woman, her face worn and tired and rutted already with deep lines.

'I'm looking for Kolya,' I said.

She grunted, and a bitter smile lifted the corners of her thin lips. Turning her head, she gazed out of the rain-smeared window.

'*Nu*, well, you're not the only one,' she said in Polish.

My Polish was not very good and I struggled to grasp her implication.

'There is somebody else looking for him?' I clarified.

'Someone else?' she said. 'Always someone else. He's been here two months and nothing paid.'

'But did somebody else come here? A man? Kirov – his name?'

She shook her head, and I was not sure whether she had not understood me or whether she was confirming that Kirov had not been there.

'Have you any idea where Kolya is?' I tried.

'The last I saw of him was Thursday. He went out for cigarettes.'

'He didn't say where he was going?'

The woman laughed at that.

'Are you not concerned?' I asked.

She shook her head despondently.

'Kolya and I grew up together,' I told her, 'in the children's home. We were drafted to Afghanistan together.'

She turned away from the window. 'You understand,' she explained, 'he is not well. He has morphine addiction, his little gift from Afghanistan. He is sick.' She shrugged. 'There is only so much you can do. What, am I to throw him out?'

She stood up and wandered over to a large old bureau. Leafing through a pile of letters, she took a pen and wrote something on a scrap of paper. Handing it to me, she pointed to a woman's name and an address.

'It'll be as good a place to start as anywhere,' she said.

I thanked her and drank the last of the bitter coffee. As I stood she was staring out of the window into the darkening, rain-swept street. Standing in the doorway, I told her I was leaving. She glanced back over her shoulder.

'If you see him,' she said, 'tell him . . .' but she turned away and didn't finish the sentence. When I emerged into the rain, she was standing there still, a ghostly shadow behind the window.

The address of the woman was on Pylimo, which was not far so I decided to walk, even though the rain had grown steadier. The clouds had fallen so low they snagged against the roofs of the city. The church spires had disappeared. The traffic was thick, moving slowly, lights shimmering on the wet surface of the road. The few pedestrains hurried by, newspapers covering their heads. I walked close in against the wall, crouched into my jacket with the collar turned up.

The young woman on Pylimo had a vicious bruise beneath her left eye. She was a short dark girl, no more than twenty. I thought possibly she was a Gypsy, and perhaps she was, but when she spoke her Lithuanian was coarse enough to be her mother tongue.

'I'm looking for Kolya Antonenko,' I said when she opened the door a crack.

She peered at me suspiciously through the narrow space. 'What do you want?'

'I'm looking for Kolya,' I repeated.

I tried to peer into the dark room behind her, but could see nothing.

'Who are you?' she asked.

'I'm an old friend of Kolya's,' I told her.

Ridiculously, I took out the letter Kolya had sent to Vassily and showed her. She took the paper from me and examined it.

'You're Vassily?' she asked, and something in the way she said it suggested she knew of him. For a moment I considered lying to get past the door.

'No,' I explained. 'Vassily gave me the letter. He asked me to find Kolya.'

'Oh,' she said.

'So?'

She continued to eye me, suspicious still. Finally she seemed to come to some kind of decision and nodded. 'Fine. Come in, then.'

She showed me through to the tiny kitchen and indicated I should sit at the table.

'He's not here at the moment,' she said, 'but he shouldn't be long.'

She pulled a chair around the table so she was closer to me. The sleeve of her blouse was hitched up, revealing a thin row of scars across her forearm. She made no attempt to pull it down to hide them.

'How did you know to find him here?' she asked, extracting a cigarette from a packet. She offered me one and I took it.

'I was given an address on Warsaw Street,' I told her honestly. 'The woman sent me on.'

The young woman wrinkled her nose and laughed mirthlessly. 'His landlady? That old witch! He comes here when he can't stand any more of her nagging him for his rent, among other things.' She snorted. 'I think she has a thing for him.' Inhaling the oily smoke of the cheap cigarette, she added, 'I'm a little more understanding of his needs.'

The apparatus of Kolya's heroin addiction was scattered about the small apartment.

'Kolya has been waiting for this Vassily to contact him,' the young woman said. 'Reckons he owes him money.' She looked at me as though I might volunteer some.

'Vassily's dead,' I told her.

She looked disappointed rather than upset. I smoked the cigarette while the girl chatted inanely about her life. She fell silent suddenly and I heard a faint scuffling sound as somebody tried to insert a key in the lock of the door. It clicked open and a few moments later Kolya appeared in the kitchen. Seeing me he stopped short, a startled look passing across his face. I gasped audibly. Kolya's once thick figure had shrunken away. His cheeks were sunken and his eyes had receded to dark shadows burrowed beneath his brow. His shaking hand reached out to steady himself.

'What the fuck?' he muttered.

'Kolya,' I said, standing.

'Antanas?'

He paused, gazing at me, an irritated frown furrowing the waxy skin of his forehead. In his hand he held a small brown paper package. He darted a glance at the girl, but she avoided his eye.

'You're going to have to excuse me,' he said, and turned away sharply, disappearing into another room.

'Kolya,' I said, following him.

The girl held out her hand and grabbed my jacket.

'Leave him,' she said.

I turned to her.

'He has his needs,' she said, quietly. 'Just leave him for a while.'

When I looked at her stupidly, her hand swept over to the syringes on the edge of the sink. The burnt spoons, crushed foil, straps. I sat back down by the table. The girl went out, following Kolya into the other room. I heard their hushed voices through the wall.

When she reappeared some time later, the young woman was wearing a very short skirt and a low top. She had combed her hair and applied some make-up carelessly. She pulled on a leather jacket.

'I have to go out to work now,' she said. 'He will come out soon. He asked me to tell you not to go. Wait for him.'

I nodded. She slipped a small handbag over her shoulder and left. I glanced at my watch. It was almost ten o'clock.

Chapter 20

It was a month before the opportunity arose to go into Jalalabad. The new recruits seemed hopelessly unprepared and had to be assessed and allocated to different units depending on their expertise, if they had any.

It was Vassily who suggested I volunteer to escort the supply trucks on a trip into the city. He had some business in Jalalabad, he told me.

'It's simple,' he explained in a café in the centre of the city, grinning over the rim of a steaming glass of tea. 'Hashim supplies me with jewels – sometimes it's worked pieces he gets, gold inlaid with stones, sometimes it's unworked lumps of lapis lazuli, beautiful pieces. Now, as you know, there is no way I am going to be able to get these pieces out of the country; they would be confiscated on the border. And selling them here isn't an option; here it's a buyer's market.'

'So?'

'So what we do is slip the stuff into coffins.'

'Coffins?'

I spluttered tea across the table. Vassily motioned with a finger to his lips that I should keep my voice down. I glanced around, but there were only a few Afghanis morosely sipping tea at the high tables.

'Obviously it means taking in more partners, and that splits the profits, but it's that or nothing.'

'What do you mean, coffins?'

'Kolya gets the stuff into the coffins here in Jalalabad. He knows somebody who works in the morgue.'

'That's where he is now?'

Vassily nodded and grinned. 'Don't sound so outraged. They're already dead – what are they going to care if they have a bit of company on the trip home? Back home we have a guy who unloads the coffins. He fences them and the cash is split.'

I shook my head in disbelief.

'The idea came with Chistyakov,' Vassily explained. 'Hashim had just got this beautiful piece and I could not turn it down, but what to do with it? Kolya had the idea – he is taking Chistyakov's body to Jalalabad, where it will be put into a zinc coffin and loaded on to a black tulip. *Nu, va!* And there we have it. What? Don't look at me like that, comrade, there are people doing worse. Some of those coffins are going home with top-grade opium packed in them.'

'I have to go,' I said.

'Hey!' He caught my arm as I rose. 'You won't say . . .'

For the first time I saw a dark, worried look cross Vassily's normally jovial face.

'You know,' he said, 'I tell you as a friend. Maybe you want in?'

'No,' I said. 'But don't worry, I won't talk.'

There was an old telephone at the back of the café. It was covered in dust and did not look as if it had been used in years, but when I picked up the receiver it buzzed healthily in my ear. On the back of a cigarette packet I had scribbled Masha from Krasnoyarsk's telephone number. I pulled it out and began to dial. The dial spun slowly. After two numbers I put down the receiver, and considered. Glancing back through the beaded curtain,

I saw Vassily drinking still at the table. I picked up the receiver again and dialled the Jalalabad hospital, my fingers shaking slightly.

The streets were busy. I pushed through the crowds towards the hospital. When I turned the corner Zena was standing outside the gate, talking to an Afghan soldier. She was wearing her white hospital gown, and her short hair was tidily pinned back. She smiled as I approached.

'I got your message,' she said.

I nodded mutely.

'I only have an hour,' she added.

We walked down to the tree-lined avenue running along the Kabul river, where there was less bustle. For some while we walked in silence.

'Where in Russia are you from?' she asked, breaking the silence.

We sat on the bank of the river, watching it flow past sluggishly.

'I'm from Lithuania,' I explained.

She raised her eyebrows.

'You are a long way from home.'

'And you?' I said. 'Are you really . . .'

'My father was a Tajik, my mother a Pushtun from Kabul. My father was a communist; he has family in the Soviet Union. He is dead now, he was shot in the street in Kabul on his way home one evening. I grew up in Kabul. My father had a job in the government of the PDPA so we lived in a nice apartment built by the Soviets, in the Mikrorayon. I went to the Friendship High School built by the Soviets. I loved school. I loved studying. I joined the Communist Youth Group and was top in the class and won a holiday in Moscow. Moscow is wonderful.'

'I've never been,' I confessed.

'You've never been to Moscow?'

I shook my head.

'It is a beautiful city. Kabul is just a dirty little town, and here . . .' Her nose wrinkled with disgust. 'Moscow is so cosmopolitan – the theatre, the ballet, all the latest fashions.'

'So you volunteered?'

'We have a choice here – it's the communists or the mullahs. With the communists we women are free. That is the problem the people here have with the communists, they don't like things changing. The communists say that women have rights too, that they have control over their own bodies, that they have a right to choose their own husbands and a right to educate their daughters, and that is what makes the men so mad. You know, we hate Pakistan, it is always sticking its nose into our affairs, trying to control what is happening here, but the men, they are so against the idea that women should have any rights and worried that their place is going to be taken away from them that they are accepting aid from the Pakistanis.'

She had turned on the dry earth and was facing me now, her green eyes sparkling in the sunlight. She ran her fingers through her hair, shaking it back behind her ears. Her cheeks were flushed. Down the side of her face the fresh razor wound cut from her forehead to her jaw. She touched it carefully with the tips of her fingers.

'You must hate it here,' I said.

'But I can't just run away.'

I reached out and touched the livid wound gently, where it bulged out over the top of her cheekbone. She flinched away from my fingers, reflexively.

'Not here,' she said quietly. 'You can touch me, but not here.'

For a moment I thought it was the wound she was worried about, but her eyes flicked around her, at the people, the buildings, the trees, and the slow pull of the river. 'What about you?' she said, her eyes falling upon me.

'Me?'

'Tell me something about yourself, about your family.'

I paused for a moment, gazed down at the murky water, at a woman on the far bank scrubbing a colourful rug. I thought of the children's home, of Ponia Marija and Liuba. They seemed so far away now.

'I never knew my father,' I said. 'He left when I was a baby. I lived with my mother in a small apartment in Taurage, a town in the west of Lithuania.'

I paused again, searching through the small, scattered, brittle images of my early years, which I still hoarded, like wrinkled photographs, poorly exposed, fading with age.

'My mother drank heavily. I didn't understand then, of course. She would shout and scream a lot, except when she had drunk a bottle or two, and then we would lie on the bed together and she would wrap her arms around me and cry. She would fall asleep and we would hold each other through the night. One night, when I was six, an ambulance took her away. A neighbour took me in overnight. They said she would be back in the morning, but she never returned. I was taken to a children's home. No one ever told me what happened to her. She just disappeared.'

'That's sad,' Zena said.

I shrugged. 'It was a long time ago.' I smiled. 'I did badly at school and couldn't defer my national service.

But . . .' I hesitated. 'Seeing you in the village, seeing the work you do . . . I'm glad I came here. I feel useful.'

Zena smiled and reached out and touched my hand. She pressed it briefly, then withdrew. She stood up and glanced at the small black digital watch on her wrist.

'I have to get back,' she said.

As we walked back towards the hospital, I felt the proximity of her arm beside me. Occasionally our hands touched as they swung between us.

'And when you studied at the Friendship High School, is this what you wanted? To be a nurse?' I asked her.

She glanced at me and grinned. 'No,' she said. 'I wanted to be a soldier.'

'A soldier?'

She nodded. 'My father used to take me hunting with him when I was young. He allowed me to shoot his gun. Well, you know, I was small so he held the gun, but he allowed me to hold it with him. I remember the feeling, the kick of the gun when he tightened the trigger, his finger pressing down on mine. The feel of his body around me, protecting me as we shot. He would say to me, "Zena, when you are big, we will go into the mountains and hunt a snow leopard."'

'Can I see you again?' I asked.

She hesitated for a moment and looked away from me.

'Yes,' she said, quietly. 'I would like that.'

Vassily was still in the café when I returned, Kolya with him. He looked up as I entered. On the table in front of them was an unmarked bottle of vodka, half empty. Kolya gazed at me vacantly as I sat down. He was chewing lazily.

'*Nu?*' said Vassily, eyeing me. 'How did it go?'

I shrugged and slipped into the chair opposite Kolya.

'Is he all right?' I asked.

Vassily glanced across at Kolya, as though he had just noticed he was sitting there. He slapped him on the back. Kolya looked up a fraction of a moment later and grinned.

'He's fine,' Vassily said. 'Let's get back to base before we're missed.'

Almost as soon as I had left Zena, on the corner, close to the hospital, I longed to see her again. When I returned with Vassily and Kolya to the barracks I felt little desire to join in the laughter and jokes. Now we were the granddads the burden of work had eased. The breathless, ceaseless occupation of our first year shuddered to a halt. I lay back on the low, uncomfortable bunk and stared up at the wooden ceiling. Kolya slumped on the edge of his bed, smoking a cigarette, flicking the ash irritably to the floor. When a new recruit came in with his washed clothes, Kolya eyed him bad-temperedly.

'Your clothes,' the recruit muttered, placing them carefully on the end of the bunk.

Kolya leant across and tipped them off. They landed with a dull thud on the packed-mud floor. The recruit bent quickly, scooping them from the earth and patting off the dust. He went across to the flimsy wooden cabinet that stood in the corner and, opening the door with care so that it would not fall from its hinges, placed the clothes tidily on a shelf.

'Go and fetch us some tea,' Kolya said as the recruit was leaving. He lay back on the bunk and sighed.

'Liuba sends her "love" to you.' He pronounced the

word ironically, and immediately coughed up some phlegm and spat through the open door, as though the sentiment disgusted him.

'Liuba? You've heard from home?'

Kolya took a thin sheet of paper and dropped it from the bunk. It fell slowly, twisting away from me towards the door. I reached out and took it. The paper was of poor quality; it seemed to have been carefully ripped from an exercise book. Liuba's tiny, neat handwriting filled both sides of the page. I attempted to read it, but gave up after a couple of minutes.

I tried to imagine Liuba's pretty face and found I could not. All I achieved was a hazy outline framed by the burden of her hair. I recalled her sitting with Kolya and me on the wall by the children's home, smoking gracefully, the cigarette held between her fingers in the pose she had appropriated from a television film.

For some minutes we lay on our bunks in silence. The sounds of the camp drifted in on the breeze. Kolya tossed his cigarette out of the door and I heard a match strike as he lit another.

'What is the first thing you're going to do when you get home?' he said after a while.

'When I get home?'

The idea seemed incredible. For the first six months in Afghanistan I had dreamt of nothing else. In the few hours of sleep I managed to snatch, the rolling landscapes and lush greens of our home town visited me with such intensity that the taste of them lingered long into the hectic heat of the day. I could close my eyes and summon up immediately the dark pine forests, the clear lakes, the reed beds and the taste of porridge. My senses haunted me. Now I closed my eyes and saw the dusty plain, the fields of wheat as you approached

Jalalabad swaying in the wind, orange blossom and startling bougainvillea, the mountains dark and hard against the taut blue sky. I smelt sweat and wood smoke, dust, cheap vodka. I closed my eyes and saw a young woman, a livid scar running down the side of her face, her lips slightly open, the tip of her tongue protruding as she concentrated on something. I saw the flash of her eyes, heard the sound of her laughter, the authority in her command, the guttural rasp when she spoke in Pashtu.

'Are we going home?' I said, lifting myself up on an elbow. 'Can you imagine that? Do you think it will ever happen?'

'I'm going to move to the coast,' Kolya said. 'Get a little cottage near the sea, spend my time fishing.'

The recruit entered with a battered metal pot of tea, a jar of raspberry jam confiscated from another new recruit and a couple of chipped cups. He carried them on a tray fashioned crudely from a plank of wood, which he placed on a small, rickety table beneath the window.

'Do you want me to pour?' he asked.

'No, just fuck off,' Kolya said.

Kolya heaved himself off his bunk and dropped to the floor. He was wearing sports trousers and a white vest, cleaned and ironed by one of the recruits. He poured the steaming tea into the cups and removed the lid from the jam. Before spooning it into the tea he put his nose to the jar and sniffed. He sighed.

'Just smell that,' he said, closing his eyes. 'Just smell that fruit.'

When he waved the jar in front of my face, I pushed him away. I had no desire to bring back the sensations of that other life. It was gone, there was no point thinking about it. Kolya stirred the jam into the tea and passed me a steaming cup. I sipped it slowly.

Kolya had grown quieter as the Afghan months shambled by. While his grin had always been coupled to a violent temper, we heard his laughter less and less. Often he did little more during the day than lie on his bunk, smoking cigarettes he had stolen or bullied from new recruits. His moments of animation became rarer, and when they came they were often spent producing opium tea.

Inside the hut he would pour out from a sack the dozen of poppy heads he had gathered and begin the slow, awkward process of extracting the seeds from the pods. The pods were dark, almost purple, and though brittle still had the suggestion of moisture in them. Once the pods were emptied he pounded them in a pestle, grinding them to a fine, dirty powder. He rarely looked up from his work. Beads of perspiration ran down his forehead and dripped from the tip of his nose.

'I've not seen you working so hard since you came here,' Vassily joked once, slumped back on a bunk, watching him.

'Why don't you just buy the fucking stuff?' Kirov said. 'It's not as if it's going to cost you much. They're happy enough to have us smoking it, they'll give it you for nothing in town.'

'It's not the same,' was all Kolya would say.

Young boys from the neighbouring village brought marijuana and opium to the edge of the camp. Standing on the outside of the high wire fences surrounding the base, they would call through in almost perfect Russian. Small wads of afghanis were folded into a tin can that we pitched across the two fences. The small boys would pick up the can, extract the money and replace it with the opium or marijuana wrapped carefully in paper, then toss it dextrously back, making sure it did not drop down among the mines between the fences.

When Kolya had reduced the pods to a powder he poured it into the toes of a clean sock he reserved especially for this purpose. Rigging up a kettle over a fire outside the hut, he would sit by it, poking sticks into the flames, keeping the heat high to quicken the boiling. When the water had come to a boil, he removed it from the fire and carried it carefully into the hut. Hanging the sock in the boiling water, he would allow it to infuse for fifteen minutes, while he sat back for a cigarette.

No matter how much we made fun of him for the effort he put into producing the opium tea, we never declined it when he offered. It stank. A dirty sludge lined the bottom of the cup. We drank with bitter grimaces. Kolya reboiled the kettle and more tea was produced. We drank slowly and steadily as the heat of the afternoon passed and the sounds of activity gradually ceased to irritate us and we sank back against the walls and smiled and felt the tension rise from our bodies.

'Sometimes,' Kolya said, relaxed now, and ready to join us in conversation, 'I see all our fear and anger and hatred just rising up out of the top of our heads, or through our ears like from a kettle. I can see it sometimes; it settles beneath the ceiling in a cloud.' He grinned.

Another time, later in the evening, when darkness had descended upon us suddenly and we were smoking marijuana laced with opium by the light of a candle, Kolya worried. 'Do you think it's OK?'

'What?' I asked drowsily.

'The cloud. You know, that cloud that settles beneath the ceiling, do you think it's dangerous?'

'Why should it be?'

'Sometimes when I'm lying here I can see it grow. Sometimes I worry that it's breeding evil spirits or something.'

I laughed. Sleep was taking me gently and I was giving myself to it, allowing it to siphon me off.

Kolya had started smoking opium when diarrhoea set in, sending him dashing for the stinking latrines every few minutes. A *dembel*, finishing his two-year tour of duty, advised him that the muj traditionally used opium to treat diarrhoea. He even provided Kolya with a small amount wrapped in a paper twist. Kolya smoked it and immediately went to buy more. The opium worked – worked better than the vodka binge that one of the officers tried – and Kolya stuck with it.

At the next opportunity I got, I volunteered for escort duty on a trip to Jalalabad for provisions. I managed to get a message through to Zena before I left.

She met me by the gates of the hospital. Touching my hand lightly, she moved quickly down the street and I followed her. Zena lived in a modern, concrete hostel constructed by our Soviet builders in the early years of the decade. Already it had a shabby appearance. The stairwell was dirty, and smelt of urine. The lift was out of order. I followed her up the stairs to a door on the third floor. As we entered she put her finger to her lips.

'Most of the girls are out at work,' she said, 'but a couple that work night shifts will be sleeping.'

From farther down the long corridor I could hear the slow, rhythmic creak of old bed springs. A lazy, slow rasp of rusting metal. Zena pushed me through a doorway and indicated for me to sit on one of the two unmade beds. The small room was littered with the debris of two girls' meagre life. Chipped cups, dirty plates, a crumpled newspaper, *Komsomolskaya Pravda*. A dusty window provided a view over the small stretch of Soviet apartments and a jumble of low, clay-coloured buildings.

'I share the room with Nadia, from Tajikistan,' Zena explained. She disappeared down the corridor, returning a couple of minutes later with a tray. Sweeping papers and books from a small table, she laid a clean cloth over the scarred wooden surface. From the tray she produced paper place mats and arranged a coffee pot and two cups neatly. On a plate she had arranged a few biscuits.

'Coffee?'

'Thank you,' I said, a little overwhelmed by the feminine care.

We drank in silence. The coffee was scalding, but I sipped it because I could not think what to say.

She pulled a photograph from the wall by the head of her bed and showed it to me. It was a black-and-white picture of her standing before St Basil's Cathedral in Red Square, the domes rising behind her. Her hair was longer. It hung silkily across her shoulders. She was wearing a school uniform, a blue dress that rode quite high up her thigh. Against the plain cloth of her dress, the Komsomol badge she wore was clearly visible on her breast. She had a broad grin on her face.

'When I was in Moscow,' she explained.

'You look very happy.'

'I was. I want another life. I want the freedom there is in Moscow. I can't stand it here, where to be a woman is to be nothing, to be less than an animal.'

She leant closer to me, and I placed the coffee cup back on the table. She sank down on to the edge of the bed beside me. Her skin was warm. When I touched her a gentle electrical pulse throbbed from the downy hairs, and flesh goose-pimpled beneath my fingertips. I lowered my head into her shirt, pressing my forehead against the warm firmness of her chest, tasted the sweetness, the saltiness of her skin on my tongue. Her fingers massaged the back of my head. My lips brushed each eyelid, and I traced the tip of my tongue down her scar, sucked the flesh at her throat. My hands traced the curves of her figure, pushing back the stiff cotton of her green shirt, resting on the gathered cloth of her trousers. My lips skimmed her belly, tickled by the roughness of her excited skin.

The sounds of the street faded, along with the mountains and valleys, the dust and dirt, the violent sun and the bone-shaking night. For one moment it slipped from me and I was alone with her beneath the cotton sheets. Time snagged; the minute caught its breath. The bed sighed and enfolded us in its warm oblivion. We lay side by side, gazing empty-eyed at the ceiling and felt the damp sheets dry beneath us.

When I pulled on my clothes, she stood brushing her hair, gazing into a fragment of mirror perched on top of a cabinet. I slipped a small metal cross from around my neck. It was on a thin chain. Liuba had given Kolya and me the crosses the evening before we left. Her cool, full lips had brushed our cheeks, and I had noticed the blush spread across Kolya's face.

'I would like to give you this,' I said to Zena.

She turned from the mirror and took the chain from the palm of my hand. She gazed at it for a few moments before she looked up.

'A cross?'

'Just for luck.'

She held it out for me to take from her. I glanced at her questioningly, and a small sharp pain stung my heart. She noticed the hurt flicker across my eyes and smiled.

'I would like you to put it on me,' she said.

'Oh, I see.'

I took the thin chain, and with fumbling fingers looped it around her. The back of her neck was furred with fine dark hairs that led down to her spine.

'Shit,' she said, glancing at the clock, 'I'm going to be late.'

Chapter 21

It was some time before Kolya reappeared from the back room of the apartment. Exhausted by the activities of the long day, I was dozing when he staggered into the kitchen, knocking over a basket of laundry. Waking from a dream of Laura, I sat up sharply. The dream had been bright and pleasant and it was painful to wake from it to see Kolya's emaciated figure stumbling around the kitchen and the girl's underwear spread across the floor, the cold grime of the apartment.

Kolya cracked a bottle down on to the table, pushing aside the dirty cups and plates. Sitting on the bench by the window, he opened it and took a crushed packet of cigarettes from his pocket. It took him a while to extract a broken cigarette without losing all the tobacco. He offered me the packet, but I indicated I had my own. He filled two glasses to their rim, pushed one over to me and took up the other. Despite his clumsiness, his hand shook less now.

'*Nu, tovarich*,' he said, raising his glass.

He drank quickly, smacking his lips.

'It's been a long time, Antanas.'

His eyes wandered around the kitchen, avoiding my own. Suddenly he seemed to notice the dirt, the underwear, the plates and glasses, the overflowing ashtrays, the detritus of his addiction; he scowled and rubbed his head vigorously.

'Do you remember,' he said, 'in Afghanistan, how

we talked about what we would do when we got back home?' He chuckled darkly.

I drew deeply on my cigarette, watching him, the tobacco scorching my throat.

'I had this idea I would live by the sea, in a little cottage,' Kolya continued. 'I can picture it now, still, the idea I had. Tucked away behind the dunes, the pine forest stretching away into the distance. A log fire. A little boat to go out fishing. What I couldn't eat, I would trade in the village for bread and coffee.'

He stubbed his cigarette out in the ashtray, twisting it around absently, grinding it into the ash. He leant a little closer to me.

'What happened to us, Antoshka? What happened?'

I shook my head.

He laughed. 'You know,' he said, 'I even had this crazy idea Liuba would come and live with me. A fisherman's wife. It was something we daydreamt about, idly, when we were kids.'

He paused to pour himself another drink. The sardonic smile slipped from his face as he knocked it back, wincing.

'When I got back from Afghanistan, I was so fucked up . . .' His voice trailed away. I gazed across the table at him, at the wreck of his body, already an old man's, crumbling away from the sagging structure of his bones.

'I went to see her, you know,' he said.

'Liuba?'

'It was a stupid thing to do. I wasn't fit to see anybody. I had to have a few drinks to get up the courage. She was married. Some university prick that never had to do his national service. They called the police. Can you believe that? Liuba called the fucking police.'

I could see the hurt still in his eyes.

'That was just before I went to Kaliningrad.'

Not knowing what to say, I allowed a few moments' silence before I said, 'Vassily died.'

Kolya looked up. A range of emotions seemed to flicker across his face. Sitting back, he poured himself another drink.

'Well, here's to Vassily,' he said bitterly.

He emptied the glass and slammed it back down on the table. For a few moments he gazed at it, his face dark with rancour.

'You know, don't you, that Vassily, Kirov and I smuggled jewellery, among other things, out of Afghanistan,' he went on. 'We stuffed the goods into the coffins, flew them back on the black tulips. When the stuff got to Moscow it was sold and the money was shared between us. It didn't come to that much.' He flicked his arm ruefully. 'Most of the money I made went in here.' His shirtsleeves were buttoned down at his wrists.

'Vassily mentioned one piece to me,' I said. 'A bracelet.'

'The bracelet?' Kolya paused and gazed at me malevolently. 'It must have been worth a small fortune. We got it in Ghazis, but the whole thing went disastrously wrong. Kirov and I ended up in prison, "complicity in the sale of Soviet supplies to the enemy". When I got back to Vilnius I went to see Vassily but he would not talk about the bracelet. I was angry; I needed the money. Like I said, I was in a state at that time and perhaps I said some stuff I shouldn't have. Vassily was furious. In the end he gave me some money and warned me to stay away. He threatened to kill me if I went anywhere near you.'

'Vassily threatened to kill you?' I said incredulously.

Kolya nodded aggressively, as if challenging me to

disbelieve him. 'I suppose Zinotis had already sold the bracelet for him,' he added.

'Zinotis?' I said, sitting up. 'What does Zinotis have to do with it?'

'Zinotis was our contact here. He sold the stuff once we got it out of Afghanistan. He knew the market, he had the contacts. It meant a four-way split, and that meant less money for each of us, but Zinotis was always going to get a better price and so it was worthwhile having him in on it.'

'You're telling me,' I said, stunned, 'that Zinotis knew about the bracelet?'

Kolya nodded. He rubbed his face and poured himself a fourth large vodka. 'I have no doubt about it,' he said. 'How else would Vassily sell the bracelet? Zinotis sold all of the stuff we smuggled. To sell things like that you have to know private collectors. You can't just take it down to the local market.'

My mind reeled. I thought about the way Zinotis had behaved, how he had been interested in seeing the bracelet. How he had kept turning up, digging for information.

'I talked to Zinotis about the bracelet,' I said to Kolya. 'Yesterday. Today. He denied all knowledge of it. He didn't seem to remember you.'

Kolya laughed. 'He's a bastard. You should be careful, he will double-cross you at the first opportunity.'

'I told Zinotis I was coming to see you,' I said, Kolya's revelation reverberating around my head, rearranging the events of the previous couple of days.

Kolya looked at me, his eyes dark and sunken, his forehead creased. For one moment he reminded me of the serious boy I had met in the garden of the children's home just over twenty years before.

'Why were you talking to Zinotis?' he asked.

'Vassily wanted me to find you. I thought Zinotis might know where you were.'

Kolya chuckled darkly. 'Not if I can help it. He is too close to Kirov. It was Kirov who introduced us to him in the first place; they had been involved in some business together in the early eighties. Drugs from Afghanistan. Zinotis plays up his respectable image as a university professor, but he's more crooked than a politician. When Kirov is finally released from prison, Zinotis will be the first person he contacts.'

'But he has been,' I said.

'What?'

'Kirov came to see me a couple of days ago,' I told him.

Kolya's face wrinkled, perplexed. He glanced across at me, his watery eyes examining me.

'I was in my workshop when he burst in,' I said.

Kolya got up. He paced across to the sink, spat in it, then turned back to look at me.

'What are you talking about?'

His breathing was laboured, I noticed, and fine beads of perspiration had broken out across the top of his lip, glistening among the bristles.

'He's looking for you. For the bracelet. He came to the workshop and threatened me.'

Kolya slumped back into his chair. 'Well, *tovarich*, you really are the bearer of good tidings today.' He ran a hand across his face, and when he looked at me his eyes were alight with weary fury.

'I had no desire to get mixed up in this,' I said, angrily.

'When Kirov and I were put away,' Kolya said, 'in the Pol-e-Tcharkhi, Kirov tried to kill me. He blamed me for him getting caught. There were fights in there continually, murders happened all the time.' Kolya pulled up his shirt, revealing an ugly scar that ripped up from his belly to his chest. 'He failed, though. He was transferred to a maximum-security prison in Russia and had five more years added to his sentence.'

'I told Vassily I wasn't interested in the bracelet,' I said. 'He insisted on sending me after you. "Find Kolya," he told me, "he will tell you about what happened." I shouldn't have listened to him. Tanya pressed me.'

'Vassily wanted me to tell you what happened?'

I pulled the letter Vassily had given me from my pocket, unfolded it and pushed it across the table to him. Picking it up, he gazed at it for some moments before letting it fall back on to the table. He looked at me over the top of his glass.

'How do you come to have this?' he asked.

'Vassily gave it to me before he went into hospital. Before he died he made me promise to find you. He told me there was a story about the bracelet you must tell me. I have had enough of thinking about those years, but it seemed important to Vassily that I know.'

I turned over the letter and indicated Vassily's scrawled instructions in pencil across the back of it.

'He wrote here how you can find the bracelet. He decided after all that you should have it, if you told me the story of how he came to get it.'

Kolya picked up the letter again and examined the writing.

'You mean to say,' he said, 'it's written here where the bracelet is?'

I nodded. 'Vassily never sold it. He buried it. He wanted to forget about it – the whole thing, the bracelet, what had happened. But he couldn't. It haunted him right up to his death.'

He looked up from the letter, and regarded me, his sunken gaze receding to some place I could not see.

'Kirov was responsible for what happened,' he said, slowly. 'For Zena. For that whole fucking mess.'

'For Zena?' I said, my throat tightening, the blood seeping from my face, leaving my skin cold and clammy. I stood up and paced over to the window.

'You remember, of course.'

'Of course I fucking remember,' I said, my voice brittle. I gripped the window ledge. 'Do you think I could forget?'

Kolya shook his head. He did not seem to notice the anger in my tone. He stood up and came over to me, put a hand on my shoulder.

'You don't know Antanas, you never knew.'

'I don't want to talk about Zena, Kolya,' I said. The perspiration stood out on my forehead. My heart was thudding. My hand trembled when I put it up to push him away. 'That's not what I came here for. Vassily told me you had to tell me something about the bracelet. That's the only story I want to hear. You understand?'

'But Zena . . .' he began.

I lashed out at him. He stumbled backwards, a look of surprise crossing his emaciated features.

'I said I don't want to talk about Zena,' I yelled.

I punched the window frame hard. The pain that shot up my wrist was blissfully sharp. My knuckles were bloodied. Biting my lip, I punched the wood again, thrilling to the fierce burst of fresh pain. The lump in my throat loosened, the bubble of fear shrinking in the darkness, in the corner of my mind.

'Hey!' Kolya said, pulling me back, his voice shaking. '*Tovarich*, stop!'

I allowed him to pull me away. To push me down into the seat by the table.

'Here,' he said, almost overturning the glass in his hurry. 'Here, a drink.'

I licked clean the torn flesh. Tasted the sweet tang of blood on my tongue. Concentrating on the soreness of my knuckles, I allowed the panic to recede. Kolya slumped into the chair opposite me. He closed his eyes and sank his head into his hands.

'So Kirov is out of prison and Zinotis is after the bracelet,' Kolya mused after a while. 'It's time I left Vilnius, I think. Do you think you were followed?'

I recalled the times over the past few days when I had been convinced I had seen a flicker in the shadows when I looked behind me, sure somebody had been watching me but seeing no one. Remembered too how Zinotis had turned up at Tanya's apartment, then my own. A shiver ran down my spine.

'I don't know,' I said.

Kolya shifted in his chair. He turned the empty glass in his hands, not refilling it. I waited for him to say something. He picked up the letter and stared again at the instructions Vassily had scribbled on it.

'Antanas, *tovarich*, I think we are going to have to move fast,' he said, quietly. 'Help me to find the bracelet and I will tell you about it. It is a story you should hear, whether you want to or not.'

I nodded, aware of the danger I had placed Kolya in.

'We'll have to go back over to Warsaw Street,' Kolya said. 'I need to get some things.'

Chapter 22

I saw Zena as much as I could, volunteering to escort the supply convoy into Jalalabad as regularly as it went. Vassily laughed at my enthusiasm to take a job largely left to new recruits. The trip to Jalalabad was slow and dangerous – after dark the rebels often mined the potholed roads and would launch regular, lightning attacks along the route.

On the weekend leaves we were occasionally given I would stay with Zena, her Tajik room-mate, Nadia, sleeping in one of the other rooms. Often I would wake in the early hours of the morning and sit up and watch her as she lay sleeping, the pre-dawn air cool on our skins; the sweetest hour of the night, when I wished the day would never come.

'Hold me,' she would say, drowsily. 'Hold me tight.'

And I would hold her, feel her smooth, lean limbs curl around me, the warmth of her breath on my chest.

'I don't want to move from here,' I would say. 'The night is best. When it's dark the world disappears and it is just the two of us and this bed.'

'This bed is my world.'

'Your body is my world.'

'I like that. I like it when you look at my body. Look at me. Why should I be hidden? Why do they want me to be hidden?'

And so it should have stayed. But joy in Afghanistan was as insubstantial as breath on a pane of glass.

'Who do you think you are?' Zena said, her voice tight with emotion, one day a few weeks later.

I stood in her doorway. She had been dressing, getting ready for a night shift. A brush hung in her hand; she pointed it at me accusingly. Her face was pale, and dark shadows rimmed the underside of her eyes.

'You know what happened at the *kishlak*?' she demanded. I nodded. 'Yes, I know,' I said. 'I was there.'

'You disgust me. You are no better than they are.'

The *kishlak*, the Afghan village, nestled in a hollow by the river. There was an orchard of orange trees by the side of the village. Some months earlier, not long after we had arrived, the orchards around Jalalabad had been in full blossom, the tiny fragrant flowers shivering in the breeze, like the frills and folds of a thousand young girls' dresses. Their branches were heavy with fruit now. The mud-brick walls of the village were dark and strong, the doorways to the small family compounds brightly painted. At the edge of the orchard was a well. The first time I drove past the village, I noticed an old man seated by the side of it. I had been smoking hashish. We had been in the mountains for two nights and the hashish was a relief from the cold and fear and boredom by the small fire, well shrouded so the mujahidin would not see it.

Under the trees there were children playing. The bright colours of their clothes shimmered in the dappled shade. As we drove past, clouds of dust rose lazily from our wheels. The scent of oranges hung in the air. Security measures demanded we train our weapons on the passing village, but I could not suppress a shudder as we turned the big guns on the children. The sudden flash of their movements ceased as they saw us. They drew closer, a small group. A child pulled close to her elder brother, hugging his thin leg. The boy's arm snaked around the girl's shoulder and he folded her close, his large eyes staring out from beneath the trees.

The old man by the well looked up too, hearing our engines. He wore a grubby white turban. As we passed his eyes caught my own and locked on to them. In his hand he held an orange, given to him, perhaps, by one of his grandchildren playing among the trees. The morning was still apart from the noise of our vehicles passing. A slight breeze stirred the trees. The air was cool. The old man held my gaze.

'You look at me like I'm a piece of shit,' I commented. 'Do you have any idea what it is like to be out there?'

'What's this?' she said, thrusting her face forwards, indicating with a jab of her index finger the livid scar down the side of her face.

I shook my head. 'Zena,' I said, 'you live in this moral world, this world of good and bad. I don't know how you do it. We are soldiers, we have to do our job. We have to survive.'

'That *kishlak* was your job?'

'I'm defending your fucking country against the rebels. What do you think life would be like for you if we were not here?'

'My father fought for my country but he did not do what you have done.'

'Your father was killed,' I shot back.

Immediately I regretted my words. The brush in her hand fell to her side. She stared at me for a moment, her face twisted with contempt, then she turned away to the small broken fragment of mirror and finished tidying her hair.

*

We were mobilised late one evening after dark. As we scrambled to the helicopters, dressing as we went, we learnt that there had been an attack on a convoy close to a village at the foot of the mountains. There were casualties. The helicopters rose noisily into the night sky. Trembling, the new recruits gazed out into the darkness, eyes bright with trepidation.

Kolya undid a twist of silver paper, revealing a small quantity of opium. He flicked his lighter, a red plastic Chinese one he had bought from the market in Jalalabad, and held it beneath the silver wrapping. As I had been leaving our building on the base, I had paused for a moment in the doorway, oppressed by a sudden strange heaviness. I looked up. It was a clear night, and the sky was littered with stars. A wave of sorrow washed over me. Is this it? I thought. Am I to die? But it was sorrow I felt, not fear. I had heard of many soldiers having these premonitions. 'Visits', they were called. Death's calling card.

As the helicopters turned heavily, clattering low across the fields, flares falling away into the darkness, I looked out through the open door and realised, too late, where we were heading. Already visible, illuminated by a bright moon and nestled in the arms of its orange grove, was the village we had passed a couple of days previously. The mountains rose, ominous shadows overhanging the village. On the road a few kilometres out of the village was a short line of APCs and BMPs. The first in the line was smoke blackened. A large crater opened out in front of it. The carcass of an APC lay beside the crater, split open, as if it were a tin can. It had toppled on to its side, displaying its shattered belly to the night sky. We circled the convoy and came down on the road behind them. Wild-eyed soldiers surrounded us almost immediately, the stench of battle fresh on their skin.

'An ambush . . .'

'A mine took out the APC . . .'

'They were all round . . .'

'Half the fucking platoon is gone . . .'

'Fucking muj . . .'

They were climbing in, squeezing into the corners. A boy was pulled in on a makeshift stretcher, whimpering. As they shoved past, his leg brushed against my arm, coating my sleeve with blood.

'Close the fucking door,' the pilot shouted back, 'the rest are gonna have to wait.'

The helicopter rose unsteadily and turned above the line of vehicles, leaving behind those who had not been able to squeeze into one of the choppers. It headed low and fast across the fields towards the village. The bright light of the moon looked like a soft layer of snow fallen across the orange orchard. The village was dark and nothing stirred in its streets or small courtyards. We hovered above the low houses, the down-draught of air raising a cloud of dust and stirring the leaves on the trees.

I pushed open the door and trained the heavy machine gun on the dark doorways. Behind me the boy on the stretcher had started to howl. The pitifulness of his wail chilled my heart.

'Mama,' he cried, 'oh, Mama, please, I want Mama.'

'Shut him up,' I said, turning to the stretcher-bearers.

The floor beneath my feet was wet, and my foot slid. I looked down. It was dark with blood.

'Oh God, oh God,' the boy moaned. 'It hurts so much.'

I stared out into the darkness, my eyes searching for

movement in doorways, windows, in corners where the light of the moon did not penetrate. Were the children asleep beneath these fragile roofs? I wondered. I recalled the small girl, arm around her brother's leg, his snaked protectively around her shoulder. The old man with the bright, fresh orange in his hand. Oh God, I prayed, give my heart an eye that I may see here a family sleeping, children.

'Don't let me die,' the boy was pleading, 'please don't let me die.'

God, give my heart an eye that I may see . . .

'There!' A finger stabbed in the direction of a movement in the darkness below us. The pilot saw the movement too, and shouted out. The earth rumbled and burst into flame. My finger tightened on the trigger of the machine gun, even as I was praying. The village shuddered. The dust rose in thick, bulging clouds. The boy's cries were lost for a moment beneath the whistle and thud of rockets, the metallic chatter of the machine gun.

'It was so noisy, the machine gun, the blades of the chopper,' I said to Zena's back, 'but behind all that – no matter what noise we made – I could hear the cries of one of our boys, dying. Knowing he was dying. Pitifully fearing the approaching darkness. Wanting only to be in the arms of his mother, a little child again. Safe.'

The helicopter lurched and turned and settled by the side of the *kishlak*. As soon as it was down I was out and running. I was screaming. Unable to hear my scream, yet aware of it.

The dust hung over the village, a choking cloud

obscuring our vision. We plunged forwards into the darkness. Flames licked along wooden beams and rushed through the dry grass roofs with a hot crackle. Mud-brick walls crumbled with a soft thump. From somewhere in the darkness came the muffled sound of cries and the rattle of machine-gun fire. In a side street I came upon a locked door. I pressed my weight against it, my shoulder to the peeling blue paint. I kicked it hard with the heel of my boot and the wood splintered and fell away.

'He was just a child,' I whispered to Zena. 'Barely eighteen. Only a few years ago, if he had fallen and scraped his knee, his mother would have taken him in her arms and kissed him and soothed him.'

Zena did not turn to me. She leant against the cupboard, staring vacantly into the mirror.

'He was just a child,' I said.

Kicking the jagged edges of the door aside, I pressed through into the courtyard. Almost immediately a flicker of movement caught my eye and I turned and fired without hesitation. A dark figure crumpled into the shadows. I ran across to the door of one of the buildings, my hand feeling for a grenade.

'Come out!' I screamed into the darkness.

There was the sound of movement behind the door. For one moment I hesitated. Kicking open the door, I pulled the pin and tossed the grenade in through the doorway. I stood back, flattening myself against a mud wall, warm still from the day's heat. My fingertips dug into the dry clay. Faintly I heard the sound of cries above the explosion.

Turning, then, I ran, plunging in through the blackened cavity. The machine gun shuddered in my hands and I heard the clatter of its ejected shells bouncing on the polished clay floor.

I stood in the doorway, catching my breath. The moon was suspended over the courtyard, hazy and red behind the rising pillar of dust. Vassily entered through the small gate, Sasha close behind him.

'You OK?'

I nodded.

'What happened?'

I stepped forwards into the centre of the courtyard. There was a well and I lowered my head over it, felt the damp coolness rising from its depths.

'Shit!' Vassily turned from the doorway. I heard him gag.

'What is it?' Sasha asked.

Vassily did not answer. Sasha pushed past him and entered the room.

How deep is this well? I thought. How deep? How long would it take to fall into the water? The water would be cool and fresh. It would not be a bad way to die. I felt a hand on my shoulder. I felt Vassily's breath warm against my face.

'What happened?' he whispered, close to my ear. 'What happened?'

I shook my head.

'They are children,' he said. 'Little children.'

'I don't know,' I said, 'I haven't looked.'

The children. They stood beneath the orange trees and the light seeping through the leaves lay on their skin like refined sugar. They drew close as we passed. The little girl hugged her brother's leg tight and his arm curled around her shoulders. Their dark eyes gazed out at us as we passed. The games that had amused them, had sent their small limbs tumbling through the grass, ceased as we drew close.

'What are we going to do?' Vassily said.

'Cover this fucking mess.'

Sasha ran a hand through his hair. He scratched the palm of his hand against the stiff bristles of his new beard. 'We'll be in deep shit if this is discovered.'

I squatted down by the wall and closed my eyes. I heard their grunts as they lifted the bodies from the room and dragged them out into the courtyard. The first splashed, far down, and so did the second. But after that they landed with hollow thuds that echoed slowly up from the depths. Sasha tossed a grenade down after the last body and its dull thud shook the earth. I helped them to pour rubble from the buildings into the hole.

We discovered Kolya sitting at the corner of a street. In the light of a candle he had wound his belt around his upper arm and was preparing a syringe. He looked up and grinned.

'They found a whole stash of arms. Swiss Stinger missiles, English T-6.1 mines, heavy-calibre Degterev-Shpagin machine guns, the lot,' Kolya said, tightening the belt around his arm.

The syringe he was using was a Soviet-issue 'Rekord'. They were notoriously blunt and unpredictable and the medics preferred to use the Japanese disposable syringes we were sometimes able to capture from the Afghans. In the medical stores on base we had a store of Western syringes as well as plasma bags and bandages seized in a couple of successful raids on mountain hideouts. Kolya must have stolen the syringe from the helicopter. He winced as he plunged the needle into an engorged vein.

216

'Bring him back to the chopper,' Vassily said to Sasha.

Leaving him with Kolya, we worked our way back through the narrow dirt lanes of the *kishlak*. Dull explosions rippled across the rooftops and, turning a corner, we walked into a hail of bullets as a lone insurgent, caught behind a crumbling wall, defended his position. Ducking down, we plunged for cover in a family compound.

The room we stumbled into was dark. Leaning back against the wall, listening to the rattle and whine of machine-gun fire as the insurgent was flushed out, we became aware that the room was not empty. A dark shape moved in the gloom. A pair of shadowed figures struggled in the corner. We heard a grunt of amusement and the frightened whimper of a girl. Vassily raised his gun.

'Who's that?'

Kirov rose from the darkness, hauling his trousers up from around his knees. He grinned. Visible behind him then, slumped across a table, was a girl of no more than twelve. She seemed to have fainted for she lay dead still.

'You want her?' Kirov asked, companionably.

Mutely I shook my head.

'No?'

Kirov removed his Makarov pistol and, turning, casually fired a single shot. The girl's body bucked slightly then lay still once more upon the table.

Vassily put his arm around me and we walked out through the narrow streets to the edge of the village. In the back of the helicopter the boy we had picked up was lying quietly. Vassily raised his eyebrows questioningly.

'He's gone,' the young medic said. He was sitting beside the boy, smoking a cigarette.

*

'I want you to leave,' Zena said, not turning. 'I want you to go now.'

I went to her, tried to touch her shoulders, but she turned and the look on her face was ferocious. She brandished the brush before her, keeping me back.

'Go.'

Chapter 23

Kolya stumbled on to the helicopter, his Kalashnikov slung carelessly from his shoulder, a small, private smile playing on his thick lips. Slumping beside me, his hand clutched my knee, squeezed it. I turned to look at him. His eyelids were closed. They opened slowly, revealing tiny pupils, bloodshot whites. He grinned, catlike.

'You ever read Malraux?' he said. 'You know what he said? Opium teaches one thing only – aside from physical suffering, there is nothing real.'

The lids of his eyes slowly slid back down.

Squatted down in the corner of our room, back on the base, I accepted a bottle from Sasha. It was not the Stolichnaya we had got from Hashim, it was *samogonas*; moonshine. Water mixed with sugar and left for a week, then boiled. We drank and smoked hashish. My darkness came just before dawn. It was deep and dreamless. When I woke later the next day, Vassily placed a bottle of good vodka by my side. My fingers were not strong enough to crack open the bottle, so he did it for me.

Technically, in the medical station, where I was referred the next day, I was not allowed to drink any more. The medic preferred, however, to have me drinking something good, rather than sneaking the surgical spirits. He provided me with a bottle.

*

'Enough,' Vassily said, two days later. He bent down over the low, uncomfortable bunk and grabbed the front of my vest, pulling me up sharply. I gasped, woken from a stupor.

'That's enough now.'

Dragging me from the bed, Vassily pushed me, stumbling, towards the door. When my legs gave way and I crumpled in a heap, he pulled me up roughly. The young medic, who had raced out of his office, hearing the commotion, mounted a feeble protest. A look from Vassily quietened him; he stood back against the wall and let Vassily take me.

The brightness of the light split my skull. I begged Vassily, but he did not listen. Hauling me across the dusty parade square, he threw me to the ground close to the latrines. Turning on a hosepipe, he doused me with water. I lay on the earth, my knees pulled close to my chest, hugging them tight, burying my face in the sodden cloth of my trousers. He left me there for a while and I lay still, feeling the heat of the sun slowly warm me, feeling the cloth dry against my skin. I smelt the burnt scent of the Afghan soil, the fresh odour of wet earth, the sharp stink of my body, the heavy stench of the latrines hanging in the air like a sour cloud of gas.

'Get up,' Vassily said.

When I did not respond he kicked me hard in the ribs. Involuntarily I let out a whimper.

'Get the fuck up,' he snarled. 'It's enough. Now it is time you got on with things.'

Lifting me to my feet, he put his large hands on either side of my face to steady me and drew me close.

'Antanas, comrade, it is time to get on with life. Come on, my little brother, it's enough.'

I staggered around after him. He pushed me, prodded me, kept me working. He boiled tea and mixed large spoons of raspberry jam into it. Forced the metal cup to my lips and made me drink the sweet infusion while it was hot. I sweated hard. He sent me to shower, dressed me in clean clothes, threw my sweat-stained uniform at one of the recruits to wash. He woke me early in the morning and took me to the parade ground and forced me through exercises with the new recruits. Slowly, hour by hour, I began to improve. I threw myself into the routines of the base. Up before reveille, I exercised hard. I volunteered for extra duties. I worked and did not think.

'Our soul is cut out bit by bit,' Kolya said, smoking his pipe. 'And soon we will have none left.'

'It is better not to think about it,' Vassily said, smoking, watching one of the recruits polish our boots.

'Malraux again,' Kolya said. '"Don't think with your mind – but with opium".'

'Where did you get that fucking book?' Vassily snapped, picking up the dog-eared paperback that lay at Kolya's feet.

'The bazaar in Jalalabad.'

After Zena had told me to leave, I went angrily.

'Fuck you,' I said, as I left. 'What do you know? What do you understand?'

Almost as soon as I reached the street, though, I regretted having shouted at her. I waited in front of her apartment for her to come out. When, after half an hour, she still had not emerged, I trudged back up the crumbling concrete stairs and knocked on her door. Nadia answered.

'I'm sorry, Antanas,' she said, 'Zena left. She slipped

out through the other exit. One of the girls told her you were waiting in the street.'

I asked for paper and a pencil and wrote Zena a note, which I left on her bed, asking her to meet me the following evening, in a café not far from the river. I slept that night in the compound on the outskirts of Jalalabad.

I went to the café early, and sat outside drinking tea and watching the motorised rickshaws buzzing past. In front of the café stood an old eucalyptus. I moved my chair into its shade and thought about what I would say to her. When a soldier from the supply convoy came and sat with me, I was not able to join in with his chatter. I wished only that he would leave, fearing that he would still be there when she arrived and would carry on with his inane conversation, his stream of weak jokes and tales of his exploits with the whores from Russia.

When finally he left, in search of vodka, I breathed a sigh of relief. I waited until darkness fell, watching the street down which she would have to walk from her hostel, but she did not appear.

I found her on a street corner, head in her hands, one foot up against the wall on which she was leaning. She jumped when I touched her shoulder.

'It's not long till curfew,' I said.

She looked around, as if surprised that darkness had already fallen upon the city.

'I got your note,' she said.

'But you didn't come.'

'I was coming and that is more than you deserve.'

Her tone was softer, but she sounded tired and miserable. 'I tore it to pieces and threw it out of the window,' she said. 'I wanted to forget you. I was coming to tell you that, perhaps.'

She walked beside me, kicking disconsolately at the loose stones at the side of the road. Taking heart from the tone of her voice rather than her words, I put my arm around her shoulder. She shrugged it off.

'Don't,' she said softly.

'I love you,' I told her.

'Well, I can't love you.'

'You're all I live for,' I pleaded. 'All that I think about when I am not with you is when I will see you next. I don't know what I would do if I could not look forward to seeing you again.'

She stopped and looked at me. Her eyes were dark. She had, I noticed, put on mascara and lipstick. She was wearing a thin cotton blouse beneath a soldier's *Pakistanka*, and around her neck she wore the cross I had given her.

'They brought in some of the injured from the *kishlak*, after you had been there,' she said. 'Children with limbs missing, old people. Of course, then I did not know you had been involved. There was talk of worse, of a massacre.' She looked at me, as if hoping I might refute this. I said nothing. 'A soldier from your division, Kirov, was with one of the girls a few nights later – one of the girls who does it for money,' she said, not attempting to hide the disgust in her voice. 'He was boasting about having been involved in the raid on the *kishlak*, said that it was a rebel hideout, said that a whole arms cache had been found and that there would not be an investigation because it had been proved to be a mujahidin stronghold.'

I nodded. The commander considered the raid to have been a great success.

'The children,' Zena said, 'you should have seen them.' Her voice trembled and her eyes brimmed with tears. 'Women were raped.'

'I didn't do that,' I said, quickly.

She stared at me hotly.

'Zena,' I said, 'I don't know what to say to you. Don't blame me for this mess. When I came here, to Afghanistan, I thought I was coming to do some good. The Political Officers told us we were fighting for the revolution here, that we would be protecting the villagers from the rebels, that we would be digging wells for them, building hospitals and schools. I thought we would be welcomed. Instead everybody wants to kill us. A child might smile at me, and when I turn around he could push a knife into my back. A village welcomes us in the daytime, they shake our hands, thank us for our help, and then darkness falls and the muj use their village to shell us.

'A few weeks ago, there was a call from one of the villages. They needed help. Bandits were firing on them from the mountains. We sent a detachment out to the village to help them. When they got there it was empty. Suddenly there was shooting from all sides – rockets, automatic fire. Only three soldiers from the detachment managed to escape alive.'

Zena was shaking her head.

'I know this,' she said, 'I know. But still, these are my people.'

'They are your people? You want them to force you back into the burqa? You want them to force you out of your job? You want them to treat you like a piece of shit?'

Zena sighed. She leant back against the wall in the doorway of her hostel and closed her eyes.

'I don't know what to think any more,' she said.

'I love you,' I said.

She opened her eyes and looked at me sadly, but said nothing.

'Can I see you next time I come to Jalalabad?' I said.
She nodded.

'Maybe,' she said simply.

When I returned to the base I was sent out immediately on a raid. Afghan informants had passed on information that there were *dukhi* in a village near Hada, a centre for Buddhist pilgrims. Two divisions mounted a quick raid on the village. Information passed to Intelligence from local sources was notoriously unreliable and we entered the village with particular care.

The streets were quiet. We fanned out, shadowing the sappers with their mine-clearing equipment and their dogs, yapping and straining on leashes. Ahead of me I saw Kolya in a doorway. He motioned for me to join him. It took a few moments for my eyes to adjust to the gloom inside the mud hut. Against one wall slouched an old man, a dirty turban fastened loosely around his head. His dark skin was heavily lined, but his eyes were surprisingly bright.

The room was bare. There was no furniture, not even a chair, in the room, only a threadbare rug covering the packed-earth floor. The sole other object was a dog-eared copy of the Koran, on the floor in the corner. The turbaned man crouched against the wall. He did not attempt to fight, and he did not appear to be carrying any weapons. Kolya left me to guard him.

'Shoot the fucker if he moves.'

For some moments I stood there, watching the old man, silently. He shuffled a little, shifting his weight from one leg to the other. He smiled at me, a sad, small smile.

'I have no weapons,' he said, shrugging his shoulders, showing his dirty, calloused hands, his broken nails.

He reasoned with me gently. He spoke fluent, if heavily accented, Russian. His eyes showed no hint of fear. He watched me candidly. I shifted uneasily, the gun in my hands pointed directly at his heart. I thought of Zena, of her words the last time we spoke. I imagined her watching me. The clatter of the destruction of the village drifted in through the open doorway on the dust-clotted air. The drivers were rolling the heavy tracks of the BMPs across the demolished houses, flattening the village into oblivion.

'We are just leading peaceable lives,' the old man said. 'We have nothing against you. We just want to farm – to live without fear.'

'Are you not angry?' I asked, watching his soft smile as he talked to me of his village. He laughed quietly. 'Don't you hate us?'

'No,' he said, shaking his head. 'You are a child of God as much as I. How could I hate you?'

'Is there space left in this world for compassion?'

'Compassion?' A broad grin wrinkled his leathery face. 'Listen, child, compassion is easy for me. Compassion is the gift of the powerless – the dying.' He indicated my gun. 'Now, if it was the other way round, if I held the gun and you sat here defenceless, you might not find me so understanding.'

He coughed up a large gob of phlegm and spat on to my dusty boot. He smiled still, as though this was a normal thing to do, as though I could not mind.

At that moment there was a loud explosion. The ground shook and dirt shivered from the ceiling. For a moment I thought the building was going to come down on top of us. I ducked down, covering my head. The old man did not move. A resigned smile twisted his lips.

'Now you must shoot me,' he said. 'The village, you see, was mined. We set the mines and our "informers" gave you a little bit of information. We knew you would not be able to resist.'

He stood up. He was the same height as I, broad shouldered, and despite his years still looked strong. He tightened the dirty cotton chemise across his chest.

'Here.' He grinned again. 'Shoot me.'

I could hear, as the rumble of the explosion drifted on the breeze, rolling away across the plain, banking against the rise of the foothills and echoing back, the sound of crying, the desperate weeping of young men whose legs and arms lay detached from their bodies. Young men crouched over dead friends with whom, only moments before, they had been sharing a joke. A cigarette. The old man laughed.

'Come on, shoot,' he taunted. 'I would, if I was in your position.'

My hands trembled. I felt my heart pounding. I thought again of Zena. Of her eyes on me. The old man stepped towards me; I stepped back, waving at him, indicating he should not approach. I felt my back press up against the mud wall. A prickly sweat broke out on my forehead. I wiped it. My face was slick with perspiration. The old man's grin was friendly. He reached out a large hand, stubby fingers, grasping at the Kalashnikov.

The image of Zena's face interposed itself between the old man and me. A fleeting image of her supple body twisting beneath me, the soft warmth of her ochre skin. I closed my eyes and felt the gun shift in my hands as the old man's fingers wrapped themselves around it.

A familiar metallic chatter jerked back the lids of my eyes. The old man stepped away. He held his hands to his chest. Blood seeped through the cracks of his fingers. It bubbled up like a warm geyser beneath his hands. He coughed, almost as if he were clearing his throat. Blood spilt, crimson, from his full lips, trickled on to his white beard. He fell to his knees before me. His face twisted and his throat gurgled and for a moment, as I stood there, bewildered, watching him, I thought he was laughing. A hand took hold of my arm and pulled me roughly through the doorway.

'What the fuck is the matter with you?' Kolya rasped. 'If I hadn't shot him he would have taken your gun.'

I nodded, blindly. He pushed me forwards and we ran through the smoking, dust-hazed streets.

Chapter 24

'Warsaw Street?' I said to Kolya. 'I'm not sure that's such a good idea. If Kirov or Zinotis did follow me tonight, they might be watching your apartment.'

Kolya gazed at me for a second and I wondered if he was taking in what I said, or whether the fix he had had earlier and the vodka he had consumed since had dulled his comprehension.

'If they followed you, they could well be outside now,' he said, nodding towards the door. 'It seems you have given them more than enough opportunity.'

He continued to gaze at me, his expression remaining vacant as his tone grew more ironic.

'If Kirov and Zinotis have any idea where I am, it will be because they followed you. I don't really think you are in a position to advise me on my safety.'

'OK,' I agreed.

Kolya pulled on a thick coat, turning its collar up around his ears. We left the apartment, slipping out through the doors into the street as unobtrusively as we could. Standing in the shadow of the doorway, I checked each parked car, each shadow, each pool of darkness. There was no sign of anybody. It was late and there were no pedestrians, no cars on the road. We hurried down the side streets, taking a longer route back to the Rasa district, looping up around the cemetery and back down towards Warsaw Street from the far side. As we approached Kolya's apartment block, he touched my arm and indicated for me to follow him into the darkened area behind the buildings. A door at the back of the apartments opened on to a small yard of muddy earth, criss-crossed with lines for hanging out washing and beating rugs.

We walked up the shallow stairs to the front entrance of the apartment block, where Kolya reached for the light switch in the stairwell. I told him to wait. Pushing open the door I scanned the street carefully. There were few cars and no sign of anybody watching, lingering in the shadows. I relaxed a little.

We climbed the stairs to the fourth floor in silence. Kolya made slow progress, pausing every few steps to take a gulp of air into his lungs. At the end of every minute the light clicked off and I had to press the switch again. When we reached the fourth floor it did not come on.

'It was working when I came here earlier,' I said.

'They're always going,' Kolya muttered. 'It's the cheap bulbs they buy.'

The door to the apartment was open slightly. Kolya pushed it gingerly, to see whether the safety chain was on. The door swung open with a squeak. He looked up at me. I raised my finger to my lips. We stood in the silence of the early hours of the morning, listening for noises coming from within. There was none.

'It looks like there have been visitors,' Kolya said, his voice low.

'Your landlady . . .' I said, but he had turned away.

The apartment was in pitch darkness. Kolya edged around the door, his trembling fingers feeling along the wall for the light switch. Beneath our feet, papers were strewn, barely visible in the pale light of the street lamp glowing through the dirty windows of the stairwell. Kolya's fingers found the switch and pressed it. I heard the hollow click, but no light came on. From somewhere deep inside I heard a strange low muttering.

I felt Kolya's hand on my arm, his fingers gripping my sleeve tightly, the nails digging through the damp cloth and biting into my flesh. It was impossible to see his face in the darkness. We moved forwards, together, down the corridor. Beneath our feet shattered glass crunched; a large sharp object scraped my ankle painfully. We moved slowly, listening. The muttering had ceased and, apart from the soft crunch of our footfalls, the only other sound was of water running in the bathroom.

Kolya flicked on the bathroom light switch and immediately the square around the door was illuminated brightly. Seizing the handle, he pulled the door open, the slab of light falling painfully brightly across the chaos of the corridor. The bathroom floor glistened, the old linoleum slick with water dripping from the overflowing sink. A mirrored-door cabinet hung from the wall, askew, disembowelled, its contents filling the sink, cotton-wool plugs stopping the flow of tap water escaping through the drains. Pills were scattered colourfully in the stained bath.

'Shit,' Kolya muttered.

He turned from the bathroom and crunched quickly to the front room. The light from the window was enough to indicate the uselessness of trying to switch on the lamp. Its bulb was shattered. The old sofa on which I had been sitting only a few hours earlier had been slashed; its stuffing poured out over the floor. The large bureau was overturned, its contents spewed around it.

'Kristina,' Kolya called.

The low muttering began again, closer, a little louder than before. I turned, trying to place where it was coming from. Kolya stepped away across the debris. He opened the door to a side room and disappeared inside. I followed him.

The bed was rumpled, sheets strewn across the floor, the mattress slashed, stuffing exploding out, pictures wrenched from the wall, the nails pulled out along with lumps of plaster.

In the corner Kolya was bent in the darkness. The muttering was louder, more pitiful. A moan, a thin wail, a sob.

'Who was it?' Kolya was saying, his voice impatient. He gripped the shadow and shook it.

The shuddering wail grew louder, more strident. Kolya stood suddenly and turned. He pushed past me, hurrying back into the sitting room. For a moment I lingered, staring down at the small area of darkness in which the woman was hunched, listening to the sharp catch of her breath, her wail, the soft thud of her head banging against the wooden cabinet by her side, then I turned and followed Kolya.

He was standing by the window, gazing out into the street. When he turned his face was twisted with tension. He ran his hand through his thinning hair and surveyed the damage done to the apartment.

'You little bastard, Kirov,' he said with venom.

He stepped over the papers and fallen bureau, the sofa stuffing and the overturned chairs, out into the corridor. In the bathroom, he knelt down in the water pooling on the linoleum, wetting the knees of his trousers. Fitting his fingers into the corner of the wooden panel beneath the bath, he tugged it away. Reaching under the old bath, he pulled out a small parcel. A cloth wrapped tight and tied with string. With trembling fingers he untied the knot and opened out the flaps of the cloth. Inside the parcel was a Makarov pistol. Oiled and gleaming. Beside it a clip of ammunition.

He weighed the gun in his shrunken hand. Slotting the clip into the pistol, he checked the mechanism. He lifted the pistol and sighted it on the tap. Turning to me, he gazed into my eyes.

'Antanas, *tovarich*, we grew up together.' He put his hand on my shoulder. Through my jacket I felt it trembling. 'We were boys together, we were called up together. We went all the way together, right into the very belly of hell. What happened to us there – it tore us apart. Gutted us. Every noble sentiment, every decent feeling, was reduced to ashes. We died then, on the fields around Jalalabad, in the mountains. It was not us that came back, it was our ghosts. Our spirits, forced to wander the world, empty, deranged.'

He took his hand from my shoulder and wandered out into the corridor. From a peg behind the external door he took down a shoulder holster. Clipping it on, he fitted the pistol into it, pulling his thick jacket over the top.

'Come on,' he said. 'There is nothing that will compensate for what has been lost. No jewel will pay for the pain we suffered, or relieve our nightmares. But there is one thing that will give me a little happiness.'

He grinned. In the pale light that shone from the bathroom his face looked as though the flesh had been sucked from it, like the skull of a cadaver.

'The idea of beating Kirov. The thought that I have something he wants. Come on. I will tell you about the bracelet. About what happened in Ghazis.'

Chapter 25

Ghazis lay in the east of Afghanistan, in Nangarhar province, on the road over the mountains to Peshawar, to Pakistan. The first time I heard of it was from Zena. It was a couple of weeks after the disastrous raid on Hada before I was able to see her again. When I tried to contact her she put me off with excuses. She had become involved with the Revolutionary Association of the Women of Afghanistan and was visiting villages, setting up literacy schemes, exerting pressure on the authorities to allow the girls in rural areas to be educated.

Desperate to talk to her, I volunteered for escort duty for the supply trucks. When I got into Jalalabad I telephoned the hospital and asked for a message to be passed to Zena. I waited at the café by the river for two hours but she did not come. Despondently, I wandered past the large hospital complex.

Plucking up my courage, I entered the hospital. It took a while to track her down to a ward in the east wing where she was working.

'What have you come here for?' she asked, wiping perspiration from her brow.

'I needed to talk to you.'

'I'm busy.'

'I sent you a message.'

'Like I said, I'm busy.'

Her face revealed nothing; she glanced back over her shoulder to the ward I had fetched her from.

I longed to talk to her about what had happened in Hada, to tell her that I had failed to kill the old man, but it seemed suddenly ridiculous to boast of such a thing.

'When will you be free?' I asked. 'I really need to talk to you.'

'I'm busy now,' was all she would say. 'Some other time.'

We stood for a few moments in silence. I gazed at her; the pink scar, a bead of perspiration clinging to the top of it, green eyes, her short, boyish haircut. I thought of the nights we had spent together, wrapped in each other's bodies, which already seemed so long ago. Reaching out, I touched her hand. She pulled back, away from me.

'I have to get back to work now,' she said, quickly.

And she turned and walked at a smart pace back down the corridor to her ward. The doors swung shut behind her with a sharp crack.

When I returned to the base, Kolya had, I discovered, told Vassily about the incident at Hada.

'What is going on, Antanas?' he asked, urgently.

'What do you mean?'

'Kolya told me about Hada.'

I shrugged. Lit a cigarette. Exhaled and watched the smoke rise and dissipate slowly in the heavy air. A storm was brewing. Dark clouds massed over the mountains. The weather was so oppressive it felt as if we were all being crushed into the earth.

'It was nothing,' I said. 'Kolya has exaggerated, I am sure.'

'The old man was about to take your weapon. You were stuck with your back against the wall, your eyes closed, sweat pouring from you. Like a frightened porker off to the slaughterhouse.'

'Was that your analogy or his?'

'What happened?'

'I don't know what happened,' I said, irritably.

Over the mountains the low clouds thundered ominously, and the darkened ravines flashed with lightning, heaven's howitzers opening up at last, joining in the struggle to reduce the country to total ruin.

'Comrade, I am concerned,' Vassily said, earnestly. 'We were sent here to do our International Duty. That was shit, we know it. They told us we would continue the brave and noble work of the soldiers who had gone before us, who had begun the struggle to bring peace and revolution to Afghanistan. We know what they did before we came – they dug a big fucking cesspool for us to fall into. We were deceived. Such a lot of lies they fed us. Of course they did, would they tell us the truth? Can you see it as a headline in *Komsomolskaya Pravda* – "Heroes of Soviet Union rape Afghan women"? Or a special report on the TV show *Vzgliad* about young Russian boys getting their legs blown off? Of the drugs here? Of how our girls come out here to be prostitutes for the "regimental elite"? Of the massacres? *Niet*, comrade, it was all a big fucking lie – but, Antanas, that is not the point. We must survive, we must get home. That is the only truth there is left for us now, our own fucking survival. The only way we can poke the bastards who sent us here in the eye is to make the most of our time, make a little money and get home safely.'

Vassily was absently picking at a wound on his leg, a cut that refused to scab over properly and seemed to be growing by the day.

'If you have lost the ability to kill, you have lost the ability to live,' he concluded.

'That's it?' I said. 'It's that simple?'

'You shouldn't make it any more complicated,' he said.

'But what if I don't think my life is worth the killing of innocent children and women, the demolishing of villages. What makes my life so valuable?'

Vassily's brow furrowed.

'That girl has been filling your head with rubbish,' he muttered.

'Don't bring Zena into this,' I snapped.

'She is one of them. She is trouble, Antanas. If you need a woman, fuck one of the Russian girls, pay them and do it. Anything else is not healthy.'

I flicked the cigarette away; watched it bounce on the dusty ground, scattering sparks.

'Leave me be,' I said.

Vassily grabbed my arm as I turned away.

'Comrade, listen to me. She is not worth it. She's putting you in danger, filling your head with nonsense.'

I shook his hand off my arm and left him sitting outside the hut. Already the walls we had built had begun to crumble; the roof was covered with dust and stones. It looked as if it had been there for years. Purple clouds rolled down from the knot of mountains, advancing across the plain towards us. A hot gust of wind blew up the dirt. I tasted the moisture in the air, the coming of the rain.

It reached us later that afternoon. It moved across the base like a sodden blanket dragged down from the mountains. The water ran away in a million little rivulets, pooled in every dip in the earth, battered the walls of our huts, eating them away. I sat on my bunk smoking, listening to its thunderous beat on the roof of corrugated tin, drowning out the hard rock pounding from Kolya's cassette player. Kolya lay slumped in the corner, grinning stupidly.

'Legend says opium poppies sprang from the tears of Aphrodite,' he had told me, apropos of nothing, one evening, as he smoked in the stifling heat, a thick, oily cloud hanging darkly around his head. 'Mourning for Adonis.'

The rain pummelled the earth, warm waves of water irrigating the new crop of poppy fields. Aphrodite's tears, I thought listlessly, as I lay on the bunk. I wrote a letter to Zena and gave it to Sasha, who would be escorting the supply convoy the following week. When Sasha returned he brought a reply with him. I sat on my bunk with the envelope before me, not daring to open it.

'Antanas,' she wrote, 'try as I might, I cannot erase you from my mind. You think I'm being cruel, when I am only trying to do what is right. What will become of us? I remember our nights together and long to have you here again. I try not to think these things because they can bring no good. Call me when next you come to Jalalabad.'

But when I next volunteered for escort duty, Lieutenant Zhuralev rejected me, putting me instead on guard duty. Angrily, I confronted Vassily.

'What have you been telling Zhuralev?' I demanded.

He shrugged his shoulders, turning from me. 'I don't know what you are talking about,' he said.

'You know what I am talking about.'

'Listen, comrade,' he said, 'it's for your own good.'

'It's none of your fucking business,' I shouted.

I lashed out at him. Vassily stepped back, a furious

look crossing his face. He slipped on the wet earth, sliding to his hands and knees. Standing slowly, he faced me, raising his fists. His eyes burnt angrily and his trousers were dark with mud. I threw another punch at him. It hit him hard and he flinched. For a moment he stared at me, perfectly still, like a snake on a rock disturbed in its sleep. The punch he threw knocked me from my feet. I heard the sharp smack as his fist connected with my jaw, felt the pain as my neck wrenched suddenly. Felt the mud sliding beneath my body, the dirty water in my eyes, in my mouth.

'Antanas,' Vassily said, bending over me, his voice shaking with concern. 'Comrade, are you OK? Can you hear me?'

My eyelids flickered open, and I gazed up at him; saw his large face, his dark beard quivering in the air above me. I was acutely aware that my head was resting in a puddle, the water seeping into my ear, but I could feel no pain. Vassily lifted me from the earth and carried me over to the medical hut. I heard his voice, apologetically explaining to the medic what had happened.

'Stick him over there,' the medic responded, unconcerned.

Gently, Vassily lowered me on to a bed. He bent over me, staring at me anxiously, listening to my breathing, feeling my pulse. The medic came over and pushed him out of the way. Roughly, he seized an eyelid, pressed it back and shone a torch into my eye. He repeated the process with the other.

'How you feeling?' he asked me with evident lack of interest. I could smell the alcohol on his breath.

I nodded, sending little pains shivering down my spine. 'Fine,' I said.

'Split lip.' He felt my jaw. 'Nothing broken. Concussion,

perhaps.' He held up three fingers. 'How many fingers?' he asked.

'Three.'

'Better shape than me.' The medic grinned, dropping his hand. 'Rest for a couple of hours, you'll be fine.'

Later Vassily seemed mortified by what had happened.

'It's nothing,' I said.

'About the girl,' he said. When I raised my eyebrows, he held up his hands. 'Please, I just wanted to say, it is not my business. I apologise, comrade.'

Vassily approached me the next weekend I had leave and offered to take me to Jalalabad with him. I left him with Kirov at their favourite café, and hurried over to the hospital, hoping the hurried message I had sent had got through. Zena was waiting, sheltering from the rain beneath the spread branches of an old oak. She smiled. We stood for a moment, awkward in each other's presence. Then, taking my hand, she led me out into the rain.

'Come,' she said, 'I have somebody to meet.'

We caught a tram across the town, its lights glittering in the dark, rain-swept streets, to a district close to the river. I alighted from the tram, nervous, feeling conspicuous in my uniform. I swung my Kalashnikov around from my shoulder and followed Zena, who was hurrying towards the doorway of a newly built apartment block.

A young boy of about six opened the door when Zena knocked softly. He gazed up at us, eyes wide. Zena whispered something to him and he disappeared. A moment later a young woman appeared in his place. She opened the door with a smile and ushered us into a small, tidy apartment. When I entered she looked apprehensive. She drew Zena aside and I heard the quiet, guttural tones of their whispered Pashtu. When they emerged, she shook my hand and greeted me in perfect Russian. Her hand was slim and cool.

The young woman was earnest and intelligent. Her hair, which was long, was tied back under a colourful scarf. Purposefully, she moved around the tiny kitchen, boiling water for coffee and tidying as she talked. Zena sat by the table, listening to her quietly.

'Even here in Jalalabad,' the young woman said, 'there are girls who are not getting an education, though legally their families could be punished for preventing it. But in the villages there has been little movement on the issue. And it isn't just the education, there are the clinics and medical care that women in rural areas need, and are being denied.'

I sipped my coffee and said nothing. After a while the young woman settled on a chair by the table. She folded her hands in her lap, and spoke in her quiet, educated voice. Mainly she spoke in Russian for my benefit, but occasionally she slipped into Pashtu; sometimes Zena interpreted and sometimes she did not. From the doorway of the kitchen the young boy watched me, his eyes fixed on my gun, which stood by the side of my chair. When I offered him a sweet, he ducked away, out of sight.

We left a little while later, hurrying out of the apartment block and down the wet street towards the tram stop.

'You realise,' Zena said, breathing heavily as we hurried, 'that I was putting Aisha in some danger taking you to see her. She was worried that I had brought you.'

'Why did you take me, then?' I asked, puzzled.

She stopped at the side of the road, the water running across the toes of her shoes, her hair plastered against her skull, dripping from her cheeks.

'I wanted you to understand the gulf between us,' she said, 'the risk we pose to each other.'

'I would never do anything to harm you,' I said. 'Or your friends.'

'I know,' she said, 'I trust you. That is why I took you.'

I pulled her close to me, felt her sodden clothes against me, smelt the wetness of her hair, kissed her skin slick with rain, salty.

'Aisha is a member of Rawa – the Revolutionary Association of the Women of Afghanistan,' Zena told me as she towelled her hair dry, later, in her room. 'Earlier this year Meena, who founded the organisation, was murdered in Quetta, in Pakistan. The police there have done nothing to discover who killed her. Some claim it was KHAD agents, others the mujahidin. They were probably working together.'

'And you?' I asked, sitting on the edge of her bed, wrapped in a towel, while my clothes dried. Zena shook her head.

'Her organisation can do little here around Jalalabad, there is too much opposition. It's ridiculous for them to be taking a stand against the communist government; they are tying their arms behind their backs. It makes more sense to work with you Soviets.'

'Is that why you were willing to see me?' I joked.

'No,' she said, softly. She reached over and stroked my cheek. 'I have missed you.'

*

'There is a small school in a village,' she said later, as we lay in the darkness, our bodies close, illuminated by a sliver of moon that had broken through the thick covering of cloud. 'The village is called Ghazis. I will be going out with the Agitprop Brigade. I'll take books and paper out to the teacher there. It's not a big deal, but it really does make a difference.'

I left her early the next morning to meet Vassily. She called me back as I opened the door.

'I can trust you?' she whispered, seriously.

I stroked her ruffled hair, and kissed her.

'Zena,' I said, 'you know you can trust me.'

She smiled. 'Yes,' she said. 'I know.'

Vassily was drinking coffee and smoking when I pushed open the door of the café. In the corner Kirov was talking with a small Afghani, dressed in shabby Western clothes. They looked up when I entered, and seeing me glanced over towards Vassily. I slipped into the chair opposite Vassily and nodded across towards the dark corner of the café where Kirov was sitting.

'Who's the shady character Kirov is with?'

Vassily turned, as if he had been unaware that Kirov was sitting behind him. He shrugged but said nothing.

'Why are you such a friend of Kirov?' I asked him.

'He's an evil bastard, but he has his uses,' Vassily said. He exhaled a thick cloud of smoke. 'He has his uses.'

Chapter 26

'Do you have any money to pay for a taxi?' Kolya asked, as we left the apartment block, slipping out through the back door again.

'A little,' I said.

We walked down to the railway station, keeping to the damp darkness of the backstreets, our eyes and ears alert for signs that we were being followed. In front of the station Kolya found a taxi cab. The driver was sleeping on the back seat and Kolya rapped on the window, waking him.

'Zverynas district,' Kolya said, reading Vassily's scribble. 'Birutes Street, by the bridge.'

I climbed into the cab behind him. The driver, wiping the sleep from his eyes, started the engine.

'It was the bracelet that was the start of it,' Kolya said.

'The start of what?'

'Of everything. Of what happened in Ghazis.'

'How so?'

'What did Vassily tell you about the bracelet?'

'He did not tell me much. Only that he got it in Ghazis, from a merchant there.'

The taxi slipped into the thin stream of cars rounding the traffic island outside the railway station and sped down the hill towards Pylimo. As we passed the apartment where I had met Kolya, I noticed the young woman he had been with opening the door of the block. Kolya did not seem to see her.

'It was Hashim, of course, who set up the deal,' Kolya continued. 'Normally Hashim would approach Vassily directly. This time, however, it was Kirov who came to Vassily with news of the bracelet.'

There was little traffic on the road and we made good progress, driving out across the river on Jasinskio, and into Zverynas.

'If we had known from the beginning the true cost, I am sure Vassily would have had nothing to do with it. Kirov, of course, was not going to reveal the nature of the deal until Vassily was well and truly hooked.

'Hashim teased Vassily when Kirov took us to see him. "This piece I have found," he said, "it will wet your dick."

'Vassily was sceptical and wanted to know what kind of piece it was, but when Hashim tried to speak about it, Kirov stopped him. It came at a good time, Kirov explained. The piece was, at that moment, in a village to the east of Jalalabad, having been intercepted before it was smuggled over the border into Pakistan. Kirov had never been too interested in the jewellery – it was just one of the many things he was involved in, and was not as profitable as prostitution or drugs – but he had some other business in Ghazis that made the jewel useful.

'When Vassily pressed them to tell him more about the jewel, Hashim told him it was an amber bracelet that was thought to have belonged to the Amir Timor – to Tamerlane. This immediately excited Vassily.

'The Agitprop Brigade were going out to the villages along the Peshawar road, Kirov told us, and Zhuralev would have to put together a division to escort them. It was easy enough to volunteer; nobody wanted the job.

'When Vassily asked what they were expected to pay

for the jewel, Hashim told him they wanted an AGS-17 automatic grenade launcher, mortars and a 12.7-millimetre heavy machine gun. Vassily snorted, but Hashim raised his hands, as if the demands were nothing to do with him. Finally Vassily sighed and shrugged his shoulders. "This stuff your friends have unearthed had better be worth my while," he said.

'"It will make you ejaculate," Hashim told him with a grin.'

The taxi stopped at the end of Birutes. The road was quiet. Few lights illuminated the windows of the large houses. A dog barked, woken by the noise of the taxi. I paid the driver.

'Should I wait?' he asked.

Kolya shook his head.

The earth sloped away from the road, down towards the river, invisible in the pitch darkness. It was possible to hear its faint murmur as it flowed swiftly around the edge of the forest. On the high footbridge spanning the river, street lamps burnt dimly. The trees of Vingis Park were darkly visible against the gloom of the cloudy night sky. After looking at Vassily's instructions a moment longer, Kolya waved his hand in the direction of the other side of the river.

'We need to go over there,' he said.

The taxi pulled away from the side of the road and drove slowly back down the hill towards the centre of the Old Town. Above the sound of its engine, the bark of the dog and the ripple of water washing against the muddy bank, I heard the sound of another car engine approaching. It turned into Birutes, at the bottom of the hill, and, pulling up at the side of the road beneath the trees, cut its lights.

'Just some girl earning her keep,' Kolya said, following my gaze.

He set off towards the footbridge. I stood for a moment longer, peering down the hill, my eyes straining to pierce the darkness.

'Come on,' Kolya called quietly.

I followed him, carefully picking my way across the wet earth towards the path. Kolya's footsteps echoed in the night's stillness as he hurried on to the bridge, the metal railings reverberating softly. In the shadow of a tree I paused and looked back: nothing stirred down the long hill. I stepped into the light of the street lamp and followed Kolya on to the bridge.

'Where in the park is it?' I asked, catching up with him halfway across.

'Not far, according to this,' he said. 'Just a little way into the woods.'

Above us, the trees rose darkly now. Below, obscured by the night, the river ran swiftly, tumbling, revealed only by the small, glittering, globular reflections of the street lamps. Kolya was breathing heavily, and as we passed beneath a lamp I noticed that a thin film of sweat coated his forehead, even though the night was cool. Across the centre of the bridge rainwater had pooled in the cracked and sunken concrete, forming a puddle of some depth. We waded through it and hurried on towards the shadow of the trees.

On the far side of the bridge the bank rose up into the woods. The footpath branched off in two directions. Kolya took the left fork, running parallel with the river, along the edge of the park. I followed him as he paced up the track, muttering under his breath, casting his eyes from side to side in the gloom, seemingly searching for some object.

'Is there a marker?' I asked.

He waved his hand, irritably, for me to be quiet. A few moments later he paused and dug a lighter from his pocket. In the dim light of its small flame he read from the back of the letter. Turning from the path, away from the river, he plunged in among the trees. Glancing back along the path, deserted and quiet, I followed him, hurdling low brush, ducking beneath the branches, arms up to protect my face from the sharp back-slash as Kolya pushed through them before me.

'How can you be sure this is the right route?' I called to Kolya impatiently, as my shoes sank in the soft earth.

As if in response Kolya stopped dead, looked around, glanced back towards the path, and turned. He brushed past me and made his way back to the path. There he stood, as a stray beam of moonlight broke through the heavy layer of cloud, illuminating the woods with a cool light, looking around him, hand against his forehead.

I glanced at my watch. It was two o'clock. Kolya slipped down the bank from the path again and examined the bark of the closest tree. Turning from it, he examined those on either side. Shaking his head, he moved off, down the tree line, feeling the rough bark.

'*Blyad!* Are we going to have to examine every single tree in the park?' I complained.

Kolya ignored me, working quickly from the bark of one to another. A few metres along the path, his fingers found what they were looking for. He gave a little cry of pleasure.

'Found it,' he said, and plunged once more into the wood.

He progressed more cautiously this time, working his way from one tree to another, following the signs carved into the trunks of the thick pines. Occasionally he would stop, unsure, moving from one tree to the next, discovering small clearings where trees had fallen, having to work past them, picking up his trail on the far side.

'Two trees,' he said, turning to me, his face obscured in the darkness. 'There are two trees marked in a particular way. Between the two of them, exactly halfway, it is buried.'

I caught up with him.

'Here.'

He took my hand and placed the tips of my fingers on the cool, coarse bark. I felt the grooves cut deep into it, a cross, thick and long.

'Stand here,' he said.

He moved, feeling his way from trunk to trunk until he had found the one he was looking for. He stood with his back to it, resting, his face a pale blotch. There in the earth between us, the box was buried. I felt a childlike thrill at the thought of it. And Kolya, I noticed, as he paced deliberately across the space towards me, was grinning.

Finding the spot, Kolya knelt down on the damp earth and brushed back the thick drift of pine needles that had settled across the ground. I knelt beside him, my heart beating fast. Kolya took a penknife from his pocket. Opening out the blade, he dug it into the earth, loosening the soil.

'It's buried not far beneath the surface,' he explained, his voice quivering a little.

He was scrabbling with his fingers now, pulling up clods of soil, his hand cupping the loose earth and swooping it out of the small hole. His fingernails scratched against metal. Working quickly, he cleared the earth from the top of the box and worked his fingers around it, prising it up from its shallow grave.

He laid it on the slippery bed of pine needles by the hole and for some moments we sat in silence, gazing at its rusting surface. Blue paint flaked from it.

He shook the box gently. There was a soft knock as something moved inside. Taking out his penknife again, Kolya slipped it under the lid and pulled it up. The rusted metal gave easily. He slipped his fingers inside the box, which was barely visible in the gloom, and grinned.

'Let's go,' he said.

'When we got to Ghazis,' Kolya explained as we worked our way back through the trees towards the path, the box tucked beneath his arm, 'we slipped away from the platoon, into the backstreets where Kirov had arranged to meet his contact. The man we met took us down a passage into a courtyard. Vassily feared we were being lured into a trap. We were taken up to a large room at the top of some stairs. To our surprise, we found Hashim was there.

'Three or four other men were in the room. Shady-looking characters. Kirov's friends. KHAD, as we were to find out later. To begin with Hashim took out some pieces of jewellery, lapis lazuli, nothing of any significance. I could see Vassily was beginning to get restless. He threw the pieces contemptuously across the floor.

'And then Hashim took a leather pouch and went and squatted down by Vassily. Taking his hand, he shook out the contents of the pouch on to Vassily's palm. We could all see it was just one bracelet. Vassily sat perfectly still, the bracelet resting on his palm, hardly breathing. Kirov, noticing his expression, wandered over. Slowly Vassily turned it over and examined it carefully from every angle. He asked whether Hashim knew what it was, whether he had any idea what he'd given him, Hashim told him that it was stolen from the Kabul collection.

'Kirov nodded to the KHAD agents and they left. We didn't realise its significance then; we didn't know the full price we were paying for the bracelet. You see it, wasn't just the arms they wanted.'

'What do you mean?' I said. 'What was the price?'

'The government was trying to crack down on the anti-Soviet revolutionary women's group, Rawa. They were, as you know, orchestrating campaigns against the activities of the government. They were stirring up trouble everywhere they went.'

'What are you trying to say?' I felt my heart flutter with fear.

Kolya paused. He looked at me for a moment, then turned away. 'KHAD wanted Zena.'

I stopped on the path. I felt my knees tremble and begin to give. Kolya paused and looked back. The frail light of the moon, which struggled still against the rain-heavy clouds, cast a waxy sheen over his thin face. He looked apologetic.

'She was sold for the bracelet?' I whispered.

Kolya nodded. 'Kirov had organised it all,' he said. 'It had all been planned before we got to Ghazis.'

Chapter 27

We met up with the Agitprop Brigade outside Jalalabad and headed east towards the border with Pakistan, passing Qala Akhuud and Gerdi Kac. The convoy moved slowly, negotiating the broken road with care. On both sides the mountains rose jaggedly. The rain had moved off, leaving the sky clear, sparkling, as beautiful as lapis lazuli. Sitting on top of my APC I could see Zena a few trucks behind.

The road cut through barren plains, greenery sprouting from rust-red rocks. Cerulean lakes mirrored the sky. When we passed villages, the children chased behind our vehicles, screaming, begging, hands reaching out for sweets, money, their eyes full of menace. Beside the road lay the charred corpses of APCs, cars and the shattered skeleton of a helicopter, picked clean by village vultures.

In the afternoon we pulled cautiously into a small town a little off the road, where the loudspeakers were set up to pump out local songs with rousing revolutionary words. While we kept the heavy guns trained on the village and covered the milling crowd with assault rifles, the medics doled out an array of medicines, examined the diseased, pulled rotten teeth, then stretched a large sheet between two trees, erecting their portable cinema.

'If I have to watch *Anna Karenin* one more time!' Kolya moaned.

Occasionally new films were sent out to us from the Union, but usually it was the ageing *Anna Karenin*, Tolstoy's tortured story of love, or a Second World War-era patriotic film. This time, though, the images flickering faintly against the stretched cotton sheet were those of a propaganda film, showing grinning Afghan workers, new apartment blocks, roads, parks, peasants working in the fields, looking up and waving, and a soldier grinning back from the turret of an APC. The children ran around in excited circles, shouting obscenities in perfect Russian; old men limped up the queue for half a tablet and a small bag of rice. There were few healthy young men to be seen.

We were not able to relax until we pulled out in the late afternoon, back on to the main road. Lieutenant Zhuralev kept up a continual, voluble, muttered protest about the exercise and snapped at anybody who addressed him.

That night we were stationed at a small base close to the road. The barracks, a large stone building, was surrounded on three sides by linked trenches. The latrines, ornately constructed from green ammunition boxes, stood some fifty metres away by a clump of eucalyptus. Sand-filled barrels dotted the base at regular intervals, providing cover from the bullets and shell fragments that were a regular feature of everyday life there.

The small company stationed at this far-flung base consisted of a wild-looking group of Uzbeks. They greeted us cheerily, especially when they discovered we had brought them rations of vodka. They stared at Zena, who was one of only two women in the Agitprop Brigade's company, with ravenous eyes, and I feared that all their military discipline would be an inadequate check on their obvious needs.

The darkness was punctuated by the regular zip of sniper fire from the mountains, and the occasional thump of mortars. The Uzbeks paid little attention to the gunfire. Occasionally their conversation would falter as they cocked their heads to listen to the mortars, ascertaining the level of threat, but once they were sure they were not going to score a direct hit, they immediately picked up the thread of their conversation and didn't even blink when the ground shook and the plastic covering the windows billowed out.

'Don't you fire back?' Kolya asked, crouching on the floor as another shell exploded less than a hundred metres away.

The Uzbeks drew our attention to a deep thump. 'One of ours.'

'Don't worry,' the bearded commander of the garrison commented, 'we are at the edge of their range when they are shooting from the mountains and they rarely venture down on to the plain where they would be able to score a direct hit.'

Later, seeing that Zena had left the stuffy, smoke-filled room, I slipped out into the darkness. She stood outside the door. The night air was fresh and clear, sharp with the scent of conifer and the cool dampness of the river that bordered the base. Zena felt comically large when I wrapped my arms around her. She was wearing the bulky standard-issue flak jacket, which like most of the equipment issued to us was more of a hindrance than an aid to survival. Dodging from barrel to barrel, we worked our way through the darkness down towards the river. Beneath a eucalyptus we made love quickly and fiercely, afraid only that someone would stumble upon us, or a shell would disturb us before we found relief.

'I long for our bed,' she whispered, as we sat, backs pressed against a wall of sand-filled barrels. My heart jumped with delight that she considered her hostel bed ours. Later we wound our way back to the barracks, avoiding the drowsy Uzbek on sentry duty, squatting by a small hut, one of our vodka bottles nestled between his legs.

The next day followed a similar pattern. We set up warily in several villages and provided cover while the Agitprop Brigade did their job. In the early afternoon we arrived in a larger village called Ghazis. The mountains rose steeply behind the village and the area was heavily wooded, with ash and juniper and an orchard of walnut trees.

Lieutenant Zhuralev cursed as we wound up the low foothills away from the main road to the village. On the crest of a hill, a little lower than the village, was a small hamlet, a few households surrounding a dusty square.

'We're a sitting duck!' Zhuralev muttered furiously. 'Why do we have to do this? Fucking Agitprop Brigade!'

Unlike in the majority of villages we had visited, a large group of young men milled around among the jostling crowd in the marketplace as the cinema screen and distribution tables were erected. Seeing them made Zhuralev more jittery than ever.

'I don't like this, I don't like it one fucking bit,' he snarled.

The afternoon passed quietly, though. Strolling about the village marketplace, keeping a sharp eye on the crowd, I glanced frequently at Zena, who worked at a furious pace with the young bespectacled medic, distributing pills and examining yellow-faced elderly men and sickly children. The young men, who had been boisterous when we first arrived, settled down and sat in the dust, watching the faint, flickering images of the propaganda film with rapt attention.

Lieutenant Zhuralev breathed a sigh of relief when the Agitprop Brigade began to pack away their gear. I brushed by Zena as she stood by the Agitprop's APC. She caught my arm.

'I want you,' she whispered in my ear. Her breath was warm and dampened my skin. I felt a blistering burst of desire in my groin.

As we organised the vehicles into a convoy, and the first BMP rolled out of the village, I noticed Vassily emerge from a doorway. He loped across the market-place and jumped up on to the back of an APC. Behind him came Kirov. Their heads ducked together in conversation.

Chapter 28

'It can't be,' I protested to Kolya.

He gazed at me in the moonlight, his expression troubled. Shifting the metal box from beneath one arm to the other, he nodded solemnly.

'That's how it was, Antanas, *tovarich*. That was the deal.'

'But . . .' I said. 'I don't understand.'

'It was Kirov,' Kolya repeated. 'It was he who organised everything. They wanted her, Zena. KHAD wanted her out of the way. They considered her dangerous. Kirov had organised with KHAD that she would be arrested; they would cart her off to the Pol-e-Tcharkhi prison. She had relatives in high positions. Her uncle, her father's brother, was a figure of some importance in the government. They would not be able to keep her long.'

My mind raced back to those events, events that for years I had tried to forget, events that tortured my dreams. I saw them playing back across my mind. Every movement caught in slow motion; an indelible looped videotape. Playing, playing, playing.

'But it didn't happen like that,' I whispered.

'No,' Kolya agreed. 'It didn't.'

Winding down the low hill, the convoy passed with care beneath the overhanging trees, the telescopic radio antenna projecting from the turret of the APC clicking

257

against the branches above. The Agitprop Brigade's APC was towards the end of the convoy. Behind, protecting it at the rear, was a BMP with a grenade launcher and a heavy machine gun fitted on top. At the foot of the hill, the track twisted through a clump of trees and forded a shallow stream thick with reeds. Close by the road stood a pair of ramshackle, isolated buildings. The mud walls had begun to crumble, and the windows were blackened holes. Close to the buildings was a small cemetery, coloured rags, faded by the weather, fluttering from sticks. On the low hill behind them was the family compound, its modest buildings huddled around the little square.

The first vehicles forded the stream and disappeared from view behind the thick undergrowth the drooping foliage. The APC I was seated on slowed as it approached the stream. I clung tight as it dipped into the hollow. Glancing back, I glimpsed Zena laughing with the bespectacled medic. She closed her eyes as she laughed, throwing back her head.

The APC splashed into the stream. The water shimmered in the dappled light that broke through the thick canopy of oak and ash. The water had run off the mountains, and was icy cold. The coolness rose from its surface. The APC had slowed sufficiently for me to leap from it. I landed on the sandy bank of the stream. Crouching down, I dipped my hands into the water and threw it up against my dusty face.

'In Kirov's plan, we would be ambushed as we forded the stream,' Kolya explained, quietly, coming to me and resting his hand on my shoulder. I knelt down, felt the path dampen the knees of my trousers.

'It was a good place for an ambush,' Kolya continued.

'The curve in the road that put the last vehicles out of sight of the first; the fact that we had to slow down to ford the river; the vantage point of the village on the hill.

'Zena was travelling in one of the last APCs, that had been organised. On the last BMP were the armaments Hashim's friends wanted. It should have been easy. The road was mined. The last two vehicles would be cut off, quickly surrounded, and the objectives achieved with minimum fuss.'

When I glanced up from the stream, wiping the freezing droplets of water from my cheeks, brushing them up through my hair, I noticed a sudden movement in the blackened window of one of the abandoned buildings. It was so fast, so fleeting, I could not be sure it had not been a trick of the light. I stood up, retrieving my gun from the river bank.

Experience had taught us excessive caution, and I called to the driver of the next APC, which was slowly negotiating the steep slope to the bed of the stream. His head bent out of the APC and he shouted to me, but the roar of the engines, the crunch of gravel and the splash of the water drowned out his voice. I stepped into the water and jogged over to the APC.

The water detonated with an ear-shattering crunch. I pitched back. Fighting for breath, I choked and gagged. Rising from the water long enough to grab half a breath before my arms gave way, I plunged down again beneath the icy surface. Confused and panicked, I rolled on to my back. The water was not deep. I grabbed another breath and struggled to my knees. I glanced around.

In the centre of the ford the APC billowed thick black smoke. Its guts had been wrenched violently open. The air whistled and the ground danced. The stream flamed. My gun was lying close, submerged beneath the flickering surface of the water. I reached for it.

Though it was perhaps only a moment, time stretched elastically as I fought to make sense of events – to incorporate them so that I might react. My eyes flicked from the hulk of charred metal that had been an APC up the incline to the BMP and the Agitprop Brigade's APC. The vehicle was accelerating towards the stream, bodies tumbling from it, scattering into the undergrowth, bouncing on the dusty earth. The BMP reversed furiously back up the slope, its machine gun spitting pink-blue flames randomly, spraying the hillside, ripping through the foliage, bullets pinging from the trunks of the trees and dancing across the mud walls of the buildings. Figures emerged from the undergrowth. They scrambled over the BMP. The heavy machine gun jerked up, sending its stream of fire into the sky.

In the window of the abandoned house at the foot of the hill, flames flickered menacingly. I saw Zena, crouched foetally in a shallow hollow, beneath the mud wall. Her face rose, crumpled with despair. She shouted out, but her voice was lost. I stumbled forwards, the icy water spraying around me. My right arm throbbed. As if in a dream, my legs seemed to paddle in soup, barely moving forwards. Distinctly I heard the zip of bullets slit the air around my head; saw the hollow beneath the trees shiver and swell with light, dust and stones splaying out, a wall vanish.

Behind Zena the air billowed with flames. Her mouth opened and she screamed. Her beautiful ochre skin puckered as she cried into the blistering sky.

Among the dark figures that had emerged from the shadows, I noticed a familiar face darting across the track towards where Zena lay huddled. For a moment I could not place where I had seen his sharp features before. Kirov stood, as if bewildered, on the far bank of the stream, his automatic slung loosely, staring across the water at the mayhem. I waved for him to move across with me, but he did not react. I shouted at him, and, as if only then noticing me, he brought up his rifle. It struck me suddenly that I had seen the sharp-featured man in the café in Jalalabad talking to Kirov.

When I glanced back across the water Zena had gone. I stumbled towards the bank, eyes searching the undergrowth. Farther up the track the BMP was disappearing over the crest of a rise. From the way the blackened APC lay twisted in the stream it was evident it had hit a mine. A group of our soldiers regrouped on the far side of the stream. Setting up a heavy machine gun, they opened up on the brush higher up the slope. The ground rocked as a grenade exploded close to the Agitprop's APC.

A movement on the hillside caught my eye. Glancing up, I saw Zena being pushed by two figures, advancing up the hill through the heavy undergrowth towards the family compound. Ducking into the trees, I worked my way around the side of the hill and, finding a path on the far slope, advanced to the summit cautiously. A goat was tethered by the wall of the first hut. It gazed at me nonchalantly as I approached. Chickens cackled and fluttered across the dusty earth. From the ford in the hollow, machine-gun fire rattled. Dark smoke curled up through the tops of the trees.

As I reached the square in the centre of the family compound, Zena emerged, pushed from behind by two Afghans in civilian dress. She stumbled and fell heavily to the ground. One of the men, the one I recognised from Jalalabad, shouted. He kicked her and, bending, grabbed a handful of her hair, pulling her face from the dust. While his short, bearded colleague watched, he shoved the nozzle of his pistol against the back of her head.

Without pausing to consider, I raised my rifle, sighted it and fired. The bearded Afghan looked up, surprised, as his colleague pitched violently to one side. I shot another round immediately and the second Afghan twisted around and fell backwards. Zena squealed.

She turned to me, her eyes wide with fear, uncomprehending. I called for her to come across the square. She nodded and stumbled to her feet. As she staggered across the dusty square, her shirt became entangled in some stray wire.

'Keep low,' I shouted as she straightened to untangle it.

'What?' she mouthed, turning.

A dark hole opened in her throat and she gasped. A look of intense surprise flickered across her face. A second hole opened in her cheek. She spun around as if she had been slapped violently and fell to the earth. For one moment I watched as her fingers scrabbled in the dirt.

'Zena . . .'

I lurched forward. Out of the corner of my eye, I saw a movement in the dark shadow of one of the huts.

'Zena,' I called again.

My body lay across hers, protecting her. I grasped her tight, felt her body buck beneath my own. Her eyes did not shut. I closed my hand around the wound in her neck, my palm slipping on the soft wet flesh. The blood pumped hotly between my fingers. She gazed up, a look of astonishment on her face.

'Zena,' I whispered into her ear.

She moved, but it was her muscles twitching. Her skin paled. The blood pooled in the dirt. The weight of my body, as I shifted, pressed the air from her lungs so that she gasped and spat bloodily, her unblinking eyes staring fixedly into eternity.

From the shadows I heard the shuffle of footsteps and the click of a magazine being slotted into place. I looked up into the shadowed doorway of one of the huts. An elderly man gazed out, Kalashnikov raised. Rising from the earth, blood dripping from my hands, my shirt dark and wet, clinging to my chest, I faced him. He shouted something in Pashtu and waved the gun. I stepped towards him. He shouted louder, pointing the gun at me threateningly. From my belt I took my knife. The old man tottered out into the sunlight. He pointed at the girl and shouted. He pointed at the two men and shouted again. He waved the gun at me and shouted some more. His pale, old eyes were wild with fear.

Knocking the gun from his hands, I grabbed the front of his tunic. He fell to his knees, gabbling, pointing at his hut, at the three bodies strewn across the centre of his little village. I wound the dirty white cloth of his turban in my fist and jerked his head back. He looked up into my eyes, his lips moving continually, words pouring forth incomprehensibly, his arms jerking back and forth between his hut and the bodies. I took the knife and, with one hand holding his head back, slit his throat. He gargled, his lips moving silently, working still as the blood fountained out across the front of my shirt.

Kneeling beside me, Kolya stroked my back. I pressed my forehead against the sharp gravel of the path. I smelt the earth beneath me, felt the small stones biting into my flesh. I dug my fingers into the soil, turning it, clawing at it.

'It's over,' Kolya murmured. 'It's all over now. It's finished.'

He placed the metal box on the path beside me, and attempted to pull me up from the ground.

'Let's get a move on,' he encouraged. 'We have the bracelet. It was for this that Kirov sold her. He betrayed us all. We lost half the battalion in that ambush.'

When the old man was dead, I stood for some moments in the centre of the square. Below the village, in the hollow where the road forded the stream, the battle was still raging. Rocket fire shook the ground, automatic gunfire chattered among the trees. I knelt beside Zena and gently lowered her eyelids. I kissed her forehead. Her skin was cool and clammy.

Birds had begun to gather on the roofs of the houses. Insects swirled in dark clouds, settling already on the bloody pools, on the stained earth, on the warm flesh of the bodies. I picked Zena up and moved her to the side of the square, laid my jacket over her face and shoulders.

I worked quickly, moving from hut to hut, gathering wood. Tables, chairs, wardrobes, roofing, doors. I fashioned a pyre in the centre of the square, stuffing dry grass into the gaps between the wood. I worked with care, as if building a bonfire at home, making sure that when I lit it, it would go up. When the clumsy pyre was finished I took a can of fuel I had come across in one of the huts and poured it liberally over the wood. For some moments I stood back, surveying my work. It gave me grim satisfaction to see the sturdiness of the table on which I would lay her.

Her body rested on the ground, by the hut, her limbs carefully arranged, my jacket covering her, keeping away the flies. I knelt by her, pulling back the khaki shroud. She could have been sleeping. She did not look so different from those times when I had awoken in the morning to see her face by my side in her room in the hostel in Jalalabad. A little paler perhaps. There was a smudge of dirt on her forehead. I took the corner of my jacket, dampened it with my saliva and wiped the soot from her skin, cleaned the neat wound in her cheek, washed away the blood from her throat.

Looping my arms beneath her, I lifted her from the dust. Her body was strangely stiff, resistant to my touch. She was heavy and I struggled slightly under her weight.

Carefully I laid her on the pile of wood. She looked fragile in death. I pressed my lips to the scar running down the side of her face. A breeze had picked up, blowing from the east, from Pakistan. It rustled the dry grass in the pyre and whistled across the roofs of the huts.

I knelt before the pyre. There should have been something fitting for me to say, but I had no prayer – no prayer any god would find decent, would consider bending an ear to listen to. A poem, a couple of lines, would have done, something to sanctify the moment, but my mind was dark, a blank fury. I knelt in silence, my head bowed, my hands trembling.

When I rose I took the can of fuel and went quickly to the farthest hut. There, without pausing, I sloshed the fuel around the dark interior. There was little in the hut, just a table and a rug. In the corner was a Koran, and I took that and ripped a page from it. Taking from my pocket the Chinese lighter Vassily had once given me, I lit the crinkled yellow paper and tossed it to the floor. A small flame rose from the packed earth. It ran quickly along the rug, and as I turned the fuel exploded with a dull thud, knocking me forwards with a warm burst of heat. Without turning back, I hurried to the next hut and doused that with fuel, taking care not to use too much. Tearing another page from the Koran, tucked beneath my arm, I tossed the flaming, crinkled ball into the hut and watched it explode in flames.

When all the huts were burning I stood once more before the roughly fashioned pyre and drank in her form. She seemed shrunken in death. Reduced. Childlike and vulnerable. The dry grass and wooden beams crackled as they burnt around me. Dark smoke billowed up into the clear air, then, caught on a draught of suffocating wind, bent back down and swirled around the village. Ships of flame sailed the currents of air, descending beside me lightly, smouldering in the dust.

Slowly and with care I tore each remaining page from the Koran. I clothed her with the sheets, spread them over her, weighted down with dust. As I worked, the fire descended softly upon us, settling on the dusty pages, on the grass that stuck out like unruly whiskers from between the planks of wood. The pages darkened, wrinkled and curled along their edges. Blue flames rushed along them, joining, spreading. The grass withered, pulled itself into the cracks, smoking, charred. A gust of wind blew low across the hilltop. There was a gasp, like a sudden intake of breath, a moment's silence, and then a belch of flame jumped from the wooden mound. The pages lifted into the air, sailing on the updraught, into the smoke-darkened air, as if God Himself were drawing His Word up into His hands.

The heat knocked me back and I staggered and fell

into the dust. I felt the flesh on my face blister. The air tore at my lungs; my throat burnt. I crawled beneath the billowing clouds of smoke, my hands and knees shredding themselves on the sharp stones. At the edge of the village the path descended a sharp incline. In my hurry I stumbled from the path and, blinded by the smoke and my tears, I fell.

'Come on,' Kolya urged. He thrust his hands beneath my arms and pulled me up. 'We can't hang around here all night. Let's get moving.'

The smoke plumed from the hilltop, like a volcano. From nowhere, then, the cry of a child arrested me, catching all at once the hate, the raging anger in my heart. Shrivelling it. I stopped; the dust rose in swirls around me; the smoke, forced down by the wind, curled into the trees. The scream froze my legs. I looked back up towards the village, barely visible, the sun behind it dark and brooding. The choking smoke burnt the back of my throat; the fire crackled in my ears as it rushed along the dry wood, through the grass roofs, consuming the village.

Scrambling back up the bank, madly, I thought it was Zena crying from her pyre. Crawling forwards on hands and knees, struggling for breath beneath the thick clouds of smoke, I worked my way into the centre of the village once more. The cries came from the hut in which the old man had been standing. I crawled over his inert body and stumbled around the back of his crumbling home. Smoke poured from a ventilation window high in the wall. I clambered up to it. From inside I could hear a hoarse low cough, the sound of a child struggling to breathe. I called through the opening. I clawed at the mud, pulling away dry handfuls, enlarging the hole.

I pushed myself through into the darkness. Landing heavily, I immediately felt the movement beside me. Squeezed tight into the corner was a child, eyes pressed tightly shut, face dark, lips blue, throat gasping, groping for oxygen, tearing painfully, choking on the smoke. I scooped the girl into my arms and staggered out through the flames.

Chapter 29

A sharp breeze rustled the branches of the trees in Vingis Park. The sudden noise startled Kolya and he turned quickly on his heel, his hand reaching beneath his jacket. The moon had disappeared, covered by another thick layer of cloud blowing in from the coast. The only light came from the lamps on the bridge, just visible through the trees.

I pushed up the sleeve of my jacket and unbuttoned my shirt. My fingers trembled so that it took a while. It was so dark that it was hard to make out the crinkled pink skin. The scars. I felt the skin's odd hairlessness, its wrinkles. Tentatively Kolya reached out and placed his fingers on my arm. They were cold and trembling too.

I felt again the weight of the fragile child's body in my arms, recalling how I had stumbled down the hill, the branches of the trees lashing my face, my arms numb with pain. How I fell, headlong, tossing the child aside. Crawled through the undergrowth, picked her up and staggered on. And fell and gathered her and stumbled on.

'We're pulling out,' a voice shouted close to my ear.

Vassily was perspiring, his face black with dirt, glistening with large beads of sweat. He loomed over me, blocking out the light. His hand reached down and brushed my cheek. I tried to turn my head, but it would not move.

His hands gripped the front of my flak jacket. He pulled the child from my arms. I struggled to hold on to the small body, pulling it close to my chest. Crushing it against me. Another set of hands pulled at my arms. The pain seared through my body, vibrating in my head. It was as if somebody were pushing hot iron against my flesh, tearing the skin away from my bone.

'He's badly burnt,' somebody said.

'Come on, let's move,' Vassily said, his voice tight with fear. 'They may come back and we're totally fucked. Zhuralev has taken a bullet, and the radio operator is dead.'

I tried to struggle to my feet, but Vassily pushed me back down.

'Just roll over,' he said. 'Let's get you on to the stretcher.'

Hands reached out and tugged at me. Pulled and pushed. Lifted and dropped. Sick with exhaustion, I lay still as they hoisted me up. They ran, jolting me so my teeth rattled. I heard the splash of water as they forded the stream and their heavy breathing and curses as they stumbled down the line. My head throbbed and my arms burnt.

'Zena,' I murmured, my voice hoarse, barely audible above the noise of the engines of the armoured vehicles.

There was a strong wind blowing. The sand was whipped up from the track and swirled in dark, choking clouds around the stationary vehicles. The wind was accompanied by a heavy throb, a clattering pulse. My stretcher was lifted and slid along the floor of a helicopter.

A medic looked down at me, gently pushing my head to one side, digging strong fingers into the side of my neck, eliciting a pain so sharp it brought tears to my eyes and a cry to my lips. A look of wearied annoyance crossed the medic's face and he pushed my head roughly back into place. He turned and extracted a syringe from his bag, took a small glass vial and snapped off its nipple. Inserting the needle, he sucked the morphine up into the syringe. The tip was white from where it had been boiled. Its rubber looked dark and perished. He injected me and turned immediately to deal with another casualty.

Sitting above me, on one of the metal seats along the side of the chopper, was the medic with the spectacles.

'Zena,' I said.

He glanced down at me. His spectacles were cracked and a yellowing bandage had been wound tightly around his head. Blood had begun to seep through it, a dark stain.

A rush of warmth flooded my senses, entirely at odds with the desperate darkness of my thoughts. I fought it. My eyelids flickered. When they slid closed, I opened them again, lifting the skin with deliberate effort. The metal beneath me lurched suddenly and somebody cursed. Somebody else was crying. My eyelids fell heavily and I could not lift them, though I tried.

'Zena.' The helicopter dipped as it turned so that my stretcher slid across the metal floor, coming to rest against the legs of the seats. Darkness enfolded me.

'Let's go now,' Kolya said softly.

I nodded and pulled down the sleeves of my shirt and jacket. We turned in the direction of the bridge and trudged along the dark path in silence, feet crunching on the gravel. On the back of my neck I felt a drop of rain. Glancing up, I saw the dark shape of an owl swoop down across the sky and settle at the top of a tree. From the far side of the bridge it was possible to hear the dog barking still, disturbed by some other nocturnal soul. On the bank of the river, by the end of the bridge, work was being done to create a new path through the centre of the woods to the auditorium. The earth-working equipment cast weird shapes in the darkness. Kolya shivered and hurried on towards the light of the lamp on the footbridge.

Chapter 30

I did not wake as the Mi-8 skimmed low through the pass, ruffling the sky-blue lakes, tossing the branches of the trees. Nor did I wake in Jalalabad when they hauled me off and lined me up on the tarmac in the darkness, with boys with missing limbs, shattered skulls, boys already zipped into bags. I did not wake on the plane that transported us across the narrow fissures, the broken-backed mountains, the jagged teeth of Afghanistan, to Kabul.

It was dark when I came to. I could not breathe. I was tied and bound and choking. I struggled and tossed around. I have been captured, was my first thought. My grenade. One for the muj, one for yourself – our first lesson in Afghanistan. I could not move my arms. When I threw back my head to clear my windpipe a searing pain scalded me and detonated a series of mini-explosions behind my eyes. I cried out.

I heard the clatter of footsteps. The slap of rubber on tiles. The slop of slippers. Hands were pulling at me, lifting me.

Leave me – no – oh fuck, oh fuck.

'Sedate him,' somebody muttered.

Lying on my back I could breathe more easily. My head continued to thump and I could not feel my limbs. Figures swam in front of my eyes.

Zena.

A hand reached out and clamped itself tightly over my lips.

'Get it in quick before he wakes the whole fucking ward with his screams.'

Light. My eyelids slid open. The brightness hurt, forcing me to squint. The walls were hospital green. A low rumble sounded softly in my ears. Carefully I peered from side to side. I could not turn too far without setting off the pain. The room was lined with metal-framed beds. Two nurses lounged against a wall, one gazing out of the window. As my mind cleared a little, I realised that the low rumbling, which I had taken to be traffic on the road outside, or the murmur of an old fan, was in fact the quiet moans of a hundred men. The moans rose and fell, a continuous stream of pain ebbing and flowing around the hospital ward. It took me a few moments more to realise that I too was a part of this current, my moan joining theirs, escaping my throat involuntarily, rising to float beneath the high ceiling, with the fat flies and spiders that nestled darkly in corners.

The nurse, noticing I had woken, wandered across to me. She took a cloth and gently dabbed the side of my face, wiping spittle from my cheek. She examined me for a moment, then straightened and turned away. I gazed after her as she wandered, seemingly aimlessly, down the ward.

It was growing dark again when next I woke. My eyelids flicked up and my mind seemed at once to be preternaturally clear. In vivid detail I remembered Zena turning as I called to her. She straightened slightly. I noticed the look on her face, the way it was twisted with fear, with the desire to hear what I had said. The look of surprise. I saw the dark hole suddenly materialise on her smooth throat. The way her eyes opened slightly wider, astonished that death had caught her so cleanly. Saw the second hole and the flick of her head as the impact knocked her to one side. I felt her beneath me, her body bucking.

I stared up at the ceiling of the ward. A large spider moved slowly across it towards a hole in the plaster where a light had been fixed clumsily. She straightened. The bullet pierced her throat. Her cheek. The spider made it to the dark hole and hesitated for a moment before disappearing.

The low hum of suffering had begun to rise, led by a single voice. It was a thin wail and it rose higher and higher. As it rose the other moans followed it, snaking up towards that small dark hole in the plaster of the ceiling, after the spider. The thin wail reached a peak and broke, became a sob, a heart-rending cry, which jerked and rasped. The chorus broke with it. The ward echoed to the sound of the screams, the lonely, tortured wails of the sick. The moans and keening of the frightened, the lost.

Feet slapped across the cold tiles. Angry voices shushed and hushed.

'The new one,' somebody said, their throat tight with panic and annoyance.

They surrounded me. A male nurse sat on the bed and pressed down on my chest. By my side another was clumsily fumbling with a syringe, filling it, holding it to the light.

'Shut the fucker up!'

I felt the soft warmth of a pillow descending across

my face, pressing down, smothering me. A stab of pain in my arm. Other memories were surfacing. They broke through the skin of my consciousness, rising like divers, spluttering for air. Children dark with blood, wide eyed, thrown back against the walls, their clothes rumpled and ragged and disarrayed. Their bodies ill placed, wrenched into positions they could never have achieved in life. I wailed into the pillow.

Sleep was not a release. My muscles twitched and prickled torturously, my legs cramped and my arm throbbed. The scent of disinfectant became orange blossom, wild rose. Beneath the trees I saw the sudden flash of their movements. The child pulled close to her brother, hugging his thin leg. The boy's arm snaked around her shoulder as he folded her close. The old man by the well looked up. His fingers played, I noticed, with a small sprig of blossom. The old man held my gaze.

'I was following orders,' I said to the young doctor.

He nodded, feeling my pulse. His eyebrows were furrowed and he looked exhausted.

'I didn't know,' I said.

The doctor shook his head, monitoring the steady throb of my pulse.

'There was a sound behind the door.'

He let go of my arm and let it drop on to the sheets. He did not place it gently on the bed, he dropped it and stood up quickly, indicating for a nurse.

'Don't let her sedate me,' I said to the doctor as the nurse approached.

The doctor did not look at me; he was turning his attention already to the boy in the bed by my side, the boy who waved his legless, armless stumps continually, weeping through the darkness and the light.

'Don't let her,' I begged. 'I have such dreams.'

The nurse frowned angrily. As if I were a disobedient, tiresome child.

'Don't. I will be quiet,' I said to her. 'I promise, I won't shout. Please?'

'Doctor,' she muttered, and he turned back to me and nodded.

I tried to raise myself from my pillow. I was slick with sweat and my skin prickled irritably.

'Don't put that fucking needle anywhere near me,' I warned her. 'I said I didn't want it.'

The doctor sat on the side of my bed. He soothed me. He laid a hand upon my forehead and pressed me down into the pillow.

'It's fine,' he said. 'Don't get upset. If you get upset we will have to punish you. You don't want that, do you? You don't want to have to be punished, do you?'

From Kabul I was flown to a hospital in Tashkent and from there to Moscow. From Moscow, some time later, I was flown to Vilnius and admitted to the New Vilnia. From time to time I surfaced from the warm darkness in which they kept me imprisoned. Haloperidol was my guard; it kept me from myself.

My thoughts wandered idly down dark passages, going nowhere. My fingers turned to rubber, and I could hardly pick up the spoon to feed myself. As clumsy as a two-year-old, I lifted the sticky porridge to my mouth, sometimes making it, sometimes waking from some dark place to find it there, still halfway to my lips, cold and jelly-like. When, punished for my lack of progress, I bent, shivering, to clean the toilets, my hands trembled so that I could barely rub the dirty cloth against the cracked ceramic bowls.

My lips split and I found it hard to speak. I sat on the edge of my bed, transfixed by a shaft of light that broke through the ragged curtains. For hours I would stare at it, drool soaking my pyjama trousers.

When occasionally the haloperidol loosened its fingers, as the doctors considered releasing me, my brain tunnelled its way towards the light like a worm, working its way through the earth. My tongue untied.

'Fuck Sokolov. Fuck Brezhnev and Gromyko and Andropov. I'll fucking kill the lot of them. With my own hands.'

'You can't kill the dead,' the doctor said, laconically, reintroducing me to my neuroleptic guard.

At other times the doctors, frustrated by my lack of progress, tried other treatments on me. The Quiet Room was at the end of a long corridor. The windows in the corridor had been whitewashed, making it impossible to see out. The room was bare. The plaster walls were unpainted and crumbling and in the corners dark with damp, green with mould. It was unheated. In one corner was a broken sink and in the other a mattress, soiled and damp. Leather straps restrained my arms and legs. High on one wall was a small window. Dingy light filtered through a thick film of dirt.

'You can't kill the dead,' I murmured to myself, my teeth rattling, my whole body convulsed with shaking.

'You can't kill the dead.'

And the dead were not killed. Under the influence of the medication, though, they retreated slowly, along with all my emotions. They withered as my muscles withered. They became no more important than anything else: the mote of dust, the crack in the wall, the shaking of my hands, the swirl of whitewash on the window, too high to reach. I ceased to exist except in these tiny fragments of attention. I became a quivering shell enclosing nothing.

Sometimes I was aware of the passing of shadows upon the wall. Sometimes I smelt the sharp stink of urine, or heard the bark of a nurse, the clang of a spoon against a metal bowl, the thump of feet on the torn linoleum floor. Laughter. Whoops of terrifying laughter that pierced the darkness and would not stop. And then for long days, weeks, I would hear nothing.

Chapter 31

I became aware of Vassily by degrees. At first I was conscious only that the figure beside me was not a doctor, nor a nurse. He spoke to me, his voice a quiet murmur in my ear, like a brook, like a breath of air in the linden trees. Sometimes he was there, sometimes not.

As the weeks passed, I surfaced slowly. The doctors reduced the dosage of my tranquillisers and I did not shout or curse or threaten. The blankness, the emptiness induced by the drugs, stayed with me, even after the medication had been withdrawn completely. Vassily came frequently, sitting with me in the chilly hospital ward, talking to me, caring for me.

'Just look at you,' he said, dabbing the spittle from my chin. 'Just look at the state of you.'

Vassily's face was drawn and tired. Beneath his eyes, dark sacs hung like vials of poison. His hair dangled over his forehead, his beard was unkempt and his eyes were bloodshot. His hands shook as he touched me.

'Just look at you,' he mumbled, dabbing and wiping. 'What a fucking mess.'

'Where am I?' I asked him one day.

'You're home,' he said. 'Back in Lithuania. I'm going to take you with me. Look after you.'

When, after a couple of months, the doctor considered me, if not well, then at least not dangerous, I was discharged. Vassily met me in a taxi at the gates of the hospital and we drove into Vilnius together. We stayed in a small apartment belonging to a friend of his for a couple of days before Vassily moved me to the coast to stay with a family in a small village close to the sea. Jurgis and Vaida lived with their granddaughter, Tanya, a student.

Vassily worked with Jurgis, making pictures from chippings of amber. As the summer passed, I sat in a wooden chair Vassily had placed in the shade of a tree, smoking cigarette after cigarette, the cheap tobacco scorching my throat, watching the heron poke around the pond, the family's dog wandering back and forth across the parched grass on which it was tethered, the quiet rhythms of village life.

The smells and sounds of the small cottage comforted me. The scent of the wood and the dust. The sound of the rain as it beat against the roof, the wind as it crooned in the tips of the pines. The pain and nausea began to subside. I felt like a child laid up in bed, sick with fever.

Whenever I awoke, my heart beating rapidly, the scent of smoke in my nostrils, the echoes of screams in my ears, Vassily was beside me, watching over me.

'Shh,' he would whisper as I cried out in the darkness.

'Where are we?'

'You're home, comrade, you're safe now. It's OK. Sleep.'

'All I can see is darkness. What is going on?'

'It's night-time.' He stroked my head. 'You are sick,' he said. 'You are tired and sick. Sleep now, tomorrow you will be fine. You will feel much better.'

Only Tanya disturbed the stillness of my existence. Her presence acted like the dropping of a smooth pebble into the shallows of a pond; the ripples fanned out slowly, making the surface shiver, splintering the mirrored tree-tops and layered clouds. Guarded as I still was by the effect of the neuroleptics, perhaps I was unaware of her physical resemblance to Zena. I was aware only that I longed for her and feared her in equal measures. I explained my confused feelings to myself as guilt for being attracted to her when it was so obvious Vassily was in love with her and their relationship was budding.

When I was feeling stronger Vassily took me on a walk through the forest to the beach. The grassland rolled down from the thick woods to the sand dunes. The land was boggy, criss-crossed with little streams. There were endless low hollows and sudden sharp inclines up the sides of hillocks. I was exhausted by the time we had covered half the distance. We sat for some time on top of a grassy knoll, looking down at a cottage close to the beach, sheltered by stubby maple and birch, bent by the winds blowing up off the sea. We did not speak. The silence was broken only by the cry of a gull, the rush of the breeze as it riffled the long grass and the sound of the waves breaking on the beach.

Vassily shuffled along the water's edge, bent double, his eyes not rising from the sand at his feet. I followed just behind him, watching his back, keeping close. He stopped and lightly lifted a heap of dark, tangled seaweed with the toe of his split shoe. A gull landed on the damp sand. It, too, rooted about, with its beak, hopping on a couple of paces when Vassily got too close, then foraging once more.

Vassily stopped suddenly. I squatted beside him.

Picking a pebble from the sand, he examined it, cleaned it on the cuff of his jacket and held it up.

'It's *gintaras*,' he said, using the Lithuanian word. Amber.

I held out my hand and he dropped the dirty lump of ancient resin into my palm. It was light, and warm, quite different to the feel of a pebble.

He was standing at my side, looking down at the amber in my hand. I could feel his warm breath on my skin. He seemed nervous. He rubbed his hands together and peered at me from beneath his dark fringe. He took the amber from me and wrapped his thick fingers around it, pressing it into his flesh.

As the summer passed, I quickly began to recover my strength. I walked along the beach every morning, going a little farther each time, easing my legs into an easy pace along the soft sand. One morning, waking early, I saw Tanya slip out through the room in which Vassily and I were sleeping. I followed her, pulling on a thick jumper. She was in the kitchen, tying back her hair in the dim pre-dawn light. Seeing me, she smiled.

'Where are you going so early?' I whispered.

'Out to milk the cow,' she said. 'Why don't you come and help?'

I followed her. The air was cold and damp. A mist rose from the dark earth, dissolving in the sharp, clear sky. The last stars were faintly visible. The pond was sheathed with a smooth, milky skin, unstirred by even the faintest breath of wind. Tanya mounted her bicycle and I walked beside her, through the village to the one narrow, metalled road that snaked away through the fields. Their cow was tethered outside the village. Tanya left the bicycle at the edge of the road, and I followed her through the wet grass, and across a brook. The cow's breath rose in pale clouds. She lifted her head as we drew closer and Tanya hugged her affectionately. I squatted down beside Tanya as she placed the metal pail beneath the cow's straining udders.

'Have you done this before?' she asked.

I shook my head. 'No.'

She reached out and took my hand, guiding it to the cow's teats. Her hands were warm and strong. I pressed my forehead against the firm flank of the cow, as Tanya did, and allowed her to guide my fingers. A jet of milk splashed into the pail. It trickled from our fingers and Tanya laughed and put her finger to my lips. When I sucked it, it was sweet. For a moment I held on to her hand and our eyes met and my heart lurched fearfully. Tanya pulled away and we finished off the milking.

The pail was heavy with milk and we carried it together back across the field, our red fingers touching on the cold metal handle. Tanya hung the pail on the handlebars of the bike and we walked back to the village.

'You're looking much healthier,' she said, appraising me as we walked.

I smiled. 'I feel great.'

The sun had risen above the tops of the trees and the unruffled surface of the pond reflected its dazzling rays. The early morning mist had begun to dissolve but, in the shade, the grass was still white with dew.

'And yet . . . ?' She hesitated.

We stopped on the road. I looked down into the village, which was beginning to stir with life. Across the glittering pond, I could see the low cottage. Vassily had come out of the door and stood stretching. He lit a cigarette and a pale puff of smoke rose slowly into the air above him.

'And yet you still dream,' Tanya said. 'You have nose bleeds and migraines. If an engine misfires in the village, you turn rigid. You refuse to mention the past – as if nothing ever happened to you before you came here. Don't you think it would be better for you to talk about it?'

For some moments I did not reply. I watched Vassily smoking his cigarette. I felt my chest tighten and shivered involuntarily. Icy tendrils coiled about my insides. Tanya reached out and laid one of her hands on my arm.

'I'm sorry,' she said, 'I've upset you.'

I shook my head. 'No,' I said. 'It's fine.' I took care to speak calmly, to hide my fear, but still my voice was thin and pitched too high. I tried to smile. 'It's better, I think, just to forget about it all.'

I could see the concern in Tanya's eyes.

The past was like a movement in the deep shadows of night. I turned from it. Curled within the bright sunlight of the present I could ignore it. I longed for Vassily's company; for the comfort he was able to give me. His laughter and stories, the craft he was beginning to teach me. I walked on towards him and Tanya followed.

'Come with me,' Vassily had said one morning. 'I am going to teach you how to work amber. Amber will heal you. Amber has always been used for medicine, you see, comrade, my friend, as far back as ancient Rome. You can wear it for things like jaundice and goitre, and it will heal them. It's also good for the kidneys and the heart.'

In the village workshop he showed me the basics of

shaping amber on an old lathe, taught me how it is polished, hardened and coloured. Told me tales and taught me about the folklore connected to it.

'Amber powder mixed with honey is a traditional recipe,' he told me, 'for the eyes and the ears, or taken with warm water it's good for healing the stomach. There is even one I heard of where amber powder is mixed with vodka – and this, my friend,' he gripped my shoulder and grinned, 'this would improve your sexual potency, yes? Give you some drive, eh?' And he laughed. 'Ah, but you are not needing it. *Blyad!* How happy I am for you, my little comrade. I brought you from the hospital and you were a shadow, empty, and now look at you!'

Chapter 32

Moving out from the darkness of the tree canopy in Vingis Park, I followed Kolya back on to the footbridge. He walked quickly, the soles of his shoes clicking against the cracked concrete. The metal box was gripped tightly beneath his arm. He seemed excited to have it. There was something about his story that did not quite add up. I wondered for one moment whether he had been lying to me; whether he had invented the story. Quickly, though, I dismissed this idea. There was no reason not to believe him.

As we approached the city side of the bridge a figure emerged from the shadows. Kolya's pace faltered. I had been gazing down at my feet as I walked, lost in thought, and almost walked into Kolya's back. The dark figure stopped at the end of the bridge and leant against the metal railings. Kolya inhaled audibly; a sudden, sharp intake of breath.

'*Zdrastvuy*, Kolya,' Kirov said calmly. His tone was so pleasant, I half expected him to hold out his hand for Kolya to shake. He nodded to me, and smiled. He took a long, slow drag on his cigarette and exhaled the smoke into the darkness. I stood rooted to the spot. He seemed to have stepped straight out of my thoughts, a phantasm. I felt bile rise in the back of my throat. My breath caught and my muscles tensed with fury.

Kolya backed away, clutching the metal box to his chest with both hands.

'Kirov,' he muttered.

'It's been a while,' Kirov said, moving towards us slowly. 'What is it, eight years now, Kolya?'

'You bastard,' Kolya snarled.

I noticed Kolya's hand moving beneath the metal box, feeling slowly inside his jacket, his eyes not leaving Kirov. He pulled out the pistol. Clumsily, releasing the safety catch, he pointed it at Kirov's chest. His hand trembled so much he had difficulty keeping the Makarov level. Kirov glanced down at the short barrel and his lips twisted into a sardonic grin. He stepped forward, closer to Kolya.

'Oh, come on,' he said. 'You haven't got the nerve, Kolya. You were a coward then and you still are.'

A bead of perspiration rolled down Kolya's forehead. He wiped it away with the back of his arm, holding the box tightly.

Kirov turned his attention from Kolya, nonchalantly ignoring the pistol directed at him. He tossed the stub of his cigarette over the rail of the bridge. I watched as the bright point of light twirled down through the darkness to the water below.

'He has told you about the bracelet, then?' he said. 'He has told you what your friend Vassily forgot to tell you?'

'I've told him how you sold the girl to your friends in KHAD,' Kolya spat at him. 'How your deal cost us half the platoon.'

Kirov did not look at Kolya. He gazed intently at me. His eyes were the colour of steel. Ice blue.

'It wasn't like that, Antanas,' he said. 'After all these years you have a right to know.'

He came closer. His eyes did not leave mine for a moment. He did not blink. I felt a shiver of disgust run down my spine. Kolya advanced, suddenly, waving the pistol, pressing it up against Kirov's chest. Kirov brushed him aside angrily.

'Get out of the way, you useless little shit,' he barked. 'You see,' he said, his eyes turning back to me, 'you didn't know. You didn't see his face. You didn't know how much he longed for this one. From the time Hashim put him on the scent of it he was like a dog at a bone. He was like a bitch on heat. He would not let it go.'

'What are you talking about?'

'I'm talking about Vassily. Oh, I know, he has been a real friend to you, yes?' Kirov sneered. 'You can't imagine Vassily might have done something to hurt you? It was him, you stupid fucker. It was Vassily.'

Feebly Kolya once more tried to step forwards, but Kirov spun around angrily, his hand balling into a fist, his lips a tight line. Kolya shrank back.

'We slipped away in Ghazis, Vassily and me and this little shit.' He waved his hand dismissively in the direction of Kolya. 'Oh yes, it was all a set-up, right from the start. As soon as Hashim told Vassily about the bracelet, he was obsessed. He had to have it. He kept saying, "If this is what I think it is, it must be worth a fortune." But it wasn't just the money with him, he knew about the bracelet, had read about it before. He went on and on. "Just think, Nero wore it! Tamerlane's wife!" And his eyes would light up and he would almost salivate. It was the same time as KHAD were after that little girl of yours. Vassily had never liked her. She was trouble. Why couldn't you just fuck one of the whores like any normal person? When they explained how he could pay for the bracelet, that it would just take the "accidental" shooting of Zena in the confusion, he agreed straight off. The generals and Political Officers

289

in Jalalabad were so keen to lick the arses of local sympathisers that it didn't take much persuading to send the Agitprop Brigade out and make sure she was with them.

'We agreed to meet Hashim in Ghazis. He would have the bracelet there for us and we would make sure the girl was shot in the ambush. I had a little business of my own with the muj, a few small armaments. Everybody would be happy.

'We fed details to KHAD about when we would be arriving in Ghazis, and I told Hashim how many vehicles there'd be and where the vehicles would be in the convoy. The plan was they'd mine the road from Ghazis and pick off the last two vehicles, which would be the BMP with the grenade launcher and the heavy machine gun they wanted, and the Agitprop Brigade's APC.

'We met Hashim in a room above a shop away from the market. When Vassily set eyes on the bracelet, he couldn't speak.

'That was it,' Kirov said. 'That was what it was all about, that was what he sold her for. You should have seen his eyes, you would perhaps have understood then. There was madness in them. He had to have the bracelet.

'Things went wrong when we crossed the brook, coming down from Ghazis. The mine was supposed to be detonated as the last two vehicles entered the water. That way there would be the least casualties. Hashim promised that any of our soldiers captured would be released without harm. But then things fucked up. The mine detonated too early. It all got confused.

'And then there you were, racing back across the brook into the thick of the fight. Vassily and I were trying to organise a retreat, Zhuralev had taken a bullet and you were heading back into the shooting.

'What a mess,' he said, shaking his head. 'When we had regained control of the situation, you were missing. Vassily went off looking for you. They found you at the side of the road, a little girl in your arms. Ten were killed, and fifteen wounded. Vassily brought you back raving. Physically you weren't in bad shape although your arms were burnt, but you were a fucking mess up here.' He tapped his skull.

'An investigation was launched into the whole fuck-up. Intelligence wouldn't have come up with anything if Kolya hadn't squealed. We were convicted for trading Soviet army goods.

'We were taken to the Pol-e-Tcharkhi prison. It was a fortress – the walls were so thick you could drive a car along the top of them.' Kirov nodded at Kolya. 'This little shit paid someone inside to finish me off. It wasn't difficult. There were continual fights inside – knives, boiling water. There were killers who would do it for a dollar or two.

'But he did a bad job and I went after him. For that I was given another five years on my sentence and transferred to a maximum-security prison.

'When I got out six months ago, I wrote to Zinotis and he let me know the bracelet hadn't been sold. Vassily, it seems, went a little crazy too, after Ghazis. Flagellating himself like some fucking Catholic monk. He was looking after you and refused to talk about the bracelet. Zinotis had stayed in touch with Vassily, but had heard nothing of Kolya. I tracked down some old vets, but nobody had heard anything about him. Somebody thought they'd heard he'd died of an overdose, years back. Then a few weeks ago Zinotis wrote to say he had seen Kolya in Vilnius.

'When I got here last week, I couldn't trace him. I went to see Vassily, but he told me fuck all. He was dying, of course, so when I threatened to kill him, he just laughed.'

Kirov grinned, as if amused by Vassily's attitude.

'I kept an eye on you, after I visited you at the workshop. Zinotis got very excited after you visited him, so I kept my eye on him too. When I caught up with him a couple of hours ago, he was at an apartment up behind the railway station. He seemed to think Vassily had sent Kolya instructions on how to find the bracelet. He could find nothing in the apartment.'

'It was Zinotis?' I exclaimed, astonished. 'I don't believe it. You're telling me he trashed Kolya's apartment? Beat the woman? Professor Zinotis?'

Kirov nodded and chuckled. 'You didn't think he was capable?'

'I don't believe any of this, Kirov. I knew Vassily, I talked to Zinotis . . . I know what they were capable of.'

'Do you?' he asked pleasantly. 'And you, Antanas? Did you know what you were capable of? Did you know you were able to do what you did? Does your wife know what happened to those children? Will you tell your child when she is older? None of us are the people we seem, Antanas, you should know that. Afghanistan did that to us.'

An icy tremor ran down my spine. Your child. She. Had Kirov been watching Laura? What did he know?

'We are capable of anything,' Kirov continued. 'We hide it from the world, pretend we are like normal people, but slowly the knowledge of our history poisons us. Zinotis was just better at hiding it than most. He was a slippery bastard.'

'Kirov,' I said, my voice tight with fear and fury. 'If you should do anything . . .'

Kirov brushed my words aside with a flick of his hand and a nod. He had not finished.

'Zinotis wanted to do a deal with me, but as he hadn't bothered to tell me what you had told him about the bracelet, I could see he wasn't to be trusted.'

He raised his right thumb to his lips and licked it. His tongue was fatly red, disgusting. I noticed the thin cut down the soft pad of his thumb. Remembered it.

'When I slit his throat, he moaned like a girl.'

Kirov spat out into the darkness, as if repelled by Zinotis's fear in the face of death.

'Back in Afghanistan not one muj I killed showed any fear – not even the boys.' He laughed then. 'When you come back to the apartment, you almost tripped over his body in the darkness. What? Don't look so disgusted – we are all the same, you, Vassily, me – we are no different.'

I opened my mouth, but found that no words would come out. I gaped, the blackened little bodies of the children twisting in the darkness before me. The thought of Laura.

Kirov paused for a moment, as if appreciating the effect his words had on me, playing with me, then he turned and addressed Kolya. 'And now, at last, I have found you,' he said. 'And the bracelet.'

His voice was quiet, but menacing. He moved towards Kolya. A single, sharp retort cracked open the night. The sound echoed from the walls of the houses on the hill, waking the dogs, and hummed down the metal rails of the bridge. Kirov gasped and stepped backwards. Trembling, Kolya raised the pistol and fired a second shot that sent Kirov tumbling. His head hit the railings and bounced off. As he lay sprawled across the concrete, his arms flailed in a puddle.

'Fuck,' I gasped. 'Kolya!'

Kolya said nothing. He stood shaking, the Makarov hanging loosely in his hand by his side. The metal box had fallen from his grip and opened on the bridge, disgorging its contents.

For some few seconds after he had fallen, Kirov's arms splashed feebly in the dirty puddle. I knelt beside him. The two shots had both entered his chest. He had been dead in a matter of moments. As the juddering subsided, the slight breeze lifted his hair, giving him an air of animation still. His neck was twisted awkwardly against the rusted metal railings.

Along with the sharp retort of the Makarov, his words echoed in my head, 'We are all the same . . . no different.' I shuddered. We are the same. No, I thought, no, Kirov, not the same.

Instinctively my fingers reached out to feel for his pulse, but I drew them back, unable to touch him. 'Not the same,' I whispered. And I thought of Laura and how much I loved her and needed her. The horror that had stopped my heart, as the bullets flung him back, dissipated then, leaving me suddenly calm. He's gone, I thought, and felt no pity.

'He's gone,' I said to Kolya. 'You killed him.'

Kolya knelt beside me. In the light of the street lamp his face looked pale and waxy.

'We'll push him over the railings,' he said. 'Into the river.'

Kirov was heavy and awkward to handle. As we hoisted him up, his head lolled backwards and cracked hard against the top of the railings. Ridiculously, I winced and lifted him more carefully. The dogs continued to bark in the houses on the hill and I was afraid somebody would come out to investigate.

We settled the body on the waist-high railing. For a moment he teetered there, the look of surprise frozen on his face. And then gravity did its work, dragging his body down. It broke through the surface with a heavy splash but in the poor light it seemed for a moment that he had not submerged. His dark shape hung on the water, moving fast with the strong down-river current. As it passed across the glittering discs of reflected street lamps, though, it became evident that it was his coat which was sailing away towards the city. Of Kirov there was no sign.

Kolya stared down into the darkness, pale faced, hair plastered to his forehead with perspiration, trembling violently from the exertion.

'The bastard deserved it,' I said, laying my hand on Kolya's sleeve. 'If anyone ever deserved it that evil bastard did.'

Kolya nodded slowly, his eyes not leaving the coat as it slipped away into the darkness.

Kneeling down, I took the bracelet from the metal box. I fingered the large amber sphere, took in the glorious inclusions. It was for this Zena died, I thought. For this she had been sold. I felt a huge wave of sorrow wash over me. Its waters encircled me, foaming around my ears. The heavy suck of its withdrawal pulled me with it. A dark clenched fist held my gut tightly in its grip.

The amber seemed to be unusually warm – my palm tingled, and when I ran it across the back of my hand the hairs rose. Vassily's words came back to me with startling clarity. I pictured him before me, sloped forwards in the armchair, the pained, weary expression on his face. *You will not hate me, when you hear the story*, tovarich – *comrade, you will forgive your friend*? I looked down at the bracelet.

I must be holding a fortune in my hand, I thought then. My mind spun dizzily for a few moments. The inclusions were beautiful. I had never seen such good examples. The amber was large and clear, shining even in the light of the street lamps with brilliant warmth. The metal was heavy, ornate, gold lace. *Sometimes*, Vassily had said once, and I tried to remember when, *sometimes great beauty is a terrible thing*.

As my fingers tightened around the bracelet, I felt my thoughts twisting, spiralling away from me. I glanced up at Kolya, who had turned from the railing and was looking at the jewel in my hand. There was a hungry look in his eyes. He moved towards me, his thin hand reaching out. I stepped back.

'Wait,' I said.

A look of surprise crinkled Kolya's forehead, followed swiftly by annoyance.

'What?' he said.

My mind tried to struggle towards some sort of revelation which I felt shivering in the darkness, just eluding me.

'Did Vassily ever tell you the story about Freyja?' I asked. 'About the Amir Timor?'

Kolya held out his hand. He shuffled forwards, grasping for the bracelet. I took another step back and found my spine pressed up against the railings. The sky had begun, barely perceptibly, to lighten. The thick darkness was dissolving and the flowing water was faintly visible. I held out my hand, suspended the bracelet over the drop.

'No!' Kolya called frantically.

I opened my fingers and released the bracelet. It clung

to my flesh, a sharp sliver of gold ornamentation snagging on my skin. Kolya jolted against me as he tried to grab it. The sudden jerk released the bracelet and it fell smoothly through the blue air, breaking the surface of the river with barely a splash, disappearing immediately, swallowed up in the darkness.

A thin howl escaped Kolya's pale lips. He hung over the edge of the railings, eyes desperately searching the water, vainly hoping it might reappear.

'It's over, Kolya,' I said.

I felt a weight lifting from me. Kolya turned, a look of absolute fury twisting his features. He hurried away, breaking into a shambling run. Dropping from the end of the bridge, he slithered down the muddy river bank to the water's edge. I stood watching him as he rushed up and down the bank, wading knee deep in the fast-flowing water, his arms reaching out to its depths, his low moan carried up to me through the cool air of the gathering dawn.

Chapter 33

Passing the glittering domes of the Russian Orthodox church under a dawn-flushed sky, I crossed Zverynas Bridge on to Gedimino. An elderly man swept the wide cobbled street, working his way slowly and steadily into the centre of the Old Town. A flock of pigeons broke from the square by the parliament buildings as I passed, rising up into the sharp, clear air, bursting into flame as the first rays of sun touched them.

That was what it was all about, Kirov had said, *that was what he sold her for.*

I shook my head, ran a hand through my hair. I pictured Vassily as I had last seen him, the night before he died, frail and thin, his beard hanging limply on the blanket.

When they explained how he could pay for the bracelet, he agreed straight off.

His chest had risen and fallen in a steady, slow rhythm. His hands, punctured by drips, lay by his side on the sheet. I had taken his fingers between my own, felt the hard calloused flesh, the faint, warm pulse.

You should have seen his eyes, you would perhaps have understood then. There was madness in them. He had to have the bracelet.

Before I left, I had bent to kiss him, and smelt then the stench of approaching death above the smothering scent of disinfectant. Had it been for nothing, then, those years of friendship, that companionship which had kept

298

me alive? Had it all been a deception? He had been my brother, my friend. He had taught me to live again.

You have a right to know, Kirov had said.

The street cleaner looked up as I passed, resting on his broom. He watched me, unabashed. A truck stopped outside a bar. The driver jumped from the cab, whistling. He rolled up the canvas sides, revealing barrels of Danish beer.

You have a right to know.

My mind skittered over the years, skipping like a stone across water, touching and moving on. Zena. The *kishlak*. Ghazis. Vassily patiently showing me how to clip the amber on to the lathe. 'There is something you need to know,' Vassily had said, 'something I should have told you many years ago, but didn't. Should have, but couldn't.'

Lukiskiu Square was quiet. The rising sun lit up the spire of the church behind it. Far down Gedimino, the cathedral sparkled brilliantly. A police car was drawn up at the side of the road. Inside a policeman was sleeping, his green cap pulled low over his forehead, his window half open. An elderly woman opened a window in one of the apartment blocks on February 16th and shook out a sheet.

You must not hate me.

An aching sense of loss gripped me – scraped the flesh from my heart with its fingernails. I paused on the pavement, gazed up into the sky, dizzy, as if I were standing on the edge of a precipice. The loss of his friendship. The loss of his love. The loss of his presence in my life. The loss of our lives, which he had bound together by the strength of his presence, of all that we had enjoyed, Daiva, Tanya, Vassily and myself. That life was gone now and would never be again.

I found myself crying, then, for the loss of him, as I stood at the edge of the pavement unable to cross the street. Tears slipped down my cheek. My chest rose as I gulped for breath.

'Antanas!' Tanya cried, as she opened the door of her apartment. She was sleep-ruffled, wearing one of Vassily's large old shirts, her hair tied back with a ribbon. 'Where have you been?' she demanded, taking my arm and leading me into the apartment.

'It's a long story.' I sighed, feeling suddenly very weary.

'Come and sit down,' she said. I followed her through to the sitting room and collapsed on the sofa.

'You look terrible,' she said, kneeling beside me.

'Kolya shot Kirov,' I told her.

Her eyes widened and her hand went up to her lips. I shook my head. Already the events of the previous few hours had begun to recede and an air of unreality clung to them, as if I were waking slowly from a nightmare.

'And Kolya?' Tanya said. 'What happened? Did Kolya tell you what Vassily wanted you to know? What was it all about?'

I paused before I answered. As I looked at her, it struck me with renewed force how much she resembled Zena. The short dark hair. The colour of her eyes. The animated passion in her movements. I nodded slowly.

'There were things he told me,' I said, 'about the bracelet, about how they got it.'

I found I was reluctant to tell her, reluctant to talk about it and so, through my own words, make more real the story I had been told; to validate it with the retelling.

'We dug up the bracelet,' I said instead.

'You have it?'

Tanya sat up, a startled, excited expression brightening her eyes.

'I threw it in the river.'

'You what?'

I shrugged. She gaped at me, bewildered.

'It's hard to explain,' I said. 'When I held it in my hand, I got the strangest feeling. I thought of all those who had died because of it. I don't know. I can't explain. I saw Kolya's greed, his hunger for it, Kirov's, Zinotis's. The effect it had on Vassily. It seemed right to put an end to it.'

Tanya stared at me and I could see her struggling to grasp what had gone on, struggling to understand what I had done. What Kolya had done. And perhaps also what Vassily had done.

'I need to get out of these clothes,' I said to deflect her attention.

'Of course,' Tanya said, solicitously, getting up quickly. 'Go take a shower. Freshen up.'

She looked embarrassed at having been so insistent. Putting a towel in my hand, she pushed me in the direction of the bathroom. I stood for a long time beneath the shower, enjoying the feel of the stiff jets of hot water pummelling my flesh. After I had towelled myself dry, Tanya gave me coffee and I smoked a couple of cigarettes.

'How are you feeling?' she asked tentatively.

'Better,' I said.

I looked across at her, curled in the armchair, legs tucked beneath her, chin resting on the palm of her hand.

'Did Vassily ever say much about Afghanistan?' I asked.

She shook her head. 'He spoke of it sometimes,' she said. 'I thought we were so open with each other. When he jumped in the night hearing something, when he had his headaches and when I found him sitting alone in a room, we talked about it. He told me what was important. That is why I was so bewildered by all these secrets.'

I considered what I should tell her. I longed to talk to her, to probe her – to demand from her the answers her husband could no longer give. To ask whether she knew how much he had betrayed me.

'There were things that happened there,' I said.

I paused. She had let her hair loose, and it fell around her face, its rich curls accentuating the rosy swell of her cheeks.

'There was a girl I met there,' I said.

Tanya looked up, surprised. She smiled. 'Really?'

'Her name was Zena.'

It was strange to hear the name on my own lips; it had been so long since last I had spoken it. When I said it, I felt my tone soften, deepen, and recognised the cadence of my younger self, felt momentarily the gentle happiness spring from my tongue, as though the very act of saying her name had the power in some tiny way to transport me back to that time.

'She was a nurse,' I said, feeling Tanya's eyes on me. 'She was an Afghani girl. Beautiful. She had short dark hair and was full of energy, of life. She was a lot like you. In the middle of all that horror I fell in love.'

'You never said.' Tanya leant forward and took my hand.

'When I first saw you, standing outside your grand-parents' cottage, it was a shock. You were so like her. What I felt for you then confused me.'

302

Tanya was trying, I could see, to understand what had happened, what I felt.

'What do you mean?' she said.

I did not answer at once, struggling to find the words to explain to myself as much as to her.

'You frightened me. Attracted me. Both at once. When it became clear Vassily was in love with you, I explained my confused feelings to myself as guilt. When I met Daiva she was so different; her coolness, her reticence. She felt safe to be with. I fell in love with what Daiva was not. I used her to defend myself.'

'I had no idea,' Tanya said, leaning back in her chair. 'I mean, I knew you were attracted to me and I was flattered by that, but when you met Daiva . . . you were so in love.'

For some moments then we sat in silence.

'What happened to the girl? The Afghani nurse?' Tanya asked, breaking the silence.

'She was killed.'

'Tell me.'

'I know only what Kirov told me a few hours ago.'

'What did he tell you?' Tanya's voice shook a little, as if she was afraid, as if she knew what I was about to say.

'Vassily sold her for the bracelet,' I said. 'There was a deal – they sold Zena to the KHAD, to the secret police, to buy it.'

'No,' she whispered. She withdrew her hand from mine, wiped it across her forehead and closed her eyes.

'Do you think it is true?' I said. 'Do you think Vassily could have done that?'

She opened her eyes again, looked at me, squarely. 'Do you?'

'I don't know what to believe.'

Tanya sighed. She buried her face in her hands. 'I don't know what to think any more,' she said.

A little later Tanya announced that she had to go to work for a few hours. She ran her fingertips across my face, gently. 'Will you be OK? It won't be for long. You can stay. There is food in the kitchen and you can sleep in the bed.'

'That's fine,' I said.

The apartment was quiet when she had gone. I did not move from the sofa. The room ticked and sighed, exhaled into the silence. Ever since he had taken me from the New Vilnia hospital Vassily had been a friend to me. He had nursed me back to health. He had taught me how to work amber; had given me a trade, a purpose, to hold back the darkness. And yet he had never told me, never even intimated, the part he had played in the death of Zena.

Leaping up from the sofa, I kicked out at the chair he had been sitting in that last evening. 'You bastard,' I hissed through teeth clenched tight. 'You fucking bastard.' I kicked it again, harder. Felt the pain shuddering up my leg, exquisitely. 'You fucking bastard!' I shouted, feeling the blood rush to the surface of my skin, feeling the heat rise in my face. I fell upon the chair, kicking and punching it. Screaming until my throat tore and my lungs scraped for breath. The armchair overturned and I toppled with it, sprawling across the floor, the rug grazing the skin from my cheek and the palms of my hands.

'You bastard,' I muttered, feeling my cheek throb. Feeling the cool smoothness of the parquet floor by the door, the smell of wax filling my nostrils.

*

Leaving Tanya's apartment, I went straight to Daiva's mother's. When I knocked, it was Daiva who answered. For some moments we stood in silence. She leant against the door frame. She looked tired and unhappy.

'You'd better come in,' she said.

She kissed me awkwardly on the cheek. In the kitchen Laura was sitting at the table, strapped into a child's chair. I paced quickly across the tiled floor and scooped her up, pulling her clumsily from the straps. I held her close to me, burrowed my head into her clothes, inhaled her smell. Tears welled in my eyes and I felt a sharp pain in my heart. Laura cried in my arms.

'You're holding her too tight,' Daiva said softly, extracting Laura from my grasp.

'I'm sorry,' I said.

I took a seat at the table and Daiva sat on the other side of our daughter.

'I've called the apartment a few times, but you weren't there,' she said. 'I got a little worried.'

'I've been away.'

Daiva spooned porridge into Laura's mouth, and when she became restless took her into her arms. She muttered and struggled in her mother's embrace.

'I've had some time to think,' Daiva said.

'Don't,' I said, holding up my hands. 'Don't tell me you've made a decision, don't tell me your mind is made up.'

She leant back, her arms folded around Laura, drawing her to her breast tightly.

'Why not?'

'I've messed things up, Daiva, I know that. Things have been hard and I haven't coped. I know I don't really have the right to ask you to wait before you make any decisions. I know we have talked about my problems many times already, but please let's wait a while. Let's wait a little while before we make any decisions about what we are going to do.'

'Are you suggesting you are about to change something? I mean, something significant?'

I stood up and walked around behind her. I put my hands on her shoulders and rested my forehead against the back of her head.

'I don't know what I am capable of changing,' I said. 'I want to be honest. But I feel as if I have lost so many things, I don't want to keep losing those things that are so precious to me.'

'There are things that have happened, Antanas . . .' she said quietly. 'There are things I can't . . . won't live with. I don't know if I can believe you are capable of changing now, after all this time.'

I turned her head and held her face between the palms of my hands. Her pale blue eyes gazed into mine. I saw the fear hidden in the tiny creases beginning to web her skin.

'I'm sorry, Daiva,' I said. 'I'm so sorry.'

When I returned to my apartment, I called Tanya at work. We met in a bar on Jewish Street.

'How are you doing?' she asked.

'More lost than ever,' I confessed. 'We did so many things there, Tanya. Things we never spoke about. When I first went to Afghanistan I really believed we were doing some good. I believed all the propaganda and lies. But the political instruction we were given and the ideals they pumped us full of just bore no relation to the situation. The longer we were there, the worse things got.'

'It was war.'

'Is that an excuse? Does that alter anything?'

She shrugged. 'It's not about excuses. We can't change the past; we can hide from it, we can accept it or we can let it chew us up. There are only so many choices open to us, only so many things we can do.'

'Is it that simple? Does that answer the wrongs we did? There are wider implications.'

'There are? What, like the fact that Russian boys are doing the same in Chechnya now, having the same done to them? That in all wars everywhere people do things they could never have conceived they were capable of doing? That afterwards they could never conceive of how they did them?'

'Do you want, now, to start paying for the things you did? Are you going to demand too that those who did things to you pay also?'

'It's not just about the war,' I said, sighing. I buried my head in my hands. 'Why did Vassily want me to hear this story? What good did he think it would do? In the end it was only Zena who kept me sane, there was nothing else for me to cling to. How could Vassily have done what he did, Tanya? Is it possible? I loved him. Was Kirov telling the truth?'

'Look,' she said, 'it's like this.' She reached over and took my hand. 'If Kirov was right, what then? Will you hate Vassily, your friend, who did so much for you? And if Kirov was lying, will those years once more seem to have been good ones?'

She squeezed my hand. Her eyes burnt intensely. She shook me gently.

'It is in nobody else's power, Antanas, to say whether Vassily betrayed you or not. Not Kirov nor I nor Kolya can do that. We cannot validate or invalidate the years you shared with him. That is something you need to decide for yourself.'

'But how can I do that if I don't know the truth?'

'I don't see what the truth has to do with it,' Tanya said. 'Either you loved him or you didn't. What does truth have to do with that?'

She paused and we lapsed into silence. A young man was sitting in the corner of the café, near the window. As I watched him, a woman came in and he got up to greet her. I felt a little pang of envy at their easy, careless affection. Ten years younger than I and they had been born into a different world.

'Have you been to see Daiva?' Tanya asked, following my gaze.

I nodded. 'I remember something Vassily said to me once,' I said. 'When we had been drinking too much, moaning to each other. "We have had the surface seared from our souls," he said. "We are naked and everything hurts us, but we feel more too. Every feeling we have is sharper. Richer."'

Tanya smiled. But then her lips twisted and tears sprang to her eyes. She pulled a handkerchief from her pocket and squeezed it tightly to her face. Her whole body shuddered and she cried quietly. I got up, went round to her and embraced her.

'God,' she said after a while, wiping away her tears. 'God, how I miss him.'

The workshop was cold, and I could smell the dampness and mould in the air. I lit the paraffin heater and sat down at my desk. For some time I remained slumped there in silence, gazing around – at the lathe, the bulging hessian sacks, the tubs of worked amber, Vassily's desk.

In ancient times, in Lithuania, I had read in the writings of the philosopher Vydunas, it was the custom to inscribe upon a piece of amber a thought, a sentiment, that would accompany the dead on their journey to the other world.

Switching on the lamp above my work table, I pulled forwards a large bowl full of amber. Digging my hand into the beads, I felt their warm weight, the pull they exerted. Sifting through them, I found a large piece, clear as water, the colour of the sun at the end of summer, at its softest.

Clipping it carefully into the small vice at the edge of the desk, I began to engrave it. *A threefold cord is not quickly broken.* I smoothed the fine dust from its surface, rubbed it clean with a rag. Held it up to the light and watched its heart explode with fire behind the words.

Chapter 34

On Friday morning the cemetery was busy. The gravel and dirt paths around the graves were carefully raked; there were flowers and a throng of candles glittering in the low yellow light. The temperature had plummeted suddenly in the night, and we woke in the morning to find that the rain had hardened to frost on the leaves, and the paths were slippery and hazardous. Halfway through the service it began to snow – light, dry flakes that danced in the air and blew like paper confetti around the graves. A young boy looked up, joyfully. He pulled his mother's sleeve and pointed into the sky. When she brushed his arm away, he opened his mouth and wandered off, head held back, trying to catch a flake on his tongue.

I took Laura in my arms and held her tight. She had fallen asleep. I watched the boy as he wandered between the graves, arms high, chasing the flurries of snow. When I kissed Laura's cheek, she opened her eyes for a moment. Looking up at me grumpily, she murmured something and then her eyes closed once more and she slept on.

When the service was over I handed Laura back to Daiva. The mourners picked their way carefully towards the gates of the cemetery, through the gravestones, the cold marble slabs, the trees whose leaves had still not been fully shed, the metal railings.

Standing at the foot of the grave, I looked at the

picture of Vassily etched upon the gravestone. I squatted down. The earth was cold and damp beneath my knees. In my palm I pressed the amber, felt its smooth warmth against my skin, and, with the tip of my thumb, the sharp edge of the words I had engraved.

I dropped it on to the top of the coffin. It bounced on the lid and settled against a knot in the wood, above his heart. The snow had begun to fall harder, and already a thin white sheet had spread itself across the grave. A flake fell on the amber, but dissolved immediately. As I watched, a pale cold sheet formed, but the amber, warm from my palm, melted its own small space.

The workmen began shovelling earth into the grave. For some moments I gazed down silently, listening to the soft, rhythmic thud as it scattered heavily across the wooden coffin. The thwack of shovels biting into the wet soil, the grunts of the workmen, their knuckles blue with cold – the sounds followed me as I walked slowly back along the path to the gates.

Daiva was waiting with Laura in her arms. When I reached her, she slipped an arm around me. I pulled her close and we stood for some moments as the snow fell thickly around us. When I took Daiva's face in my hands and drew her to me, her eyes opened a fraction wider and a small smile parted her lips. In her eyes I saw a kind of light.

Acknowledgements

For advice, support and encouragement, thanks to Almantas Marcinkus, Petras Marcinkus, Arunas Slionys, Dalia Slioniene, Arunas Stumbra, Loreta Stumbriene, Kristina, Gabriele and, of course, Lukas.